A MALICE

Love

3

A NOVEL BY

BIANCA

PREVIOUSLY...

Kade

*M*y seat was laid back, and this bad broad I met at the Playa's Ball was giving me some of the best top I ever had in my life. She raised up and stared at me with an attitude.

"Your phone keeps fucking ringing. I thought you said you ain't had no hoes," she said.

"Lency... I swear, I ain't got no hoes. I don't know why my phone keeps ringing. My boss knows I'm with you," I said, pulling my phone out my pocket.

I looked at my phone, and I had ten missed calls from Shelly and ten missed calls from a number that I didn't know. I didn't have any voicemails, so I ran the number through a system, and it came back to a gun shop.

"Watch out, Lency," I said to her.

I pulled my pants up and stepped out the car to call the gun shop back. I thought that Mayhem had stopped through there, or something.

"Yeah, this is Kade Lewis. Accountant for Mayhem," I said.

"Uh, Kade, this Ron. I know I'm the last person you want to hear from, but it's important. If I remember correctly, is your sister really dark skin, with really big hair?" he asked.

"The fuck are you asking about my sister for nigga? She's married," I let him know right off the bat.

"Nah, it ain't nothing like that, but I think you need to go check on her. She came in here a few minutes ago wanting to buy a gun. She looked distraught. I tried to call you while she was here, but she ran out before I could put the phone to my ear. Check on her man," he said, and hung up the phone.

My heart instantly started racing because Kam ain't never shot a gun in her life, let alone seen one, until she got with her husband. I jumped back in the car and told Lency that I had to take her to Starbucks up the street and call her an Uber, because I needed to get home, quick.

"Don't be like that. My sister is my heart, and I need to go check on her. You can't come to my house yet, ma! Don't be mad. I'll make it up to you," I said to her when I pulled up to the Starbucks.

I pecked her on her pouty lips and unlocked the door for her to get out. As soon as she was safe inside of the Starbucks, I dialed the house phone and it rang twenty times, and no one answered. I weaved in and out of traffic trying to make it home. Sitting at a red light, I started getting anxious. Gripping the steering wheel as if I was getting ready to take off like a Nascar driver, I burnt rubber as soon as the light turned green.

I made it to the house, rushed into Kam's room, and screamed like a little bitch. My sister was shaking violently and foaming at the mouth.

"Kam, baby, what did you do?" I cried, rushing to her side.

TO BE CONTINUED...

Kade Lewis

$\mathcal{P}$acing the waiting room floor of the hospital that the nurses told me to wait in, I was going crazy. The doctors had been working on Kambridge for what seemed like forever, and I was starting to become irate. No one would give me answers. Every few minutes, I was walking up to the desk asking them if they had heard something from the doctors.

When I rushed into Kam's room, I acted quickly. Snatching the pill bottle, the letter, and stuffing it in my pocket, I scooped Kam into my arms, bridal style, and ran out the house. I had never driven my Ferrari that fast. She was still seizing and foaming at the mouth when I ran into the hospital doors, and they snatched her away from me. I gave them the pill bottle that I found; hopefully, it would help them. I tried to go to the back with them, expressing that she was my sister, but they ain't give one fuck about that.

While I was pacing the floor, I called and left several voicemails on my parents' phones, but they ain't called back, nor have they shown up, and that's been two hours ago. I didn't want to call Shelly, but she is Kam's best friend; and not even twenty minutes after I called her, she was here, crying harder than me. I know my dad ain't give a fuck about my sister, but for my mom to switch up like that, is troubling. Very troubling.

"Kade, babe, you should sit down. You have been pacing for hours now. I know you are tired," Shelly said to me, but I ignored her.

I reached into my pocket and toyed with the letter that was in there. A part of me wanted to read it, but a part of me was scared to know what would be my sister's last thoughts. I kept taking it out and putting it back in my pocket. Taking it out, and putting it back. Would you want to know your sister's last thoughts?

"Kade, I know why she did it. It's why I was calling you all those times," she whispered.

"Shelly, stop with all the other shit! You let my sister do this shit to herself? What the fuck you mean you know WHY she did it? Tell me!" I yanked her up by her collar, and she started wheezing and clenching her chest. I didn't care that the people in the waiting room were looking at us.

"Your mom," I dropped her, and she fell to her knees, crying. "Your mom... fucked Phoenix!"

I stepped back to look at her like she had grown two heads out of her shoulders. I was shaking my head in disbelief. Hell nah, my mom is a lot of things, but she ain't a cheater. She loves my dad. That got to be the only reason why she let Dad get away with the shit he been doing to Kam. I stepped back, and looked at her with the meanest scowl ever.

"Shelby! Stop fucking lying. My mom ain't never cheated on my fucking daddy. Where the fuck is your proof?" I snapped on her.

"Read...read the letter Kade. She probably put something in there. I saw it with my own two eyes. Kam received a certified package today at work. She told me to open it, and I did. There were pictures of several different women and him, leaving hotels. There was even a video of him fucking some white woman. It was a picture of him and your mom… your mom walking out of a hotel together. Kade, I would not lie to you. I promise," she pleaded.

I picked Shelly up off the floor and put her in the seat. I sat down next to her and leaned my head back against the wall, and let the tears flow freely down my face.

"My sister has had the hardest life, and I couldn't save her. I feel like such a fuck up. It seems like Kam had it all, but nothing at all. Sure, she had a rich life, but at what cost? She got her ass beat, daily. She found love, and I told that nigga not to hurt her. I told him not to step to her if he wasn't going to be one hundred with her," I said.

"She's going to pull through this. Kam is the strongest person I know. Trust me. She is not going to let this beat her. I promise you," Shelly assured me.

I took a deep breath and pulled out the letter and unfolded it. Shelly and I read it in silence.

Dear Daddy,

For as long as I can remember, you beat me. Sometimes to the point where I would bleed, and my sores would get infected. I never thought that a father could do such things to someone that they love, but then I realized that as far as I can remember, I can count on one hand how many times you told me you loved me. I don't know what I did for you to treat me this way. I have done everything that a daughter could do, and it still wasn't enough. You treated Kade and Kalena like children of the year, but if I looked at you wrong, I got a smack across the face. It seems like the only thing I did wrong was be born into your family. I can't apologize for that. I loved you. I still loved you, up until the day you had someone place a pistol to my husband's head, and made me choose. Now, I will go wherever I go with hate in my heart for you. Seek help.

Dear Mom,

What a sorry excuse for a fucking mom. You were the one person I counted on to keep me safe…keep me safe from everything, but you didn't. You chose to keep me in the house with that monster to unleash all his gruesome tactics on to me. You watched this for years, and I still loved you. STILL. The easiest… THE EASIEST…thing that you could have done is told me that you fucked my husband the day you laid eyes on him and knew we were together. You fucked a prostitute. Smh, and you let me marry him. Hell, you could have saved me a tiny piece of heartache. Fucking scum. Wherever I go, I'm going with pure hatred in my heart for you.

Dear my Kade!

Please don't hate me. Please don't hate me. Please don't hate me. I could write that twenty thousand more times. I know you tried to save me. I know you did the best you could. I love you so much. Please leave Dad's house, and take Kalena with you. Take care of her, and continue to show her how men should treat her. Talk to her about little boys, and tell her to save herself for marriage. Something I should have done. I love you so much! Please don't hate me.

Sweet Kalena,

Please be stronger than me. Please be better than me. Continue to make good grades, and keep singing. You are going to be the next

7

Beyoncé. Listen to Kade. He's very smart and knows a lot. Also, Shelly. She's a wild child, but she will never lead you astray, or have you doing things she knows I wouldn't approve of. I love you so much baby girl. This is not your fault. Your sister got weak. The world made her weak. Please forgive me.

Shelby Jean,

I love you so much. I got weak, and I'm sorry. Please don't come to my grave and curse me out, because I will hear you. Please take care of my store. It's yours. Your white ass needs something to keep you out of trouble. Please help Kade take care of Kalena. She's going to need you both, ok? And don't you fuck with Malice, because I know your crazy ass. LOL! You are my very best friend. Always and Forever.

Malice,

Congratulations. You broke me.

After we finished reading, I crumbled the letter in my hand and tried not to cry again. If ain't one thing, it's another. My sister was tired of life. She has gotten thrown curve ball after curve ball. I couldn't believe my fucking mom. I wonder how long she been fucking around with that bitch ass nigga.

"Maybe you should try your parents again. Can you call the school so I can go pick Kalena up? I'm sure she would want to be here when she wakes up," Shelly said to me.

"Mane, fuck them! After reading this. Fuck this. We all Kam got. Kalena don't need to be here. I will go get her later," I snapped.

I walked back up to the desk, and before I could even get halfway there, the woman slid the glass open, and told me that they didn't know nothing, and the doctor would come out and get me once they're done. I went and sat back down. Shelly laid her head on my shoulder, and I could feel the water sliding down my arms. This was taking a toll on me. On us.

I took my phone out to text Lency to let her know what was going on, but the shuttering of flashes interrupted me. I looked up to see my dad, mom, and Kalena coming through the door looking like the perfect family; like Kam is only in here for a broken toe. My heart rate started to rise. The cameras… the flashes… the attention. It seems like this nigga gets off on fucking attention, but what he won't do is use my sister for it.

"Judge Kason, can you tell us what is going on with your daughter?" one reporter asked him.

"Judge Kason, is there any word on your daughter?" another reporter asked. "Sources from inside the hospital say that it was suicide. Is your daughter alive, Judge Kason?" he continued, and my dad never flinched when the reporter said that.

These fucking weak ass people will do anything for a fucking buck. No way that the reporter should know about my sister's diagnosis that fast…before a fucking doctor can come out and talk to us. I had e-fucking-nough of this shit. The anger that was running through my body damn near had me levitating off the seat. My body started shaking. The grinding of my teeth is the only thing that I could hear in my ears. I was clenching the arms of the chair that I was sitting in so hard, to the point where I was damn near about to pop my fingernails off.

"Kadddeee," Shelly whispered, and topped my hand with hers. "Think about what you are getting ready to do. You have to remember who your family is. Kade. Kade. Kade. Answer me. Say something. Anything."

"Listen, guys, I can assure you that my daughter is just fine. There is no love like a family's love. We will get through whatever is going on together. Now, leave me and my family to handle this matter pri⊠"

Before he could finish his statement, I flew over there and pushed him with all my might, making him and my mom fall. He jumped back up, but security was over there in an instant in between us. I know my father, and he would not act a fool in front of cameras, but I ain't give not one fuck! Not a one! It's time the world knows who the fuck my father is.

"HOW FUCKING DARE YOU COME IN HERE WITH CAMERAS AND SHIT LIKE MY SISTER NOT BACK THERE FIGHTING FOR HER FUCKING LIFE! I CALLED BOTH OF Y'ALL MOTHAFUCKAS TWO HOURS AGO, AND YOU SHOW UP WITH CAMERAS, LIKE THIS SHIT IS A FUCKING REALITY TV SHOW," I shouted at them both.

I turned and looked into the cameras, and said "My father is a⊠" I was cut off by an arm being wrapped around me.

"Emotions are running very high at this moment, and we can assure you that Judge Kason takes his daughter's suicide attempt very serious. Judge Kason was in a very important meeting when the phone call was first made, and Judge Kason left his office as quick as he could. Traffic was very backed up; even with the police escort, it was very hard to get here. Please understand. Let the Lewis family handle this matter privately. Thank you," Elliot Stone, our family lawyer said boldly to the cameras.

"Smile into the camera, and walk the fuck away, you fucking disrespectful idiot," Elliot spoke through gritted teeth in my ear.

I gave a small fake smile, and walked over to my seat where I was sitting next to Shelly, with Kalena in tow. I'm sure the camera people wanted to follow me, but they probably didn't know what would happen next.

"Damn, Kade, I ain't expect you to do that shit," Shelly laughed.

"Kade, why did you do that on live TV? Do you know how that's going to look for Dad☒"

"Kalena, I'm sure you can look at me and tell that I don't give a fuck about your dad, and what the fuck he thinks. He ain't nothing but a fraud ass nigga, and don't get me started on your fucking mom, but you know what? Since you wanna be grown so fucking bad☒"

"Kade, chill," Shelly nudged me, cutting me off.

"Nah, fuck that. Here, Kalena. Read the note yourself," I said pulling the letter out, and stuffing it in Kalena's hands.

She's a smart girl so she read the letter quickly, and hurriedly gave it back to me. She sat down on the other side of me as if the wind had been taken out of her. After the cameras left out the hospital, my parents and Elliot made their way over to us and took the three chairs in front of us.

"Son, did she leave a note?" my mom asked as if she was really worried about Kam. I ain't see an ounce of remorse on her face, so I didn't reply, but I waved her off letting her know not to ask me that question again.

"Kade Lewis, do you hear your fucking mother talking to you?" Kason hissed through gritted teeth, but I ain't reply to him either. I just stared at them.

Elliot and my parents glared at us, and Shelly, Kalena, and I gave them glares back. If my sister didn't survive this shit, I swear my list of people to get revenge on was long, and it was going to start with that mothafucka, Malice Bailey. Someway, somehow, he was going to have to see me.

Pryor 'Mayhem' Bailey

*I*f love is what got my brother in his room crying like a bitch, then I don't want it. Keep that shit fifty feet away from me. I need some Lysol for that shit. Disinfect that shit. I damn near had to put Malice over my shoulder and bring him over here to our parents' house, after Miss Lady Sammy Sosa'd our place the fuck up. It was only going to take the decorator a day to get everything back the way it was. Mane, I ain't never seen a girl use a bat that damn good. I didn't feel sorry for my brother at first, but when he broke down and started crying, my heart went out to him. My brother is twenty-eight years old, and he has never been in love before, so he is taking that shit hard as fuck.

See, the biggest problem in this situation is the fact that Kam told my brother that she wanted a divorce. My brother was so excited that he got married to her, he couldn't stop bragging to me about her being his wife. He was wanting to get their own place and shit, but Kam wanted him to wait until he got his place up and running. That's a solid ass bitch, and I can't even lie. I really pray that Kam forgives him and gets this shit over with, because for the simple fact that Malice ain't going to ever let that girl go. That's the one thing he kept saying to me the whole way over here. He told me out his own mouth that he would kill every nigga that she encounters. He told me that he ain't signing no divorce papers, and I believe him.

What people don't know about Malice is the fact that he is a hothead. He has learned to control it over the years, but my brother is a HOTHEAD! He can control that shit, and it really takes a lot for him to get mad, but when he does, he is liable to kill you. So, if you ask me, I'm afraid for Kam. Malice is liable to kill that girl if she thinks she is going to divorce him. One thing that happened many years ago that Malice never speaks of, and will probably never tell a soul, is that when he was fifteen, he snapped a nigga's neck in half in two seconds. Shit, even if one of Malice's closest friends asked him if he killed someone, he would say no. He puts that shit so far in the back of his mind.

Malice and I were at a court playing basketball, randomly. This dude approached us with a gun, and was going to try and rob a Bailey boy. We both had our hands raised, and I kept my eyes on my lil' bro, making sure he was alright, but his chest was rising and falling fast. I wasn't sure if he was scared or not. I looked at him, blinked one time, and Malice was behind that nigga, with his neck twisted. I didn't even know that my brother could move that fast. That was the day I knew that my brother was a hothead, and that was the day he knew the streets wasn't for him. He knew the streets weren't for him because he would have to keep killing people for doing crazy shit, and he said that his heart is not built that way. We are two totally different people, because I'll bless a nigga with something hot in a millisecond.

"Son, you need to go talk to your brother, man. He still in there crying. I put my ear to the door, and I heard him sniffing. Ya' mama said that he won't stop crying," my dad said, and sat down on the couch across from me.

"Pops, you need to understand. That boy is cut from a different cloth. That girl is his first love, and that's just how he is handling it. He will get over it, but I don't know when."

"Nigga, the way you laid on the couch with the fucking blinds closed and the TV off, I would swear you in here trying to get over a broken heart too."

I laughed at him and grabbed the remote to turn the TV on. As soon as I turned the TV on, I saw CNN running a clip of Kade and his daddy, damn near pushing his daddy through the TV.

"Yo, turn that shit up," my dad said.

Here you are watching a clip of the famous Judge Kason Lewis and his son, getting into a fight over his sister, who recently allegedly committed suicide. There is no more information being released. The audio is not good, but what we got from the clip is that Judge Kason and his wife Tracey showed up to the hospital two hours after getting the call that Kambridge Lewis allegedly committed suicide, and his son, Kade Lewis, was not happy about it. We will keep you updated.

I raised up and turned the TV off.

"Dad, we have to get Malice to the hospital," I said to him. "Dad, don't give me that look. At the end of the day, that's still his wife, and he deserves to be there."

I got up and slid on my Gucci shoes, and walked upstairs with dad in tow. When we made it to his room, I could hear him sniffing. This nigga was still crying. I turned around and put my hand on my dad's chest, stopping him in his tracks.

"Dad, don't go in here on no shit. Don't go in the hospital on no shit. Malice needs his father. Don't tell him to get over that shit because he's not, and he won't no time soon. Don't tell him a nigga don't cry over no bitch, because that ain't what he need to hear right now. As bad as it's going to pain you, he needs his father, Paxton Bailey. Not Korupt the kingpin, but Paxton Bailey. Understand me?" I told him.

"Yeah, son," he chuckled.

"Dad, I'm dead the fuck ass," I got close to him, damn near nose to nose. "If you say anything that a father wouldn't say to a son that is going through something like this, I'mma knock your ass the fuck out, and I mean that from a place of love. Now, again, do you understand me?"

He got serious, and he nodded his head slow. There is no way that I could knock my dad out, but I'm sure that he got the message. I turned around and knocked on the door.

"Yeah," he answered. His voice sounded like his nose was stopped up.

"Me and your dad is coming in, and we have to talk, ok?" I said.

I turned the knob and pushed the door in. Malice was across his bed diagonally with his head halfway hanging off the bed, looking at his phone.

"You've reached Kambridge Bailey, please leave a message," the voicemail said.

"Baby, pleasssseee call me back! I love you so fucking much. I just need five minutes to explain. Come on, Kam, please! I'm begging you. I'm losing it without you, and it ain't even been long. Please," he begged.

I sat down next to him on the bed and patted his back.

"Bro, we need to get you to the hospital," I said.

"For what? I ain't sick, and I ain't suicidal...yet," he murmured the last part, getting ready to call Kam's phone back.

"It's about Kam. I'll explain it to you on the way to the hospital. So, I need you to get up brother."

He raised up, sat on the bed, and turned towards me.

"What's going on, Mayhem?" he asked me.

"Put your shoes on, bro, we need to get to the hospital, NOW!"

He got up and slid on his shoes. We went downstairs to the car and left. We zoomed through traffic towards the hospital.

"Um, Malice, Kam tried to commit suicide. The news⌧"

"NO, no, no, no, no, no, no," Malice said, while shaking his head at the same time.

"The news didn't say anything more than that. So, we don't know anything other than that. We don't know if she succeeded or not. We just⌧"

"Don't say that shit. My wife is still alive. Don't even speak that shit into the world," Malice snapped.

When we pulled up to the hospital, and there were news crews outside, and I'm sure they were waiting to hear some news about Kambridge. We rushed into the hospital.

"What room is Kambridge Bailey in?" Malice asked the woman at the desk.

She clicked on the computer and turned her nose up, like she was about to say they don't have a Kambridge Bailey.

"Try Kambridge Lewis," I said to the woman, and her face lit up.

"Are you family?" she asked.

"That's my wife. What the fuck you mean are we family?" Malice snapped.

My dad moved my brother to the side.

"Listen, Mama," my dad said, and the woman looked up at my dad, and her mouth halfway opened. The women loved my dad. "We just found out through the TV that my daughter-in-law allegedly committed suicide. We need to know what's going on with her," he spoke smoothly to the woman.

"Well, her other family is in the family waiting room. I can escort you there. The doctors are still trying to get her stable," she said and stood up.

We followed her to the room, and her family was already there. The minute we stepped into the room, Kade stood up.

"YOU!" he pointed and shouted.

He rushed Malice and put him on his back. He wasn't even trying to fight back as Kade rained blows on him. If one thing I knew for sure, my brother was broken. My dad grabbed Kade and threw him off Malice.

"THIS IS ALL YOUR FAULT MALICE! EVERYTHING IS YOUR FUCKING FAULT," Kade screamed and started crying again.

"WHAT THE FUCK ARE YOU DOING HERE?" Kason stood

his bitch ass up like he was about to do something.

"I'm here to support my son, Judge Kason, and I suggest you bring your voice down a notch, sir," my dad said.

Security ran into the waiting room, looking to see what was going on, but by that time, Kade was already back in his seat.

"Everything alright in here?" security asked, but no one replied to him.

"He's right! Judge, you should calm down. Look around," a nigga in a suit stood next to him and said.

There were people in here with their cameras ready for drama. Malice was still laid on the floor. He wasn't passed out; he was just lying there staring at the ceiling. My brother was fucked up, and I felt so bad for him.

Malice

*M*y world fucking flipped over when my wife showed me that video and threw those pictures in my chest, but my world crashed and burned when Mayhem and my dad came into my room at my parents' house, and told me that my wife committed suicide. That's the only reason why I let Kade rain his blows down on me, because I knew he was frustrated. He asked me to do one thing, and that's protect his sister, not hurt her. I failed on both ends. I don't even deserve to be her husband right now. She gave her ring back to me, but I'll never sign anything regarding a divorce. I'll beg and plead until my knees bleed, but I ain't never divorcing her, and it will be a cold day in hell if she thinks for one second that I'm going to let her be with another man. That shit better not even come across her fucking dome, to be honest. She has only gotten the nice side of Malice. Just because I'm not in the streets, or a thug, don't mean I can't get down with the best of them; I just don't want to.

"Kade," I called his name. "Did she leave☒"

"Don't fucking ask about my sister, my nigga. Sit your stupid ass over there, and look crazy, and be glad that I'm even letting you sit here, while my sister is fighting for her fucking life."

Before I knew it, I ran over to him, and yanked his ass up by his throat, lifting him in the air. Sometimes I be forgetting how strong I am, and I be surprising my damn self sometimes.

"PUT HIM DOWN!" Tracey screamed.

"Everybody shut the fuck up before it be some more furniture moving up in this bitch! Do yo' thang, son!" my dad said from behind me.

"Look, Kade, I let you whoop my ass the first time because that's your sister, and I failed you. I was wrong, but⊠"

"HE CAN'T BREATHE!! OH MY GOD! YOU ARE GOING TO KILL HIM!" Tracey yelled again.

"Yell again up in this bitch!" Mayhem growled, and the room got real quiet, because I'm assuming he raised his shirt up and showed his piece.

"Like I was saying, Kade, I know you love your sister, and I do too! I take full responsibility for hurting her, and I'm going to spend as long as I can to make it up to her, but if you come at me again, I'm going to snap your fucking neck into several pieces," I spoke to him. "Now, did my baby leave a note," I asked him again.

"Phoenix Allen Bailey, put him down! NOW!" I heard my mom scream, but I ignored her. She must have just walked into the door.

"Lewis fam⊠oh," the doctor said, and I threw Kade to the ground, trying to catch his breath. I helped him up and patted him on his head, while he was still rubbing his throat.

We all rushed in front of the doctor, and he was looking around at all of us. His eyes landed on my face and dried up blood on my t-shirt that I used to wipe my face with.

"I'm Dr. Compton, and sir, maybe someone should look at your face," he said.

"No, I'm fine. Talk to us. What's going on?" I replied to him.

"Well, I need to speak with immediate family only. We need to talk in the privacy of my office."

"We are all immediate family except for that Poindexter in the suit," I said to the doctor.

"My name is Elliot Stone, and I am the family lawyer, and I need to go back so I can stay in the loop of everything, and make sure the right thing is said to the press," he said.

"Nigga, you ain't finna use Kam and her situation for some fucking camera time, ol' square ass nigga. You got me fucked up. This shit need to be kept private, and I mean that shit," I eyed him.

"Y'all ain't shit to my daughter! Doctor, I don't want them to go back," Judge Kason snapped.

"Honey, calm down!" Tracey said patting him on his back.

"Yeah, calm your husband down Tracey, before he gets his feelings hurt up in this bitch!" I said to her. "Doctor, lead the fucking way."

The doctor looked a little scared, but he turned around and led us the way to his office. We all filed into his office, and he sat behind the desk. There were only a few seats in the room, so the ladies took the seats. I stood next to my mom, and she held on to my hand, while my dad stood on the other side of her. Tracey was sitting in the other seat, and Kason and Elliot were standing on both sides of her. Basically, we were glaring at each other like we were waiting for something to pop off. Shelly, Kalena, and Kade were in front of the desk.

"Well, um, we were able to get Ms. Kambridge stable. She swallowed a great deal of sleeping pills, but—"

"Doctor, did my baby survive?" I cut him off.

"Your fucking baby? Is my baby fucking pregnant?" Kason snapped.

"Hell yeah, my baby is pregnant? Anything else?" I asked him with my head cocked to the side.

"LOOK! I need both sides of the family to keep quiet. If not, I will ask everyone to leave, but the person who is the sanest and qualified to make health decisions for her. Do I make myself clear? One more outburst from either of you," he pointed his pencil at me and Kason. "You guys are gone! Kason, you may have your own courtroom, but this here office, is my courtroom where I am the judge and the jury. Understand?"

Kason nodded his head in agreement, and he looked for me to do the same, and I did.

"I was getting to the baby next. Kambridge was five weeks pregnant, but the baby did not survive."

My legs gave out from under me, and luckily my brother caught me. My mom got up, and my brother put me in the chair. My eyes were cloudy, and the tears started flowing down my face. My first chance of being a father was gone, all because of me!

"The baby wouldn't have survived anyway, which leads me to the next thing," Dr. Compton said.

"Damn, doctor! How many fucking *next things* are you going to say? damn!" Kade snapped.

"Testing Kambridge's blood, we found an extensive amount of *mercury* poisoning. Sometimes you can accidentally ingest it, but the amounts that are in her system, was no accident, in my professional opinion. Someone was poisoning her," he said, looking around the room at everyone, and then he pressed a button on his phone.

Two seconds later, two policemen and a lady in a black suit walked in the room.

"All of you are suspects in this investigation, so you guys will be questioned thoroughly, until this investigation is over."

"Doctor, I'm confused. How the fuck can somebody get mercury poisoning? I been with her months, and she didn't seem different. Well she would randomly get sick, but then it would go away. I don't know. What are the symptoms?"

"Well, Mr. Bailey, a few of the very noticeable symptoms are nausea, personality changes—"

"Dizziness and headaches?" I finished his statement.

"You would be correct, sir."

"We went to St. Maarten a couple months back, and that's when she first started acting strange. I begged her to go to the doctor, and she said that she was fine. She said the headaches come and go, so that's why she didn't go to the doctor. She almost passed out one time, and then she would snap suddenly. I shrugged it off because that's how women are. You mean to tell me, the whole time, my wife was sick!" I questioned.

"EXCUSE ME? WHAT THE FUCK DID YOU JUST SAY? YOUR WHO?" Kason yelled.

"Now is not the time for personal matters, gentlemen. Due to the extensive amounts of poison in her system, it caused her kidneys to fail. They were already in the process of failing, but the pills that she swallowed sped it up. We have her in an induced coma because she will be in too much pain if I wake her up. I am in the process of placing her on the donor list. Do either one of you want to get tested?" the doctor said.

That nigga just told me that my wife is in a fucking coma, and then casually asked us if we wanted to get tested. The room was silent as fuck; you could hear a needle drop on the floor. I'm assuming that everyone was in their own feelings, but I fucking lost it.

I stood up and pointed at Tracey, "Bitch, it was you! It was you who poisoned my fucking wife. I don't even think Kason hoe ass could do something so cynical. The most he would do is beat her until she passed out, but you... you're so fucking stupid, you would kill your own daughter," I snapped.

"You got me fucked up. I love my daughter, I would never do anything to fucking hurt her. You raggedy, dumb ass hoe! It was you who poisoned her. You couldn't have her, so you didn't want nobody else to have her," she spat right back.

"Hold up, bitch! You better watch your mothafuckin' mouth. Talking to my fucking son like his mama won't beat the brakes off your stupid ass," my mama said walking towards her, but my dad and brother held her back.

"Nigga, you better hold your fucking wife. I know that fucking much!" Kason said.

"Nigga, shut your weak ass the fuck up! You ain't gon do shit but try to have us arrested. You better be glad I won't let my wife attack her hoe ass. You better keep it together, my nigga!" my dad snapped.

"GENTLEMEN! THE LONGER YOU HAVE THIS PISSING MATCH, THE MORE YOU PUT KAMBRIDGE'S HEALTH IN DANGER! NOW, PLEASE! WHO ALL WANTS TO GET TESTED?!" the doctor shouted, getting our attention, and we all looked at him.

"You can test me!" I said, and everybody followed suit.

"Okay, I'm only going to allow one side of the family in Kambridge's room, and test the other side, and then we are going to switch."

"They ain't her fucking family, and they shouldn't be tested for shit," her dad growled.

"You know what, old man? Let me hurt your feelings right quick. Me and Kambridge been married for two months now. We got married in St. Maarten, and if you don't believe me, call your lil' buddies down at the courthouse, and see. Now, if you make one more smart remark, I will have you *and* your wife escorted off the fucking premises, seeing as how I am her next of kin. Ask your lil' puss' ass lawyer."

Kason looked from their lawyer back to the doctor, and they both were nodding their heads in full agreement with me. When he looked back at me, I was wearing a smirk that I'm sure made his temperature rise.

"Now, I'm going to test the Lewis family first, and the Bailey family is going to go into her room," the doctor said.

"We will also question the Bailey family first, as well. Oh, I'm Olivia Bradshaw by the way. I'm with Adult Protective Services. We normally only work for elders, but this case is complicated, and it seems as if everyone is pointing the finger at each other. Until this investigation is over, Kambridge is going to have around the clock protection in her room," Olivia spoke.

"Lewis family, you guys stay here, and I'm going to walk the Bailey family down to her room."

We followed the doctor down to her room, and the minute we walked into the room, I broke down. My dad and brother had to catch me again. My mom pulled a chair up close to the bed, and they helped me to the chair. I fell over her and bawled my eyes out like a bitch. I couldn't help it. It seemed like the wires were coming out of every part of her body.

"My baby," I said placing my hands on her stomach, even though her stomach was empty now. "I'm so sorry. Daddy is such a fuck up. I caused your mama to lose you. It's all my fault. I'm so sorry," I cried. I rubbed my fingers through her hair. "Kambridge, Daddy is so fucking sorry. I wanted to tell you. I should have told you, but I knew you would leave me. I just couldn't have that. I need you, Kam. None of those women meant shit to me. Please come back to me. I'll give you my heart, if you need it to live baby! Damn!" I continued to cry my eyes out.

"Son, we are going to give you a minute alone with her," my dad said, latching on to my shoulder.

I looked up at him, and he wiped my tears away from my eyes, but they kept falling. At first I thought that he was getting ready to say something crazy, like get over it, but he just stared at me.

"Dad," I whispered to him.

"Yeah, son," he answered me.

"Don't go. I need you," my voice scratched.

I had never said those words to my dad ever. It was always something along the lines of, I don't need you. The moment I said those words, Mayhem pulled the other chair close, and my dad sat down next to me. I leaned over on his shoulder and continued to cry my eyes out. He rubbed his hand through my hair, and then started patting my shoulder.

"It's going to be alright, son. It's going to be alright," my dad said.

My dad had never said anything remotely close to me, so, to hear him say that, soothed me... just for the moment.

Cat

I felt so accomplished today, and especially since I had that package mailed to little Miss Kambridge. See, I wasn't going to bother her, and I was just going to give it to Malice to let him know I had it, but when he had me escorted out of that Ball, I was pissed. I was even more pissed when I saw how everyone was fucking gawking over her when she stepped her ass into the Ball, looking how she was looking. I mean, every fucking eye was on her, which had me furious.

I was waiting for a text or phone call from Malice, because I'm sure that she has already mentioned to him that she got the package. The knock on the door was just what I was waiting on. I'm sure that it was Malice, but I was surprised that he didn't use his key. I walked to the door with a smirk on my face, with my robe halfway open, and pulled the door open. It was Connor, holding a piece of paper in his hand, with a goofy smile on his face. I had forgotten that I had given him and his co-workers my address a few weeks back to put down for references.

"Yes, how may I help you?" I said to him.

"My license came, and I just wanted to personally thank you for helping us," he said, looking me up and down. I closed my robe and let him in the house.

"You are living large as fuck! Damn, I can't wait until I'm able to retire," he said, looking around my house.

"It's really not all that it's cracked up to be. Can I ask you a question? A real serious question."

"Yeah," he turned, and looked at me.

"Did you know that Kambridge was married?"

He looked at me with a shocked look on his face.

"We must be talking about two different Kambridge's because my Kambridge is probably still somewhere crying over me because we broke up. Shit, me and her were together for ten years, and we JUST broke up not even six months ago. There is no way that she can be married," he said.

"Well, I hate to be the bearer of bad news, but she got married to my boy toy. They got married in St. Maarten like a couple of months ago. I'm so serious. At the most, they probably have been married for like two months. No more than that. I don't know how they met. I don't care how they met, but they are pretty much married. I've done everything I can to break them up, but he ain't leaving her for shit, and get this...he's fucking her mom too," I told him, chuckling at the situation.

He had a look of confusion on his face.

"You know what? The last dinner I had with her family, I eavesdropped on a conversation that they were having, and Judge Kason was telling her to use somebody for him and get information, but I honestly didn't think anything of it," he said, taking a seat in the chair that was closest to him. "FUCK! I was giving her a chance to be mad, and I was going to get her back, but it seems like it's too late," he sounded defeated.

"Nah, it's not too late, trust me. After that package I sent to her store today, she will be divorcing him tomorrow sometime. If that bitch stay with him after she finds out that he fucked her mom, then she is desperate as fuck."

"'Bout as desperate as you sound right now," he said.

I rolled my eyes at him because it probably was going to be hard as fuck to get my plan rolling. I sat in the chair across from him and let my robe come open some more. His eyes trailed my body, and I knew I had him.

"You want to come to my bedroom?" I asked him.

"You're like, as old as my mom, Ms. Jenson," he reluctantly said.

"Do you care? I don't. Are you following me or not?"

He followed me to my bedroom, and he slowly started getting undressed. I let my robe fall, and I guess I looked good to him because I saw his dick start to stand up in his briefs. I laid on the bed and spread my legs. He dove between my legs, pulling my panties to the side, and started eating me as if his life depended on it.

I tried to close my eyes and imagine that it was Malice's lips wrapped around my clit, but I couldn't. The only reason I came was because he pushed two fingers inside of me and finger fucked me. I needed that release because I hadn't had sex since Malice, and I was backed up. He pulled his dick out of his briefs, and I instantly felt sick to my stomach. His shit was kind of long and skinny. There is no way that he would give me an orgasm because I been used to fucking Malice over the last decade.

"You got a condom?" I asked him.

"Shit! No, I don't!" he said.

"Oh, sorry. No glove, no love!" I said, thankful that I had a legit reason to not fuck him.

While he was putting on his clothes, I grabbed the remote and turned the TV on. I always watch the news, and the first thing I see was Kam's face on the screen.

Three hours later, and there is still no word on Judge Kason's daughter, Kambridge Lewis', alleged suicide. We are waiting for anyone to give us a word on if she followed through with the suicide, or if she is alive. Earlier, we ran a video of Judge Kason and his son, Kade Lewis, getting into an altercation. Once again, the audio is bad, but what we could make out is that Judge Kason and his wife showed up hours later after getting the call that Kambridge allegedly committed suicide. The family lawyer, Elliot Stone, made an announcement stating that emotions are running high, as we can imagine, and that they wanted to handle this matter privately. We will continue to update you on this story.

Connor and I both looked at each other, and he leaped on me. He got his hands around my throat, and he was squeezing tight.

"It's your fucking fault! My girl could be dead because of you," he growled, while still choking me.

My eyes darted around to see if there was something that I could gather to knock him in the head with, but he's a lawyer. He knew what I was trying to do, so he moved me to the middle of the bed and started choking me harder.

"If you come near me or Kambridge again you will not live to see it," he said.

He released me, and I tried to catch my breath. I couldn't even talk momentarily because my throat was hurting.

"Now this is the second man that has walked out on you for that girl! Bitch!" he said, and walked out the house.

The tears sprang into my eyes and slowly slid down the sides. If she wasn't dead, I was going to kill her. I know that Malice can't live without her, so I was going to have to kill him. I can't live without Malice, so I was going to have to kill myself. Life is truly fucked up, but in the end, I'll have what I want.

Malice

 *T*his waiting game that we were playing with the doctors had my anxiety on a million. I ain't want to take one step out the hospital to smoke, because I ain't want to miss a thing. I needed to know what was going on with my wife. I was pacing this conference room floor so much that I had made my own tracks into the carpeted floor. After extensive questioning from Olivia, and getting tested to see if I was a match for Kam, they placed us all in this conference room. He put a rush on the lab results so we would know today if we were a match for her.

The whole room was quiet, and I assumed that everyone was in their own thoughts. My dad and Kason glared at each other, but nothing was going to pop off because we had two of the hospital's security guards, Olivia, and the two policemen that came with her, in the room with us. Dr. Compton said he didn't trust us to all sit in here and act like we got a little common sense, so that's why we had these pigs watching over us like we were some fucking kids.

"I remember when I first met Kambridge☒" I started.

"You ain't finna talk about my sister like she dead, my nigga!" Kade said, and stood up.

I stopped pacing and looked at him. The police hands went to their waist, and we instantly calmed down, but something was bothering me. I had to get it off my chest.

"Kason, why do you beat Kambridge? What did she ever do to you?" I asked him. "You have so much hatred in your heart, and it's so sad, that you are going to die a lonely old man." He ain't say nothing to me, but I noticed Olivia in the corner writing on her notepad.

"You don't know me or nothing about my life. Sit down, and shut the fuck up!" he snapped.

"I know I don't know nothing about your life, but I do know that one of your daughters got married and was terrified to tell you. No daughter should be that terrified of her dad. I do know that when I first met her she had several lacerations on her body. I do know that you keep your kids locked up in the house like they are some fucking servants, and my wife is grown, but you won't let her move out on her own. I am perfectly capable of taking care of—"

"YOU AIN'T PERFECTLY CAPABLE OF TAKING CARE OF SHIT! YOU ARE JUST LIKE YOUR PIECE OF SHIT ASS FATHER. YOU WILL DIVORCE MY DAUGHTER, AND YOU WILL LEAVE HER THE FUCK ALONE!" her daddy snapped.

"Kason, I think you have us mixed up. My kids are free to go as they please. I think you told Kambridge that her and her brother had to stay under your roof, because of people who may want to retaliate against you. I would like to think that I am an important man...much like yourself, and again, my kids are free to go as they please," my dad said, not giving him the satisfaction of getting loud with him.

He was getting ready to reply when this white boy came barreling into the door. We all looked at him, and I cut my eyes at Kason, and he had a smirk on his face. He stood and greeted him.

"Hey, son!" he spoke.

"Uh, hey, Judge Kason. I saw on the news that Kam tried to kill herself. The news is not saying anything else. I came as fast as I could," he said.

"This," he patted him on his back, "is my real son-in-law, Connor Wiles. Him and my daughter have been together since they were just teenagers. Everything she has with you, is fake. She was using you... for me. She never loved you. All of that was fake and part of the plan I had to arrest all of you, and put you behind bars where all of you wild animals belong," he said like there wasn't cops in the room, who could easily be taping this shit. His lawyer was dumb as fuck not telling him to shut up. He was talking so freely so these pigs may or may not be on his payroll, because Kason is a dummy, but I know he's not *that* big of a dummy.

I stopped pacing the floor, and I ended up between where my dad and brother were sitting. My hands clenched at my sides. I could feel my nails digging into my skin. My heart rate started to rise. This was the part of me that I try to keep hidden, but he was taking me there. Mayhem stood up and grabbed my head, leaning me into him so he could whisper in my ear.

"Look, he's just trying to get a rise out of you. Don't let him win. You know where Kambridge's heart lies, and it is with you. Don't let him win. Do...not...let...him...in...your...head. Understand me?"

I nodded my head quickly, but I was still pissed as fuck. All that is lies, or could it be? I don't know. The wheels were starting to turn in my head. I have been through her phone before, hell, I even have the passcode to it, and there were no signs of her having a boyfriend. He's lying. Mayhem is right, he is just trying to get in my head. He will say anything to get me to leave her alone, but that's not going to happen.

"He's lying," Shelly softly said, and started crying. "They haven't been together, and the last time she saw him was when he came to her store and threatened her."

"What? What are you talking about Shelly?" I asked her. "Who threatened who, and for what?"

"She's lying!" Connor said. "Kam and I had been talking quite frequently. We were even going to go on a date next week."

Before I could pop off, the doctor came in the room. I took the seat next to my mom.

"I hope everyone in here was behaving like adults should behave," Dr. Compton said, sitting at the front of the table.

"Well, we got the results back, and I'm sorry, but none of you are a match. So, we've placed her on the transplant list, but we are going to have to get those kidneys out of her body because they are going to release several toxins into her body that we don't need in there, especially since all the poison is not out of her system. Once we get both kidneys out of her body, we are going to have to do around the clock dialysis for her."

I didn't even think I had any tears left, but my eyes welled up with tears.

"Okay, so let's do the surgery. What the fuck is the problem?" Kade said.

"There is a problem. If we operate on her with all the poison that's in her system, it could kill her, but if we don't get the kidneys out of her body, it can kill her as well. MY professional opinion would be to wait until the poison is out of her body, and we can deal with the toxins later, but ultimately it is your call."

"Basically, she's damned if you do, or damned if you don't," I said.

He nodded his head, and I instantly became frustrated. I looked over at Tracey, and this bitch don't even look like she had an ounce of remorse on her face. She was staring at the spot on the table in front of her with a blank look on her face. I went slap off on her.

"Bitch, this is all your fault! Everything is all your fault!" I snapped.

"You better watch your fucking mouth, boy!" Kason said. "Kade, you gon' let this piece of shit talk to your mom like this?"

"I don't give a fuck about neither one of y'all to be honest. He can say whatever the fuck he wants to say. That's his wife. He is going through it just like the rest of us," Kade replied to him.

"Ain't this a bitch!" Kason said.

"Tracey... because you couldn't have me, you tried to kill my wife. You are such a hater, and that's not becoming of a woman," I snapped.

"My wife wouldn't fuck a scrub like you. Stop trying to piss me off because it ain't happening," Kason said. "You just mad that you got played by me and my daughter."

"Don't get your feelings hurt, Judge!" Mayhem said.

"Check your bank accounts if you think she ain't been paying me to—" I started.

"GENTLEMEN! YOUR DAUGHTER," he glared at Kason, "AND YOUR WIFE," he looked at me, "IS DYING BY THE FUCKING MINUTE, AND ALL YOU CAN DO IS SIT HERE AND ARGUE ABOUT WHO'S FUCKING WHO! I HAVE NEVER BEEN THIS UNPROFESSIONAL IN MY LIFE. CALM THE FUCK DOWN! THERE IS A BABY GIRL IN THIS ROOM WHO STARTS CRYING EVERY TIME YOU GUYS ARGUE, AND NEITHER OF YOU STOP TO THINK ABOUT HOW SHE FEELS," Dr. Compton shouted, and we glared at each other.

"Now, Mr. Bailey, you have a decision to make. Do you want us to operate now or later? I gave you my professional opinion, but ultimately, it is up to you since you are her next of kin. You still have several pieces of paper to fill out. Also, would you like to sign a Do Not Resuscitate, if in fact something goes wrong?"

He kept talking about the pros and the cons of having the surgery today, or having the surgery a few days from today. While he was talking, I was thinking about losing my wife. I was thinking about having to spend the rest of my life without her, and not even being able to physically apologize to her. I needed her to know that I apologize for what I did, and not telling her about it. I needed her to know that I never ever cheated on her since we got married. I stopped fucking with them women the minute I found out that her mother was my client. I just needed to apologize to her. If God ever gave me another chance with her, I promise I will tell her the truth about everything, even if it hurts her feelings.

Where would I find another woman like Kam. A woman who

could make me fall in love with her so fast. A woman who only wants everyone to be happy. A woman who doesn't give a damn about status or money. There would never be another woman like Kambridge...at least not for me. I will never love another woman the way that I love Kambridge. She fucked me up inside, and I don't know if I will ever be the same.

"Mr. Bailey," Dr. Compton called my name. "Did you hear what I said?"

I nodded my head slowly.

"Have you made a decision, or do you need a few more minutes?"

Before I could even respond, Kason popped off again.

"What the fuck is there to decide? It's either a fucking yes or a fucking no. Doc, do the fucking surgery now."

"If he does the fucking surgery now, then she will die from the poisoning, but then again, that's probably what you and your bitch of a wife want huh? You don't want all of your dirty little secrets to get out," I replied to him. "Because you know, once she wakes up, the whole world will know all your secrets, and they will shun both of you. Your reputations are done for."

"Fuck you! You think I give a fuck about you, your family, or the public, and what they would say about mine?"

"Yeah, I'm sure you would once they find out that your hoe ass wife pays for male escorts. I'm sure I have gotten about twenty stacks from her over the last few months. She PAID me to do something you couldn't do, and that's make her squirt. Let that sink in," I snapped at him. "I need everybody out. I need to think about this shit, and I need to do it in silence," I said.

The room got deathly quiet. Everybody's mouth was opened, but nothing came out of it. I was looking at Kason with a smirk on my face.

"Okay, Mr. Bailey," Dr. Compton said. "I understand, and I don't want you to rush and make a decision. I'll be in my office whenever you have made your decision. I'll leave all this paperwork here so you can go over it, and if you have any questions about anything, you know where to find me."

Everyone stood up to leave out the room so I can think in peace and sign these damn papers, when the door came open.

"You can test me," the deep voice said from the door.

My mouth hit the floor like I had just seen a ghost.

Trent 'Big Will' Wilson

I was in my cell staring at the ceiling with my hands clasped behind my head. My mind was on my daughter, and her husband, my godson. The secrets he dropped on me during their visit weighed heavy on my mind. A part of me wished that he didn't tell her because my daughter is fragile, and another part of me wanted him to tell her because I wanted him to be a man that takes responsibility for his actions, even though they may cause harm to the person. My phone that was under my pillow started vibrating. I took it out, and it was big bro calling me.

"What up, bro?" I answered.

I looked up to see that the door was open, but I ain't give a fuck. Nobody in here fucks with me, even the guards.

"Um, I know you probably can't do much about this shit, but I just stepped out the hospital to give you a call. Um, I don't know how to say this, but—" his voice cracked.

"Nigga, you crying," I chuckled.

"Um, I'm trying to stay strong for your godson. Um, shit kind of hit the fan with his... you know, and Kam..." I heard him sniff.

I sat up in my bed because I've only known my big bro to have cried twice in his life, and that's when the birth of his kids took place, so I was fucking worried.

"Nigga, you scaring me. What the fuck is going on?" I whispered.

"Kam allegedly committed suicide. The doctors haven't come out to give us a word yet. It's been hours. I just wanted to let you know," he said. "I know you can't do nothing in there, but... bro. I'm so sorry. I'll keep you updated," he said.

I hung up the phone and jumped off the bed to hurl in the fucking toilet. I was on my knees, trying not to cry. I walked out my cell and headed towards the Warden's office. I was walking so fast that I ignored everybody that was calling my name. I wanted to cry. I needed to cry. My baby girl may or may not be fighting for her life, and I'm in here and can't do shit about it. The CO stopped me at the warden's door.

"Big Will, what's good, man? Warden on the phone, but I'll tell him that you need to see him. Give me a minute," the CO said, and walked in the door.

Five minutes later, he opened the door and ushered me in. I didn't say anything until the CO stepped out.

"Big Will, what can I do for you?" he asked.

"I need you to let me out of here. I don't care what you do, or how you do it, but I need you to let me out of here. I will come back, you have my word," I said.

"Now, Wilson. You know I can't do that."

"My daughter has allegedly committed suicide, and I need to be there. You don't have to get the Governor involved in this. Pardon me for just twenty-four hours. I will come back. Give me an ankle monitor. A security escort. I need to be with my daughter," I begged, with tears streaming down my face. I was on the verge of having a nervous

43

breakdown.

"Your daughter? I didn't know you had any kids. Sit down, Wilson. You're scaring me."

"Look. I don't have time to go into the full spiel, but long story short, Judge Kason's oldest daughter is really my daughter, and he is the reason why I am behind bars today," I said.

"Oh wow!" he said shockingly.

He clicked on the TV, and it was playing a video of the Judge and his oldest son getting into a spat.

We have been running this clip every thirty minutes. The audio is not good, but what we got from the clip is that Judge Kason and his wife Tracey showed up to the hospital two hours after getting the call that Kambridge Lewis allegedly committed suicide, and his son Kade Lewis was not happy about it. Say what now? Alright. This just in... Sources from inside the hospital have said that Judge Kason's daughter, Kambridge Lewis, survived the alleged suicide, but is in an induced coma because of kidney failure. We will keep you updated on this story.

My heart touched my damn feet. I couldn't really think or breathe.

"Warden, twenty-four hours is all I need. I know this may be asking too much, but until they get a bed for me in Arkansas, can I be pardoned? I promise you, I won't fuck up. I won't get in trouble. Shit, I'll even come back in this bitch for the weekends. Please. This may be my last chance to get to know my daughter," I continued to plead my case.

"Wilson. You are tying my hands here. If I do this for you, I would have to do that for every prisoner in the fucking pen. Wilson, I just can't do it," he said. "I have a daughter, so I know how it—"

"NO, THE FUCK YOU DON'T! YOU GET TO GO HOME TO YOUR DAUGHTER EVERY FUCKING NIGHT. NOT ME! I BEEN LOCKED IN THIS BITCH FOR TWENTY-TWO YEARS. TWENTY-FUCKING-TWO. I HAVE NOT BEEN IN ONE FIGHT! I HAVE NOT SPENT ONE NIGHT IN THE HOLE. IF ANYTHING, I MAKE YOUR JOB EASIER AS A WARDEN BECAUSE I KEEP THE PEACE AROUND HERE. IF YOU DON'T DO SHIT ELSE FOR ME, YOU CAN DO THIS. ALL I WANT TO DO IS SPEND TIME WITH MY DAUGHTER BEFORE SHE FUCKING DIES! I JUST WANT HER TO KNOW WHO I AM. ALL I AM ASKING FOR IS SIX MONTHS. SIX! I WILL DO WHATEVER YOU NEED ME TO DO. WEAR AN ANKLE MONITOR. CALL YOU EVERY DAY. SEE ONE OF YOUR PEOPLE TO TEST ME. ANYTHING. IT WILL BE OUR SECRET," I yelled.

He had a scared look on his face, and I don't know if I got through to him or not, but he was quiet. I left out of his office and went back to my cell. I used my phone to try and call my brother, but he ain't answer, but he sent a text. I hated texting.

K: Can't talk right now, bro. Getting tested to see if I'm a match for your daughter's kidney surgery she gotta have asap. So much going on. Gotta tell you 'bout dis shit.

Me: My nigga. Thank you, bro. Knowing that you would give my daughter a kidney... I'm crying right now, dawg. I'm eternally grateful. I owe you one, family.

He didn't text me back, so I put the phone back under my pillow and laid down. I ain't know what I was feeling, but I needed to pray. I closed my eyes and said a silent prayer for my daughter. In the middle of my prayer, I felt some clothes being thrown on me. I opened my eyes to see a CO standing over me with a smirk on his face.

"Get dressed, and come in the Warden's office," he said, and walked out.

I held up the clothes, and it was a pair of Levi jeans and a polo shirt. I hurried up and got dressed, and surprisingly the clothes fit perfect. I don't know where they came from, and I didn't have time to question it. I grabbed my phone from under the pillow and slipped it in my pocket. I ran into the warden's office, and he was sitting there signing papers.

"Oh, the clothes fit nicely. I ain't know you and I would be the same size. I keep an extra fit here sometimes, but never mind all of that. My heart goes out to you, and I would die if something like this happened to my daughter while I was locked away. Now, I'm going to grant you the six months. Don't you get out there and get happy nigga, because you gotta come back. I have this ankle monitor that I wanted to put on you, but I trust you, Wilson, but IF YOU FUCK ME ON THIS, I will make sure you never see the light of day again. Twenty-four hour lock down."

"What about Kason? He will be there. He sentenced me to life in prison," I asked. "Won't you get fired?"

"No. Turns out I came across a few things that the Governor would not like for his wife or the public to find out. So, everything is squared away on my end. You just better be glad that you have been a model prisoner, and I hate how you ended up in here. Brother to brother, I wish I could let most of y'all out of here, but that's life."

He handed me a piece of paper and walked me out to the front gate. It was a truck out there, and I turned to look at him.

"A favor from me. Go take care of your daughter, Wilson. Remember six months from today, you bring your black ass back here. If I have to come looking for you, you are going to regret it," he said.

I got in the truck, and as the driver rode through the streets of Chicago, I could see that shit had changed...tremendously. I ain't even know what the fuck to make of this shit. The last ride I ever been on was being transported here from the jail downtown. I never thought I would see this shit again. When we pulled up to the hospital, there were people with cameras outside and shit.

"Treating my baby like she's some fucking freak show," I whispered to myself. "Thanks, bro," I thanked the guy who dropped me off in front of the hospital.

I walked in the hospital over to the front desk.

"Hey, my name is Trent Wilson, and I'm looking for the family of Kambridge Bailey or Lewis," I said to her.

"Right this way. I think they are the in the conference room," the lady said.

When we were headed towards the conference room, I suddenly started to feel like I was having a panic attack. I was getting ready to face the woman that I once loved, and the man that I hated for putting me in jail. This shit was happening too fucking fast for me, and I just needed to breathe. We arrived at the conference room, and I could hear my godson raising HELL! That nigga was hollering at the top of his fucking lungs. I took a couple of deep breaths, and I felt my temperature rising.

"Chill, Wilson!" I gave myself a pep talk.

Hol' up, did they say poisoning? What the fuck is going on? I thought to myself. The doctor was talking about no one being a match, and I lost it. I opened the door and walked in.

"You can test me," I startled the room.

The room was quiet as fuck. Tracey, Kason, Korupt, Angela, Mayhem, and Malice, all were staring at me like they had seen a ghost. You could seriously hear their fucking thoughts because it was so quiet in the room. There were even a couple of white people in the room, who must have been her classmates, there supporting her. I'm sure the extra policemen and security guards were in the room because they probably fought before I got here. I would get the scoop on the other lady in the room later.

"Who are you?" he asked flipping through the papers that were sitting in front of him.

"My name is Trent Wilson, and I am Kambridge Bailey's father," I spoke with pride. "Biologically. I just got out of prison, but I can assure you that my blood is okay to test. No funny business has been going on. I eat good, and I have not gotten any tattoos while I was in there," I said.

The doctor looked blown away as he sat back in his seat, and let out a deep sigh.

"Dad, what is he talking about?" Kade asked, looking at me, but addressing Kason.

"Mr. Wilson, follow me, please. It's only going to take about twenty minutes, and maybe thirty or so minutes to be done with the matching process," the doctor said, sensing what was about to happen.

I followed him out the conference room and into a cold ass room. He asked me what seemed like a hundred fucking questions, and then set me up for my blood to be drawn. I hated needles, but my daughter was in my mind. I could look him in his face, and I could tell that he had so many questions, but didn't want to ask. I was glad, because I ain't feel like talking.

"Um, Mr. Wilson, you are all done here. Would you like to see your... your daughter, or would you like to go back to the conference room and wait for testing to be finished? I'm Dr. Compton by the way," he shook my hand.

"I want to see her. I feel a little weak, though."

He nodded his head and led me to my daughter's room, and the minute I saw my baby hooked up to all those fucking machines, I started crying. I kissed her several times on her forehead and rubbed my fingers through her hair. She is so fucking beautiful. At least me and her mom got something right. He left me alone for a few moments, and brought me back some juice and some crackers.

"Doctor, I got to get out of here. I can't see her like this. Take me back to the conference room."

I kissed her one more time before I followed the doctor back out of the room.

"So, doctor, what is going on with my daughter? Like, what

happened. Give me the real, and not no doctor shit that I can't understand."

"Well, Mr. Wilson. Your daughter swallowed a lot of sleeping pills and tried to kill herself. After testing her blood, we found out that she was pregnant, but the baby didn't survive. Further testing proved that she had several large amounts of mercury poisoning in her system, which caused her kidneys to fail. I don't want to make light of the situation, but had Kambridge not tried to kill herself, we wouldn't have been able to stop the spreading of it, and she would have dropped dead. So, we had to call the police and Adult Protective Services to question everyone in the family, hence the lady in the pant suit in the room with the police officers. Her name is Olivia Bradshaw."

I didn't have anything to say, but I saw nothing but red in my eyes. I was ready to kill someone. He told me that he was about to go look at the results of my test, and he would be back. I walked back in the room, and the conversation that was taking place quickly ceased. I'm sure it was about me. I sat at the head of the table in Dr. Compton's seat. It was like all eyes were on me, waiting for me to say something.

"Uncle, how the fuck did you—"

I held my hand up to stop Malice from speaking.

"I have one question, and if I don't get an answer that satisfies me, I'm not sure how I'm going to react. Who the fuck poisoned my daughter?" I asked the room, and it got quiet.

"Hol' up! Who the fuck you think you are, coming in here talking like you some big shot, questioning us? You coming in here talking about you my sister's daddy. You ain't shit to my sister," Kade snapped at me, and I chuckled.

"Oh, lil' Kade. I remember when you were just a tyke. You and Malice won't remember this, but when your mom used to come over my house, and get her BACK blown out, you two would be in the living room playing. You guys had to be around five or six," I said.

Malice and Kade looked at each other like they tried to remember, but I'm sure they wouldn't.

"TRACEY! Say something!" Kade snapped at her. "Tell me that he is lying, right now!"

Kason looked like he wanted to blow a gasket, but had to choose his words wisely. I'm sure he didn't want this secret out, but oh well. You can't take shit to the grave, but your body. Tracey stared at the table, not looking at nobody in the fucking room. She looked guilty, and then her ass burst into tears, but I ain't give one fuck about it.

"Tracey, twenty-three years ago, those tears would have had me trying to move a mountain girl. I loved you, but why did you harm my daughter...our daughter? The one that we laid down and made from love. At least I thought it was love. Was it because you found some new satisfying dick in my nephew over there, and couldn't handle that your daughter was getting it, for free might I add, and then he married her? You were jealous of our daughter so bad that you wanted to kill her so you could have Malice, huh? Sweetie, look at me. Did you do this to our daughter? Did you poison our daughter?" I asked her.

Boom! She slammed her hand down on the table and stood up.

"I'M SICK OF EVERY MOTHAFUCKIN' BODY IN THIS ROOM TRYING TO ACCUSE ME OF POISONING MY DAUGHTER. I

LOVE MY DAUGHTER, AND I WOULD NEVER EVER HURT HER! SINCE YOU TRYING TO OUT ME, I'LL OUT MY DAMN SELF. YES, I FUCKED TRENT, AND KAMBRIDGE IS HIS DAUGHTER! YES, I LOVED YOU TRENT! YES, I FUCKED MALICE AND I PAID HIM FOR IT. IT WAS WELL WORTH IT. CALL ME ALL TYPES OF BITCHES AND HOES, BUT DON'T ASK ME AGAIN IF I TRIED TO POISON MY DAUGHTER!" she screamed through her tears.

She started gathering her things. I guess she called herself throwing a tantrum. She stomped towards the door.

"Tracey, sweetie, all we wanted was the—"

"FUCK YOU, TRENT!" she walked out the door and slammed it.

"Well, that was quite the outburst. Who's next to go? Kason, you feel like talking now? Does the cat still have your tongue? Was it you who poisoned *my* daughter?" I asked him.

I made sure to put an emphasis on 'my'.

"Trent, don't fucking say shit to me, weak ass nigga. You still ain't shit! On papers, Kambridge is my daughter, and always and forever will be. She calls me Daddy. She will never call you Daddy. Everything she has is because of me."

"Including those scars on her body," I asked looking at him. "You the weak ass nigga. Beat up on a girl who's two times smaller than you. Pathetic. Because what? She doesn't share your DNA? Shame on you."

We both stood up at the same time, and some stupid nigga in a suit grabbed him, and since Mayhem was the closest to me, he grabbed me. He was smirking at me, and I winked at him. Kason is jumping bad because it's some officers in here. He better be glad I promised the

Warden that I wouldn't get in any trouble while I was out here. The doctor walking in the room interrupted our stare down.

"Mr. Wilson, you are the perfect match. We have some papers that we would like for you to sign, and after that, we will wait a couple more days and have the surgery," Dr. Compton said.

Hearing the doctor say that made me so fucking happy. I got up and followed the doctor to his office, and started going over the paperwork. They would be taking one of my kidneys and giving it to my child. They are taking both of hers out, and we both will be functioning with one kidney. There are not many cons to having one kidney, but you can't really do strenuous activities, like wrestling and shit. My old ass is too grown to be wrestling, so he won't have to worry about that. After signing all the paperwork, I went back into the conference room.

"Korupt, how fast can you get four security guards here?" I asked him.

"ASAP!"

"Do that!" I said.

He nodded his head and stepped out the room. Moments later, Korupt stepped back in the room.

"I don't think I've had the pleasure of meeting the young ladies in the room," I said. "What are your names?"

"My name is Shelby, but they call me Shelly," she spoke.

"Um, my name is... my name is," she looked down at Kason, and he was giving her the look of death, so she put her head down and didn't finish her statement.

I shook my head at Kason's bitch ass. Always have to intimidate a girl. Can't intimidate no fucking man.

"What's your name, young man?" I asked nodding my head at the other white kid in the room.

Before he answered, Kason cleared his throat, and he shut up. Before I could rile Kason back up, four men in black suits came into the room. I stood to greet them, and they had a crazy look on their face.

"Big Will? What the fuck?" one of them said.

"No time to explain. Listen. Two of you will be in my daughter's room, and two of you will stand outside. Twelve hour shifts, and four more guys will come to relieve you. No one other than anyone in nursing scrubs, and a white coat, shall enter the room. If one of you have to take a piss, you call me. If anyone other than a nurse or a doctor tries to get in that room, you call me. No one other than who I mentioned is to enter the room. Do I make myself clear?" I asked eying them.

"Excuse me, Mr. Wilson, she already has around the clock protection. She doesn't need extra security," a sweet little voice said from the other side of the room.

I whipped my head around to her, and gave her a stern look.

"Your security may work for that buster over there, and I just need people that I can trust. Sorry, sugar lump," I said giving her a weak smile, and then whipping my head back to the security guards.

"What about—" one of the security guards started.

"NOBODY," I roared. "If they are not in a white coat, or in nursing scrubs, DO NOT LET THEM IN. Again, did I make myself clear?"

They nodded their heads quickly. I told them what room she was in, and they scattered from the room.

"Okay, who's hungry," I asked them.

I walked out the room with my family on my heels, and headed towards the exit. Tracey's ass was sitting outside on the bench crying her eyes out, while the fucking reporters were surrounding her trying to get her to say something. I wanted to go choke the life out of her. Mayhem and Angela went to go pull the vehicles around, while I just stared at her. Don't get me wrong, she has aged beautifully, but I know in my heart that she did something to her.

"HEY!" I turned around, and Kade's ass tried to two-piece me, but I side-stepped him really quick, grabbing his wrist, spinning him around, and putting him in the chicken wing.

"Oww, you can't keep me... me from... owww from seeing my sister," he yelled through the pain I was inflicting on him.

The minute the reporters realized what was going on, they quickly surrounded us, and started flashing the cameras and asking questions.

"I just did. No hard feelings, but I don't trust any of you right now. I'm going to let you go, and you are going to dap me up, and walk away," I spoke through gritted teeth in his ear.

I let him go, and reluctantly he dapped me up. He walked over to Shelly and Kalena. He grabbed them both by the hand, walking right past his mom sitting on the bench crying.

"What was that about? Are you a friend of the family?" the reporters asked me.

"Ask him!" I said nodding my head at the door towards Judge Kason and that white, suited up guy; I never got his name.

I got in the car with Mayhem, Malice, and Korupt, and we drove away from the hospital.

∞

I had just finished telling Angela, Korupt, Mayhem, and Malice the reason I got out of prison, and now they were staring at me as I smashed this fucking vegan ass food. This was what I needed because I was hungry and hadn't eaten all day. They didn't want anything from this place. Dr. Compton told me that he wanted me to drink a lot of water and continue to eat healthy, and what's healthier than vegan food. I also was stuffing my damn face because I must fast a whole twenty-four hours before the surgery.

"So, you're only going to be out for six months? What type of shit is that?" Malice asked me.

"Yeah, man! I had to beg for this shit, and you know I'm not the begging type. I just pray that my daughter will accept me as her dad, and not as her uncle-in-law," I said to them.

"Mane, I know you not supposed to get in trouble, but you may have to bro. You know the only reason Kason was in that bitch as quiet as he was, because he was plotting. There is no way he is going to let you win. You know that nigga hate losing, and you pulled his card like that in front of his whole family. You know that he's not going to let you live that down," Korupt said.

"Man, when the time comes, we will do something. I'll stay alert, but for right now, I just want to focus on my daughter and get her well."

"Malice, my daughter did that to your face?"

"Hell nah, he let Kade piece his ass up in the waiting room," Mayhem chuckled.

"Look, I sent a few people out to get a place ready for you, and it should be ready for you by the time we get there. I know you want some time by yourself right now, and I know you don't want to stay in the house with us, even though you are always welcome. The house has a bomb ass security system, and you will still have security outside the house and to drive you around if you want, but you do have a car in the garage. I don't trust Kason as far as I can see him. I had a few stylists to go to mall and shit to get you stuff that I know you would need. If you ain't got everything, there is cash in the safe that is yours," Korupt said.

I nodded my head. After I finished eating, he paid, and we headed towards the house that he had for me. When we pulled up, I was amazed. This was too much house for me, but I'll only be here for six months, so I will make it work.

"Welcome home, bro! Even if it's for a little while. This is yours," Korupt said when we got out the truck.

He gave me a brotherly hug, and I could tell that nigga wanted to cry.

"Damn, man, it feels so weird to be here with you. I thought I would never get this opportunity again. Damn! We are going to make the best of this six months. I might come back and holla at you tonight. Just to catch up on shit!" he said and dapped me up.

We walked in the house, and he showed me around. This shit had five bedrooms and four bathrooms, a pool and a basketball court. The room that I was going to be sleeping in had clothes already in the closet and underwear in the drawers.

"Those clothes and shit should fit. If not, let me show you the safe," I followed Korupt into the bathroom into the linen closet.

He squatted, moved the small foot carpet out the way, and raised a few boards. He told me the code, and when he opened it there were stacks of money. He gave me two stacks of the money, and it was ten thousand dollars. We left out the bathroom, and I set the money on the dresser.

"I know they took a good chunk of your money away from you when they seized your bank accounts, but just know that whatever you need, I got it." Korupt said as if I didn't know that shit already.

I walked with him back to the door, where the boys and Angela were waiting for him. I hugged them all and watched them back out the driveway. After I set the security system, the first thing I did was take my hair out of the thick braids they were in, got naked, and jumped in the shower. This was the hottest shower that I have taken in twenty-two years. This shit felt so good. I messed around and stayed in this bitch until the water started to turn cool. I swear this is the cleanest I felt in two decades. My hair was so fucking clean, the shit was squeaking. I used the blow dryer to dry my hair. After my hair was completely dry, I jumped in the bed in my birthday suit. I knew that I was about to get some of the best sleep that I had gotten in years.

Malice

*T*oday was the day of the surgery, and I was on pins and needles. I was praying every five seconds, and I couldn't keep still. Kam was still in a coma, and luckily over eighty percent of the poison was gone out of her body, which meant that the surgery was most likely to be a success. The last two days, I been crying on and off, asking God to forgive me for not telling Kam about what I used to do. I sat in the corner of the hospital room where they had both Kam and Trent in there. They were getting ready to take them to surgery prep, and Dr. Compton was letting us have a few moments alone with them. I was twirling Kam's wedding ring around the tip of my index finger, in my own little world staring at her lifeless-like body in the bed, wondering if my wife would at least hear me out when she woke up. I even took my wedding ring away from around my neck and placed it on my finger, where it belonged in the first place.

Dr. Compton came back in the room, and told us that it was time to take our peoples down to the surgery prep. I leaned over my wife's body and whispered in her ear, while rubbing my hands through her hair.

"Kambridge Bailey, you better come back to me. I love you more than life itself, and I will do whatever I gotta do to fix this. You are my whole world, and my life only got better when you entered it. You're my heart, and I swear to God that I am so sorry that I did this to you. Daddy loves you."

I placed a kissed on her forehead and went over to dap up Trent. The nurse ushered us back into the waiting room, where Kam's piss poor ass mama and daddy was waiting, along with Shelly, Kade, Kalena, and that white dude, Connor, who is one eye roll and lip smack away from getting his ass handed to him. Make no mistakes, I didn't have a problem with Kade at all, but if he wanted to square up then we could. I looked up to see the stupid Adult Protective Services woman and her police officers there. She was about her business, and I highly doubt she was on Kason's payroll. That bitch asked me what felt like a hundred thousand questions about my life and love life with Kambridge. She been randomly questioning us since she first brought her ass here. You know this mothafucka tried to say that it could have been one of my clients who poisoned her, and I had to curse her ass out. I explained to her that most of my clients were married, and they didn't give a fuck about my personal life one way or another. I left Cat out because I had a thing or two for that bitch for ruining my life.

Placing my hand over my eyes, the tears started falling again. My dad placed his hand on my shoulder and gave me a couple of squeezes. Surprisingly, Korupt has been acting like a father should, and I feel like this is a step in the right direction. A light tap on my knee made me look up, and it was Kalena. She held her hand out, giving me a fake rose petal with some writing on it.

"This is one of my sister's favorite quotes that she made up," she said. "I hope it helps you, Phoenix." She squatted in front of me and took my hands in her small hands. Kalena is very beautiful. She looks nothing like her sister, but beautiful nonetheless, and very smart. "I know that you would never want to hurt my sister on purpose. I feel in my heart that you love her a lot. My sister has never been happier being with you. You made her glow. Find a way to make her glow again, and she will come back to you," she said, and walked away from me.

I looked at the rose petal, and it said, *Life is not a problem to be solved, but a reality to be experienced.*

I pondered in my head what that meant to her. Hopefully, I would have a chance to ask her. I was starting to get restless only an hour into the four hour surgery. My phone vibrated in my pocket, and I pulled it out.

CJ: I never meant for any of this to happen. I really hope that she pulls through. NOT! Fuck you and that bitch! I hope she dies. How fucking dare you disrespect the woman that put you on. Fuck you Malice, and fuck her! I hope she never speaks a word to your dirty dick ass again. Hoe! You are sitting in the hospital crying over a bitch that you ain't even known a year yet. I wish I could blow that bitch up, with you and that hoe in it. That's why she lost y'all baby. God don't like ugly, and you treated me like shit. So, you deserve everything you get, bitch!

I looked at my brother, and he had just read the text too. My blood pressure had just skyrocketed through the roof. I was enraged. How the fuck did she even get that information anyway? Had to be the workers in this bitch telling my wife's information.

"I'll be back," I quickly said to him, and stood up.

"No, you ain't leaving," he said, and grabbed on to my arm, pulling me back down in the chair. I was bouncing my knee up and down trying to calm myself down. Cat really don't know who she is fucking with. I'mma end up killing that bitch. I swear to God! I had to get up and pace the floor because I was truly pissed the fuck off.

Three hours later, Olivia told us to follow her to the conference room. I knew that they were getting ready to give me the results of my wife. I was antsy, so I couldn't sit down once we made it to the conference room.

"The doctor will be in to speak with you all momentarily. Before he comes in, I want to go ahead and hand you these search warrants," she spoke, and passed us envelopes. "Those are search warrants for Paxton and Angela Bailey's residence, Pryor and Phoenix Bailey's residence, and Kason and Tracey Lewis' residence. In the search warrant, you will read what we are searching for."

"Excuse me," Kason spoke up as he scanned the document from the envelope. "You are not getting on my property, Mrs. Bradshaw. I don't care who you are. The people you need to be checking are across the table from us."

"It's Ms., and it's already in place. When Mrs. Bailey is released from Dr. Compton's care, she will be placed on a seven day hold in the Psych Ward on the third floor. Let us not forget the reason we are all in here is because Mrs. Bailey tried to take her own life. She still needs to be mentally evaluated to make sure that she is safe from herself. When she is released from the Psych Ward, she will be in the care of her father, Mr. Trent Wilson. He—"

"LIKE MOTHAFUCKIN' HELL! SHE DON'T EVEN KNOW

THAT MOTHAFUCKIN' NIGGA! HE BEEN IN JAIL ALL HER FUCKING LIFE. HE AIN'T NEVER DONE SHIT FOR HER. HE COULD BE A FUCKING RAPIST OR A PEDOPHILE OR ONE OF THOSE NIGGAS WHO FUCKS ON THEIR KIDS. I WON'T ALLOW THAT!" Kason jumped up out of his seat and yelled. "HOW CAN HE TAKE CARE OF HER ANYWAY? HE AIN'T GOT NO FUCKING MONEY."

"Now, Kason, you know better than that. You thought you took every penny from my nigga, but as long as he got me, he will never be broke. So, try again," my dad said.

The way Ms. Bradshaw rolled her neck and eyes at the same time, I knew she was about to let Kason's ass have it for that outburst.

"Mr. Wilson can also be under investigation for attempted murder of his daughter, but he's not," she said, and he slowly sat down. "Now, I said what I said, and that is how it's going to be. Until this investigation is over, neither of you will have contact with her, unless—"

"THAT'S MY MOTHAFUCKIN WIFE! YOU CAN'T TELL ME WHEN AND WHEN NOT TO HAVE CONTACT WITH HER," I yelled.

She looked at the ceiling, let out a deep and very rude sigh, and then cut her eyes at me. I was ready for her smart ass comment.

"Mr. Bailey, correct me if I'm wrong," she paused, flipped through her notepad, and cleared her throat. "The reason she shoved the pills down her throat is because she found out that you were having sexual relations with her mother," she said, squinting her eyes at me with her head cocked to the side, as if she was waiting for an answer from me.

"Bitch, you got me fucked up!"

Bam! Bam! Bam!

My mom elbowed me in my stomach three times, making me bend over in pain. She grabbed my ear and twisted it around, damn near twisting it off.

"Don't you ever in your life disrespect a woman like that? Do you understand me, Phoenix Allen Bailey?"

"Yes, ma'am!"

"Now, apologize!"

"I'm sorry, Ms. Bradshaw."

"Apology accepted," she replied, and my mom let me go. "Like I was saying before all of the outbursts, you can visit her in the Psych Ward, but it will be under my supervision. Does anyone have any questions, comments, or concerns?"

Nobody said anything, and she went back to her seat. Dr. Compton walked in and took his hat off. It seemed like everyone was holding their breath, waiting for him to say something.

"Okay, ladies and gentlemen, the surgery was a success. Kambridge and Mr. Trent did exceptionally well. She's going to remain in the hospital for two weeks so we can monitor her, and to make sure that her body does not reject the kidney, and she is able to use the restroom on her own. She and Mr. Trent are both heavily sedated, and are recovering in the same room. I suggest that you go home and come back tomorrow. They both are going to need a lot of rest. Also, please, please, don't come here and stress Kambridge out. She's already fragile because of everything she has been through, and we don't need extra stress. Understand me?" Dr. Compton said.

We all agreed with him and stood up to leave. I was so ready to come back and just look my baby in her eyes. I needed her to see that I was sorry for lying to her. We exited the hospital, piled in my dad's truck, and headed to his house. When we got there, there were police all over the fucking place, and niggas in hazmat suits. We weren't worried, because they weren't going to find anything at all, especially nothing that could have contributed to Kam's poisoning.

We got out the truck and walked up the driveway, and one of the police stopped us, and told us to wait outside while they were searching it. He said they were almost done, so we sat on the bench that was in my mom's garden.

"Y'all, I'm so scared that Kam won't forgive me. I know I should have told her from the beginning, but I had never felt anything like this before with her. I never thought her mom was psycho enough to try and kill her own fucking daughter. Also, a part of me feels like it was her mom who ruined her store," I said.

"Son, let me tell you something. That is going to be hard to get over. You see she tried to kill herself over the shit when she found out. I told your block head ass to tell her because it would hurt much LESS coming from you, but nah. You did the complete opposite, and look where it got you... got us," my mom said.

"Another thing that's been bothering me is the fact that Kason was talking about he had Kam using me, and that she never loved me."

"I don't put shit past Kason, but I know she loves you. Regardless of how it came about. She loves you. Ain't no girl killing herself over a nigga she don't love," my dad said, surprising me.

This nigga really a new nigga now. I wonder if my mom holding out on some ass or something, because he ain't never been this hands on with me like this. Having him by my side during one of the most tragic times in my life is comforting.

"We're done here," one of the police officers said.

We walked in the house through our broken door, and everything was everywhere. Chairs were turned over, books were off the shelves, and the pillows were thrown everywhere. The pigs are disrespectful as fuck. They ain't have to ransack my parents' house like this. I can only imagine what our house looked like. Mayhem said he would call in a team to put our house back together, because we were going to be staying at our parents until all this shit is over. My dad disappeared into his office.

The surround sound scared me when it popped on playing Prince's *Purple Rain*. My dad walked out of his office and told us that it was time to start cleaning up. I guess this was going to be one of our newfound family bonding moments, but I ain't have no problem with it because I welcomed any distraction.

Judge Kason Lewis

My life has been spiraling out of control since my stupid ass daughter decided that she wanted to end her fucking life. Her doing that caused more trouble than she ever will know. A part of me wanted to fucking kill my fucking hoe of a fucking wife. I should have divorced her hoe ass when she fucked Trent's ass and got pregnant. At first, I thought that Malice's bitch ass was lying the first time he hinted at fucking my wife, but then when she confirmed that she paid him for sex, and that she loved Trent once upon a time, I felt my insides cave in. If she admitted to that shit, it ain't no telling what else she would do. I ain't said shit to her hoe ass since the first time we left the hospital. We've been sleeping in separate rooms. I don't even fucking know where Kade is with Kalena. They ain't come back home with us that night, so I don't know where they are staying.

I had been calling all around trying to figure out how Trent got his bitch ass out of prison, but apparently, somebody got a lot more pull than me. His transfer to Arkansas is still a go, which was the only thing that made me smile a little on the inside. Leaving the hospital, the truck was quieter than a mouse. It was me, the hoe, Shaw, and Elliot.

"Okay, just to inform you, Judge Kason, the police are at your house. Are they going to find anything? If they are, I need to know," Elliot asked.

"Don't ask me. I ain't trying to kill her," I sniped at him, and then cut my eyes at the hoe.

"You ain't trying to kill her, but you beat her ass every other night. Please," she waved me off like a fly, while continuing to look out the window.

The rage inside of me came from out of nowhere, and I pushed her head into the window. I yanked her back by her hair and started choking her.

"JUDGE! FUCKING STOP!" Shaw screamed, which prompted me to let her go.

"You are a fucking monster, Kason Lewis, and I hate the very day that I laid eyes on you. No one likes you. You are a fucking disgrace to the fucking world," Tracey snapped through her tears.

"I'm a monster, but you are trying to kill your daughter over some dick. Fuck outta here. You are a hoe, Tracey, and I hate the day that I asked you to be my fucking girlfriend. The only reason why I didn't divorce your hoe ass when you got pregnant with that hoodlum's baby, is because I ain't want to look bad for the people who had to vote me in to be judge. Fuck you! When this shit is over, I want a fucking divorce, bitch!"

"Gladly!"

The truck pulled into my driveway, and it was filled with police and niggas in hazmat suits. We got out and had to wait outside until they were done with their search. Twenty minutes later, the guys in hazmat suits walked outside with a red evidence bag. I cut my eyes at Tracey, and she looked away from me. That bitch did something, and when I find out, it's going to be hell to fucking pay. Two police officers approached us with handcuffs in their hands.

"I'm sorry I have to do this, but Kason Lewis, you and your wife are under arrest for the attempted murder of Kambridge Bailey. You two have the right to remain silent, anything you say can, and—"

"I know my fucking rights," I snapped at him. "TRACEY, WHAT THE FUCK DID YOU DO? THIS IS ALL YOUR FAULT," I yelled and tried to lunge at her, but the policeman yanked me back.

"I'm right behind you guys," Elliot said as they placed me and the hoe in separate police cars, and took us to the police station.

I became nauseated. I have never sat in the back of a police car, let alone rode in one. The musty scent back here instantly made my head hurt. I asked them to let the window down, but they refused. My mouth got watery, and I knew I was getting ready to throw up. Two seconds later, I leaned forward, and hurled on the floor of the backseat. This was the fucking worst day of my life. I put people in jail, not go to jail.

Thirty minutes later when we pulled up to the jail cell, the fucking news reporters were already outside. Tracey walked in the jail with her head down and away from the cameras. I wonder what fucking cop ran their mouth to the press. I took a deep breath before they opened the door.

I'm Kason mothafuckin' Lewis. I do this, I thought to myself.

"Kason, did you and your wife conspire to murder your daughter because she married the son of a well-known drug dealer?" one of the reporters asked.

"This is all a mistake, and I can assure you that my wife and I will be out of here in a few hours, and back at the hospital seeing about our daughter. We love her very much, and accept anyone that she chooses to share her love and life with. This is just one big misunderstanding, and we would never ever harm our daughter. We will be out of here in no time," I said as they continued to walk me into the building.

I truly felt like a fucking criminal, and I haven't committed one crime. An hour later, Elliot and I were sitting in the cold ass room with a detective. He must be new because I had never seen him before.

"Good evening, Mr. Kason. My name is Detective Parker. How are you feeling?"

"I've been hauled off to jail, accused of something that I would never do. How do you think I am feeling, Detective?"

"So, why would you try to kill your daughter?"

"Don't answer that, Kason," Elliot said. "Detective, my clients are innocent of the crime that you had your people arrest them for. My clients are outstanding pillars of the community, and dragging them down here in front of the people who trust him to protect the community is reputation damaging. He has gained the trust of this city, and how is it going to look dragging him down here for questioning... especially regarding the attempted murder of his daughter? Are you going to charge them?" Elliot spoke for me.

"Mr. Elliot, we have evidence that implicates Kason and his wife in the attempted murder of his step-daughter."

I could feel my temper start to rise.

"She's not my fucking step-daughter, you fucking idiot. She's my daughter," I snapped on him.

"Calm down, Kason," Elliot spoke.

"On paper! Only on paper is she your daughter. According to DNA, she is the daughter of Trent Wilson. Someone you arrested over twenty years ago. Is that why you tried to kill your *step*-daughter? You couldn't help that she was getting close to meeting the man who actually fathered her, by marrying the son of Trent's right hand man. Is that why you poisoned your *step*-daughter? You already put him away for the rest of his life, or so you thought, and here he comes galloping full speed right back into your life. You wanted to hurt Trent more, didn't you? You feel like the only way you could hurt him more was to take the most important thing away from him, huh? Kason? Kason? Kason? You there? Answer me! IS that why you poisoned your *step*-daughter?"

During that line of questioning I could feel my blood boiling inside of me. My blood pressure was rising to the point where I was getting ready to jump across the table on him. He knew what he was doing, but I ain't new to this. He must have forgotten that I was a judge. Even though I wanted to jump over the table on his ass, I just stared at his ass, barely blinking. Letting him know he is not breaking me down not one second, especially since I know I ain't poison Kam.

"This line of questioning is over! Charge him, or we are out of here!" Elliot said.

"We're done here," he said, and stood up. "Stay in town, Judge Kason," he said, and walked out of the room.

"They arrested me just to question me. This is fucked up, and it doesn't look good for my reputation, Elliot. Fix this."

"You know I will fix this. I ain't let you down yet! They arrested you to apply pressure. They want you to snap out. You know since you are a prominent figure, this shit is going to be running all over the fucking United States."

The door came open, and Tracey walked her tear stained face in here. I ain't give a fuck about that bitch, and I don't care what they said to her. She had a big ass knot on her fucking forehead from me pushing her ass against the window in the truck. Elliot took his cloth out of his pocket and handed it to Tracey to wipe her face.

"From the moment you two walk out of here, every move you make, you are going to be under a watchful eye. Everything you do, everything you say, will be picked apart. You two are going to walk out of here looking like a happily married couple. Body language better not be off. Hold hands. Kiss if you must. You must sell this as if you are not fighting, and everything is perfect in the household."

Elliot pulled Tracey's hair out of the ponytail it was in, and fluffed her hair in her face, covering the knot that was shining. He fixed my blazer that I was wearing.

"One more thing, it's not a good look with Kade and Kalena out of the house. You have to get them back in the house. I'll find out where they are staying and get them back home. Now, remember what I said. When we go out here, don't say anything. Let me do all the talking. Give me a 'loving and concerned at the same time' look," Elliot spoke.

"Elliot, what is the evidence they found in the house?" I asked him.

"They found a broken thermometer behind Kambridge's computer desk in her room," Elliot said. "It's not enough to hold you because for now, it looks accidental. It is accidental, right?" he looked from her to me.

"Why the fuck wouldn't it be accidental? Won't the doctor say that it is accidental? Can we just tell the doctor what it was, and he change his diagnosis of it being intentional instead of accidental?" I asked him.

"That's something that we have to discuss at a later time, but for now, we have to get out there, and address these people that you know are standing out there."

Something still just didn't sit right with me, because why the fuck would Kam have a thermometer in her room? I squinted my eyes at Tracey, but she looked at the floor.

"What did you do, Tracey?" I asked her, but she ignored me.

I walked up on her, but Elliot jumped in front of me, and told me that we didn't have time for this. He opened the door to the room and led us out. Damn, even more reporters had shown up.

"Remember what I said!"

Tracey grabbed my hand, and I tried to squeeze her hand out of place, but I stopped squeezing it once we stepped out the door and the cameras started flashing. The questions started rolling in.

"This is just a simple misunderstanding, and the Lewis family wants to continue to care for their daughter in private. My clients are innocent. They love their daughter very much. There is nothing going on in their household, but love and affection. Thank you! That is all." Elliot addressed the crowd.

We walked through the crowd of reporters to the truck, and headed home. I got a feeling that this is only going to get worse, and normally, my gut was always right.

Kambridge

*W*arm sand squished between my toes as I walked along the shore. The water that crashed along the shore was gold and sparkly. This is very new.

Is this my walk to heaven?

Everyone on the beach is dressed in white and having the time of their life. Looking down at myself, I had on a white t-shirt and shorts.

Is this the way they dressed in heaven?

Some of them had small wings, and some of them had large wings. I touched my back, but I didn't have any wings.

Well, I'm walking to heaven, so, I'm sure I'll get my wings then.

"Kambridge Lewis-Bailey? What are you doing here?" I turned around and a very beautiful woman approached me. It was like she was the spitting image of me. She had very large wings on her back.

"I'm sorry. I don't know your name," I smiled.

"Katrina, but everyone here calls me T. Trina."

"You look like me. I mean, an older more beautiful version of me. Your hair is much longer than mine though."

"I know. I'm your grandmother," she chuckled. "Let's take a walk."

"Are you walking me to heaven?"

She shook her head, before replying, "You're not ready for that place, *yet. It's much more beautiful than here. I saw you walk in. I needed to get here before you made it to the gates."*

"Oh. Why? I'm not going to heaven."

"No... well, not now! Listen to me. I want you to know that you are very beautiful, and never let no one steal your shine. I know that everything seems so bad right now, but everything will come full circle, and you will be the happiest you've ever been in life, but there will be bumps along the way. Huge bumps, but don't allow your scars to transform you into someone you're not!"

"So, what are you saying, Grandma? You're sending me away," I started to cry. "You're sending me away to be beaten again. You're sending me away to be lied to again. I don't wanna live that life anymore. I'm tired of it. My husband cheated on me, with my mom... your daughter, and several other women. The one person who I trusted with everything I had left to give...messed me over," I cried.

"Trust me, you have more protection than you ever will need. Just go give life a try again. For me," she said. "Everyone has their day in court, my beautiful black angel. God doesn't come when you want him, but he is always on time. All He needs is just a little mustard seed of your faith."

"Will I remember you, or will you be my guardian angel, or something like that?"

"Of course you will, and I've always been your guardian angel. Some things you just can't intervene with because of how bad it will alter your life. Nope, nope, nope, no more questions. Now, close your eyes."

She pressed her hands over my eyes, and I felt a huge jolt.
Beep!

Beep!

Beep!

My eyes fluttered halfway open, and I automatically knew I was in the hospital from the sounds of the machine. The only light in the room was a few feet away from me to my left. I turned my head slightly and blinked my eyes slowly, and opened them halfway again. My eyes had to be deceiving me.

"Mr. Wilson," I whispered as loud as my itchy, very dry throat would allow me. "Am I in jail?"

"Baby girl, you're awake," his very deep voice vibrated my eardrums. He winced when he sat up and got out of the hospital bed. He stood over me and started rubbing his fingers through my hair. "No, you're not in jail, baby."

I started coughing and then yelled in pain.

"Why am I in pain?" I put my hand where the pain was coming from, and I felt a long ass line of stiches. "What happened to me?" I started crying. "Why do I have stitches?"

"Baby girl, calm down, okay. Please," he said before the doctor and nurse ran into the room, turning on the light. It burned my eyes, so I closed my eyes. I don't know why I did that when the doctor forced my eyes open, and blinded me again with his little pencil light.

"Hey, Mrs. Bailey, I am Dr. Compton. It is nice to have you back. You gave us quite a scare," he introduced himself, reminding me that I was married to a piece of scum. I couldn't wait to divorce his ass.

"Please just call me Kam, and it's Lewis. Kambridge Lewis," I corrected him. "Can I please have some water or something? My throat burns every time I talk. How long have I been here?"

The nurse that was with him left out, and quickly came back with a pitcher of water. She poured me a small cup, and I sucked it down slowly while the doctor checked my vital signs.

"You have been here for a week. How are you feeling? Do you remember why you came here," Dr. Compton asked me.

One whole week. That's seven days, I thought to myself.

I slowly nodded my head and thought about the distress I was in when I shoved all those pills down my throat. I let out a gasp and placed my hand on my stomach. My baby.

"Did I harm my baby?" I asked him.

The doctor looked at me with no expression on his face.

Regardless of how much I hated my husband, I didn't want anything to happen to my baby, because we did make the baby out of love. I loved him, hell. I'm still in love with him, but I hated him. I'll always hate him for what he did to me.

"Doctor, my baby," I whispered to him.

"Mrs... Kambridge. I have a few things I need to talk to you about. Give me few moments, and I'll explain everything to you," he calmly said.

"It's going to be alright, baby girl! I promise you, everything is going to be okay," Mr. Wilson said still standing over me. Mr. Wilson grabbed my hand into his before the doctor started talking.

"Kambridge, your brother brought you in here, and our main

focus was keeping you alive. You were seizing, terribly. After testing your blood, you were full of poison. Mercury poison. There is an investigation going on to try and figure out who tried to kill you, or if it was just an accident. The mercury poison caused your kidneys to fail, and we had to take the baby. The trauma your body was going through, your baby wouldn't have survived anyway."

"Wait!" I said, and closed my eyes. "Someone is trying to kill me, and my baby... wait, I don't have any kidneys? Is that why I have the scar?" I cried.

"Yes. You have one kidney. One very good kidney that your body responded to very well. Mr. Wilson gave you one of his. So, both of you will be connected for life. The poison is gone completely from your system, and all you have to do is use the bathroom by yourself for a few days straight, and you will be released from my care. The silver lining in all of this is if you didn't try to commit suicide, your kidneys would have completely failed, and you would have dropped dead from the poison."

I shook my head in confusion. This was too much for me to fast.

"I'll give you two a moment alone. I know that you are hungry, so I'll have the nurse to bring you some food. Also, I want you to drink plenty of water so we can get you up to see if you can use the bathroom on your own. Also, I'll give your family a call to let them know that you have woken up," he said.

"NO! No! Don't call anyone right now! I'll call them from my room phone," I replied to Dr. Compton, even though I was lying.

He left out the room with the nurse on his heels. I looked up at

Mr. Wilson, who was staring at me intensely.

"Thank you, I guess," I said to him. "I don't mean to sound ungrateful or anything. I just... this is a lot for me to take in, Mr. Wilson. You didn't have to do this for me. Wait, you got out of jail to give me a kidney? Do you have to go back to jail or something?"

"Yes! Yes! I did, and yes, I gotta go back to jail in six months. Kam, I'm going to just come out with it. I don't want to be another person keeping a secret from you."

"My life is so fucked up right now. I tried to kill myself, my baby is dead, my husband is a prostitute... who fucked my mom; there ain't *nothing* you could tell me that could shake me. Hell, the way my life is going right now, I wouldn't be surprised if you told me that you're my dad or some shit," I laughed.

I searched Mr. Wilson's face for a response to what I said, and he didn't say anything. His blank expression and the shrug of his shoulders said more than anything that could have come out of his mouth.

"No. NO. No! No! NO!" I shook my head, and started looking at the ceiling.

Hot tears slid down the sides of my face. I don't even know why I was crying. I mean, it's not like my life could get worse by knowing this piece of information. I couldn't even look him in his face.

"You don't want to be the one to keep a secret from me, but you *did* keep a secret from me. I sat across from you for hours, and you didn't say a word about me being your daughter, but you want to speak up now. Please."

"Kam..."

"Is that why you gave me your kidney? So you could ease some of your guilt. I guess that's another secret the people around me have kept from me," I huffed.

"Guilt for what? The only thing I'm guilty of is trying to make sure my daughter lives to see the age of twenty-three. That's it. The only people that kept this secret from you are Tracey and Kason. Malice didn't know either. When you were sitting in front of me, I just wanted to hear you speak. That was my first time ever hearing your voice, and I just didn't want to ruin the moment between us. I'm sorry, I should have said something. That is my fault."

"Kinda like you're doing now," I said, and turned my back towards him.

Laying on the stiches hurt like fuck, but I just didn't want to look at him anymore. I'm so sick of the people around me fucking lying to me.

"Well, I'm here if you want to talk. I ain't going nowhere," he got back in his bed.

"Yeah, but back to jail in six months," I whispered to myself.

"I'll take that, lil' mama,"

Moments later, the nurse brought me a tray full of food to eat. I swear I ate as if I hadn't eaten in years. Mr. Wilson kept trying to make small talk with me, but I didn't want to talk to him about anything. I think I liked him better when he was *just* Mr. Wilson, and not Mr. Wilson, my dad.

Discharge day...

The last two weeks have been stressful as fuck. People have been trying to see me, but I wasn't accepting visits from anyone. They would call the hospital room, but I would hang up on them because I just didn't feel like facing anyone. I didn't feel like talking about my problems. A week and a half ago, they released Mr. Wilson from the hospital, so I didn't have to hear his voice anymore. I hadn't talked to him since he told me he was my father. He would try to make conversations with me, but I would ignore him. I hadn't even been watching TV. I didn't have my phone, so I couldn't even get on the internet. I was truly disconnected from the world, and I don't think it was so bad.

When Dr. Compton gave me a good bill of health, I was happy that I would be getting released from the hospital, but then I thought about where I was going to go. I don't have any of my debit or credit cards to get a hotel, and I don't want to go back to that house where my raggedy parents laid their heads, especially since I believe in my heart that it was one of them who tried to poison me to death, or they both conspired together.

I didn't have any clothes to put on so Dr. Compton gave me a pair of scrubs to wear. I was waiting until he came back in the room with the discharge papers. My stitches started itching, and I wanted to scratch them so bad, but I didn't want to make one of the stitches come apart. When Dr. Compton came back in the room, he was accompanied with a pretty lady and two police officers.

"Hey, Kambridge, this is Ms. Olivia Bradshaw. She is case your worker. She's going to explain everything to you. I'll give you two a moment alone, while I go get you a wheelchair," he said, and walked out the door.

"How are you feeling?" she asked me.

I shrugged, "I don't know. I guess I'm feeling better than most. I woke up above ground. Why?"

"Well, I'm your caseworker, and I will be until this investigation is over. I will be in attendance if you want to have visits with any of your family members. I don't know if you've heard, but your parents were arrested and questioned, but released on the account of the evidence was not enough to keep them. There was a broken thermometer behind your computer desk, and Elliot argued that it could have been a simple accident. However, we will speak to the doctor and get his professional opinion regarding it, even though he has already said this was intentional. I'm sure Elliot argued that you were accidentally poisoned. What are your thoughts?" she spoke. "So much has gone on since you've been in here."

"Well, there is no doubt about it that either of my parents tried to kill me. If I had to bet money on it, it was probably my mom. My dad could have been killed me. Trust. After all the beatings he has put on me, brutal beatings at that, my dad could have been killed me. My mom was fucking my husband, and suddenly after our family dinner when they first met Malice, I started getting sick. She comes in my room talking about how I should get an annulment, and he has hoes. It's just way too much to explain to be honest, and I get depressed thinking about it. So, where am I staying, since I'm not staying with my parents? Well, I need my car, purse, and can I get my clothes?"

"Everything of yours has been removed from their home, and placed in the care of your father."

"My father, Mr. Wilson?" I asked.

"Yes! Is that a problem? If it is a problem we can place you somewhere else. He is the most qualified person to take you in right now, since your whole family is under investigation."

"Whatever. I guess."

Dr. Compton came back into the room with the wheelchair. I insisted that I walk, but he said it's protocol. I got off the bed and got in the wheelchair.

"Is Mr. Wilson waiting for me outside?" I asked looking up at them both.

They both gave me very crazy looks, and Olivia shook her head.

"Kambridge, you have to go upstairs to the Psych Ward and be mentally evaluated to make sure that you are safe from yourself, and others. You did try to kill yourself," Olivia said to me.

Tears built up in my eyes and started creeping down my face. I didn't want to go to a Psych Ward. I am not crazy. That's where crazy people go.

"Olivia, I was just having a moment. I'm not crazy. My mental is straight. I promise. I promise I won't try to kill myself again!" I begged, as she rolled me out of the room and towards the elevator.

"See, you say that you were just having a moment, but what if you had succeeded with killing yourself? We have to figure out why you wanted to kill yourself. We have to find you a different coping mechanism. You will only be here for week," she said.

"A whole week! I have already been in the hospital three weeks. Another week, it will be a month. I can't do this!" I panicked. "I'm not crazy. I don't want to be around people who hallucinate or talk to themselves. Please, Olivia," I begged her. "I will go see a therapist."

"Anytime you come into a hospital after trying to commit suicide, you have to be put on a mandatory hold so they can mentally evaluate you. I'm sorry," she said.

We got off the elevator, and a part of me wanted to get out that wheelchair and book it downstairs, but it would be worse, and I would probably have to stay longer. Just as I suspected, when she rolled me into the lobby, there were a whole bunch of people in there talking to themselves, clucking like a duck, and even trying to do handstands. I'm not going to make it in here.

"Olivia, I really don't belong here. Look at these people, man," I whispered.

"Well, we will see about that. There are all types of mentally ill people, Kambridge. There are people that have voices in their heads that tell them to kill people, and there are people that are obsessed with having things one way. Obsessive compulsive disorder is a mental illness, Kam."

I sighed deeply before she rolled me up to the desk and checked me in. This couldn't be life. Since they already had my paperwork from downstairs, the check in process was quick.

"Good afternoon, Mrs. Bailey. My name is Michelle Lawson. I will be your counselor for the duration of your stay. Your technician that will be checking on you hourly is Myia Warner," the counselor introduced herself while Olivia rolled me to my room. When we got to my room there was nothing in it but a bed and a few books on a night stand. I looked up at Olivia, and she shrugged.

"I'm going to speak with your case worker in private, so make yourself at home. Myia or I will be in to check on you later."

I got out the chair and sat on my bed. Olivia waved to me, and followed Michelle out the door. I laid back on the bed and stared at the ceiling, eventually falling asleep.

∞

I had been here two days, and I was just ready to go home and sleep in the comforts of my own bed. I mean these beds were okay, but I'm sure my bed at Mr. Wilson's house was going to feel better. I had been going through the motions here. I was going to the groups, but I wasn't participating. I was going to Michelle's office for my counseling session, but I ain't talk to her. We just sat there for the whole sixty minutes and stared at each other. She would ask me questions just from the information I'm sure she got from Olivia, but I wouldn't answer any of them.

"Counseling only works if you work it," is what Michelle has been saying for the last two days every time I left out of her office. I'm sure she knows everything about me whether she got it from Olivia or the TV. Yeah, I finally watched TV last night, and I swear that's all they've been talking about on the fucking TV. Like, nigga, you ain't got shit else to talk about? I saw that my parents got arrested, but were also released. These mothafuckas didn't even know if I was dead or alive, until Elliot's ugly ass mentioned it. I never really liked that man to be honest.

Today I was going to have some visitors, but I ain't know who, but Olivia encouraged me to talk to them. I haven't seen my family in almost a month, and honestly, I was missing my siblings and Shelly, but I didn't want them to see me like this. That's all I was missing. Fuck Malice, Tracey, Kason, and everybody else who has caused me hurt or harm.

"Hey little woman! Are you ready?" Olivia asked me after walking in my room.

Over the last couple of days, I have been calling Olivia on the three one hour phone calls that I get a day. We have been getting to know each other, well she's been getting to know me, and I can tell that she really has my best interests at heart. She doesn't really talk about herself, but listens to me talk. I feel like I much rather talk to her than Michelle.

"Yeah, I'm ready, I guess," I solemnly replied.

"Don't sound so happy about it. Are you still not talking to Michelle? Kam, she can really help you. Do you know that? She is not a bad person. She really wants to help you."

"I don't care. The whole world knows my business now, so I'll just let her speculate."

I slid on my house shoes and followed her to the visitor's room. She led me to a table, where she pulled out the seat for me. She sat on the other side. Moments later I looked up, and I saw my brother and Shelly walking hand in hand over to me. The moment they sat down, Kade and Shelly both burst into tears, in turn making me cry as well.

"Kam, why you tried to leave me? I can't do this life without you," Shelly said reaching across the table latching on to my hands. "You are my glue. I know I'm a fucked up person, but when I'm around you, you don't judge me. You make me feel so sane. Kam, at first I was so angry that you would try to do that, but then I understood...kind of."

"I'm sorry," I managed to whisper out through my scratchy throat.

"Sorry! Is that all you have to fucking say...you're sorry!" Kade snapped through gritted teeth.

"Kade," Olivia whispered, and placed her hand on his arm.

"Nah, fuck that! How could you do such a fool ass thing like that, Kambridge? You were going to let that nigga win... huh? You were going to let Mom and Dad win... huh? You are the best thing that has ever happened to me, and you were going to leave me here by myself to figure this shit out," he snapped on me.

He reached into his pocket and pulled out a piece of folded paper. He unfolded it, and slammed it down in front of me, making me jump a little. It was my suicide letter.

"These are the last words I would have had from you. Not a text telling me to come talk to you. Not a picture of your beautiful smile, but this! Telling me not to be mad at you. Why shouldn't I be? You're my best friend!" Kade whispered loudly.

"How the fuck am I your best friend, but you sit here, and let me get my ass drug for basically my whole life? I know what the fuck I put in the letter, so don't even try to show me. You didn't try hard enough to get me away from Kason, so fuck you!"

"Who didn't try hard enough, Kambridge? Are you out of your

fucking mind? I tried harder than you will ever fucking know! Look!" he pulled his phone out of his pocket, typing furiously while glaring into the screen.

He slammed the phone down in my face, making me jump again. I don't even know why I'm so jumpy these days. It seems like everything fucking scares me. He started scrolling a long list. All I could see was names, dates, and then the word denied right next to them.

"See! All those fucking denies. Over the last five years I have been applying for apartments, trying to buy houses, or rent anything that could get us out that house, but guess what... I was denied. Every last mothafuckin' time. I even applied for a fucking apartment in the projects... and was denied. Kam, I have a seven hundred and fifty credit score. Why couldn't I get an apartment there? Kason is much more powerful than you think he is. He blocked all of that shit. The only reason why I have me and Kalena a place now, is because of your fucking father-in-law, Korupt. He is letting us live in one of his houses... heavily secured. That... is... the only... reason. I saved you whenever I fucking could, Kam! I did! ME!" he pointed at his chest. "Me!" his voice cracked. "You tried to leave me, and your last words to *ME* were going to be, *please don't be mad at me*. What the fuck? I keep reading this shit repeatedly because I couldn't believe that my sister's last words to me were going to be, *don't be mad at me*. I can't take this shit no more. I'll see you whenever you get out, if you want to see me."

"Kade, pl—" I started.

"Come on Shelly if you riding with me!" Kade urged.

We both stood up at the same time, and she pulled me into a hug so tight.

"Kade loves you so much! He is running off zero sleep, and just... when you get out of here, you guys need to talk. I love you so much, Kambridge LeeAnn Bailey, and I swear to God, if you ever try some shit like this again, I'm going to kill myself to beat your ass in heaven," she chuckled.

She kissed me on my cheek and hurried to catch up with Kade. I fell in the chair and instantly slumped down in it.

"That was very intense, Kam! Maybe we should have saved the visitation until you got out of here. I don't want to stress you out or anything like that. Lord knows you don't need any more," Olivia said. "I can tell that Kade really loves you, though. Don't be so hard on him. He almost lost his sister."

I shrugged at her comment. I stood up to go back to my room.

"Um, there is one more visit. One more person that I would like for you to visit with," she said nervously.

"Who?" I sat back down, and eyed her intensely, and then realized who it was visiting me. "Olivia, I told you that I didn't want to ever see his ass again!" I snapped.

"You guys need to have a conversation, Kambridge. After all, you are his wife, and he made the decisions for you while you were out like a light. The least you guys owe yourselves is one conversation. That's all I ask. Okay. For me," she said.

"You better be glad that your fucking voice is sweet. I can tell you that. You sound really convincing."

She pecked on her phone a few times, and like five minutes later, in walked the man who made my heart beat fast and slow at the same time. Before he could even make it to the seat, his Issey Miyake invaded my nostrils. Out of my peripherals, I could see him slowly approaching the table. He had on a white muscle shirt and one of his jerseys that I made. He had on black jeans that fit his slim frame. I couldn't see his shoes, but I'm sure he had on a pair of black timbs. When he took his seat in front of me, I gave a quick look in his face, and I could easily tell that he hadn't gotten a wink of sleep. My eyes traveled to his neck piece, a Cuban link chain, and my wedding ring on a small silver chain. He was sporting a new tattoo that said 'Kambridge Bailey' around his collarbone, and I hated that my body let something so small, like a tattoo of my name, make my clit start throbbing. He placed his hands on the table, and he was wearing his wedding ring. I wanted to chop his fucking finger off.

It was like the whole room was quiet, waiting for us to speak. I could even see the staff glaring at us. Yeah, the news found out everything about us. I don't know how, but it is what it is. Our eyes met each other's, but we were still quiet. I loved him, but I hated him. Our marriage could never be repaired. I don't want to ever see him again after this. All I needed him to do was sign our divorce decree.

"Kam, I guess I should start... I want to start this off by saying that I love you. I'm in love with you."

"Don't start shit off lying to me!" I sniped. "You don't fucking love me. If you did, you would have told me that you were a fucking prostitute. You wouldn't have lied and said that you didn't know the woman that you were plowing your dick into ON CAMERA!" I shouted that last part, making Olivia tell me to calm down.

"It ain't no calming down, Olivia," I looked at her. "This man ruined my whole fucking life. I gave him something that I can never get back. I gave him my whole heart, and he even convinced me to marry him, knowing that he was FUCKING MY MOTHER! My mother! He was even fucking the woman he told me that he didn't even know! The lies, the fucking deceit... I hate him!" I looked at her as the tears started to pour from my eyes.

"Um, Mr. Bailey, maybe you should wait and speak to her—" Oliva started.

"Kam, give me ten minutes of your time. Just ten!" he begged me.

I ain't say nothing, so I decided to give him the ten minutes that he begged me for.

"Kam, when I was sixteen I met Cat. I was working as a janitor in the hospital. She was a newly widowed woman, and I was cleaning her room. Long story short, she asked me if I wanted to make more money. At first I was doing landscaping for her, and one day, we fucked. She paid me ten stacks, and told me that it was more where that came from."

"So, she became your pimp? Like, at sixteen, she was probably like fifty. So, she should have been in fucking jail. What the fuck are you even saying?" I sniped at him.

"Nah, nothing like that. She never asked me for any of my money. So, I wouldn't say she was my pimp, but she did put me on to more clients. That's how I was able to save up that two hundred thousand dollars. I was going to stop fucking them when I got my shop up and running, but then I met you."

"Bullshit!"

"It's not bullshit. I'm serious as a heart attack. From the day we got married, I never touched another woman. Never even looked at another woman the way I looked at you. I promise to God. I hope you believe me," he begged.

"My mom though!" I said.

"I never knew that Tracey was your mom! I swear to God, I didn't. You never told me your mom's name, and she never told me her husband's name. It was all about fucking! That's it! I didn't know she was your mom until I showed up at your door step, and that was the day I deleted her number from my phone."

"When was the last time you fucked her?"

"Kam," he called my name just above a whisper.

"Answer ME!" I growled.

"The day before the dinner. We fucked," he said looking down at the table.

I nodded my head, and the tears started flowing down my eyes, again.

"How much are you worth, huh? HOW much does your fucking dick cost?" I snapped.

"Your mom paid me between three to six thousand dollars. Would have been double that if I kept fucking with her after I found about you and her being mother and daughter."

"Wow!" I gasped. "Three to six thousand dollars. How noble of you to not take the twelve thousand dollars. I'm sure you needed it. Did you eat her pussy?"

Ignoring the jab, he replied, "Yes, but—"

"Wow! Did you kiss her?"

"No, you're the only woman that I have ever kissed. I haven't kissed a woman since my first kiss. You have been my only kiss since—"

"Whatever." I waved him off.

"Kam, let me fucking finish."

"Nah, you don't need to finish. You pretty much said everything that I needed to hear. Now we have to get these divorce papers signed—"

"Like mothafuckin' hell. You mothafuckin' tweakin'. I ain't divorcing you over this shit. I ain't never signing shit. So, you can miss me with that shit, and I mean that from the—"

"I don't give a fuck how you feel about it to be quite fucking honest."

"Guys, this conversation is getting a little heated. Maybe we should try—" Olivia started.

"Did you ever love me, Malice, huh? Did you ever think to tell me that I was marrying a hoe?"

"I tried to tell you several times, but I cowered out, and sometimes you would cut me off when I would tell you that I had something to tell you. What the fuck you mean did I ever love you? Kam, look at my fucking chest. Your name is forever embedded on me. I wouldn't have married you if I didn't love you. What the fuck are you even saying? That was the happiest day of my life."

"You ain't try hard enough to tell me shit. Nigga, everything we had was built on a fucking lie. You think that lil' ugly ass tattoo is going to move me, and make me jump on your dick again? Fuck you! I hope that infected mothafucka falls off."

He cocked his head to the side and stared at me momentarily.

"Funny that your black ass talking about what we had was built on a lie. You got that right. You asking me did I ever love you, but shit, did your black ass ever love me? Yeah, I was put up on game about your lil' white boy, Connor. Ten years, was it? You were with him when you got with me. You were with him when you were fucking me and sitting on my dick. Kason said that you were using me from the beginning... for HIM! The man that beat you damn near to death several times, and you want to use someone for HIM! Talk about that!" his voice elevated.

"Guyyysss, let's not do this!" Olivia interjected, but we were both ignoring her.

"We can talk about it, Malice! Sure in the fuck can! You are absolutely right! I never loved you! Connor is the only man that I have ever loved and want to spend the rest of my life with. I was using you for my dad so he would let me be with Connor," I lied my ass off, but this was the only way to ensure that he would leave me alone for the rest of my life.

His eyes turned to slits, and I could tell that his eyes were burning from the pain that I had inflicted on him just now. He needed to feel how I felt. Hurt. Pain. Anger.

"At least you were honest," he spoke through gritted teeth.

"At least I didn't fuck your dad!"

Malice's jawline was flexing hard. I could tell that he was trying to contain his anger. I had gotten the best of him, and as far as I was concerned, I was winning this round.

"You know what Kam, let me be honest too. I never loved you, either. I was using you for my dad too. Your dad has something that my dad wants, and he felt like he could only get it through you. I married you because I felt sorry for your ugly ass. You think a man of my caliber would fall in love with an insecure black bitch?!"

SMACK!

My hand went across his face so fast, I could have sworn that I heard his teeth clink together. The hot tears were flowing down my face. How fucking dare he use my insecurity against me.

"This visit is over!" Olivia said and stood up.

"I KNOW I'M NOT YOUR TYPE... RICH AND WHITE!" I screamed as I scooted the chair back and stood up.

"YOU FORGOT BLACK AND MARRIED TO JUDGES!" he yelled back at me, and stood up.

Before I could smack him again, he dodged it. Myia rushed over and started to escort me back to the back. I finally realized that we had put on a damn Jerry Springer show in front of these people. I'm pretty sure that we would end up on somebody's blog site by this afternoon, and I didn't care.

"MAKE SURE YOU SIGN THE FUCKING DIVORCE PAPERS, YOU FUCKING PROSTITUTE!" I screamed at his back while Olivia escorted him out to the elevator.

"GLADLY YOU STUPID HOE!" Malice yelled before the elevator doors closed.

The minute the doors closed, and I was back in the hallway of this stupid Psych Ward, I broke down and started crying my eyes out. I had to tell the guy that I loved the most in the world that I never loved him. I had to watch him walk out of my life for good. I knew that we would never speak again, but what he did was unforgivable. The nasty things he said to me was unforgivable. He hit below the belt. I slid down the wall, pulled my knees into my chest, and sobbed into my knees.

"Kambridge, would you like to talk now?"

I looked up to see Michelle standing over me with a very concerned look on her face. At this point, I needed to let out all my frustrations. I slightly nodded my head. Myia helped me up, and I followed Michelle in her office and slowly closed the door behind me.

Olivia Bradshaw

That heated exchange between two people who clearly are still in love with each other, hurt me to my core. This is the most complex case that I have ever had in my life, and I just want it to be over. Once we were on the elevator, Phoenix placed the back of his hand to the bridge of his nose and started sniffing. I could tell that he was trying not to cry in front of me, but was doing a hard job of hiding it. His tears were sliding down his face, and I couldn't look at him because my eyes were already watery. His tears were more out of anger than sadness. He was pissed. The way he was taking breaths, I could tell that he wanted to punch some shit, kick some shit, and/or kill some shit. This young couple was going through it, and I'm not sure they were going to make it out.

When the elevator dinged to the basement, I followed Phoenix towards a truck where his dad, mom, brother, and Mr. Wilson were waiting for him. Phoenix saw a trashcan, and he kicked it over, spewing trash everywhere. He kept kicking it, and then he managed to kick over another one. He kicked them both until they were by the wall. He was alternating with kicking them both against the wall like he was playing soccer. The way he was grunting and screaming while he kicked them pained my heart. I bit down on my tongue to keep from crying, but it was no use. I was too wrapped up in this case.

I was intensely watching Phoenix and didn't even hear his family walk up behind me. Mr. Wilson handed me a napkin, and I wiped my eyes.

"What happened up there, Olivia?" his mom Angela asked me. "Was it that bad?"

"A bloodbath. A really big bloodbath...but with words. They both cut each other so deep with their words. It was one of the worst sessions I ever had to sit in on. I couldn't stop them. Every time I tried to redirect the conversation, it got worse. The tongue lashing they gave each other, hurt me," I said to them.

We all watched Pryor walk over to try and comfort his brother, but it was no use. He kept screaming and kicking the trashcans.

"What did Phoenix say, Olivia?"

"I don't want to repeat any of those things out loud."

"OLIVIA!" she shouted my name.

"Well, it started with Phoenix trying to apologize, and then it went on to Kam asking him about her mom, which started heating the conversation up. Kam started talking about a divorce, and he got upset. Phoenix then mentioned that young man Connor, and Kam told Phoenix that she was using him for her father, and that she never loved him, and Connor is who she wanted to be with. Even I knew that was a lie. Then, Phoenix told her that he was using her as well, and that he would have never fell in love with a... with a..."

"Spit it out, Olivia!" Mr. Wilson said.

"An insecure black bitch! A man of his caliber would never fall in love with an insecure black bitch! Everything went downhill after that," I cried.

Angela walked her ass over to where Pryor and Phoenix were standing and talking. She turned Phoenix around and smacked him up twice.

"For her to be so short, she has a lot of fire power," I whispered.

"Trust me. You don't know the half to be honest," Paxton spoke.

"HOW DARE YOU SAY THOSE THINGS TO YOUR FUCKING WIFE, PHOENIX ALLEN BAILEY! I RAISED YOU BETTER THAN THAT. YOU CALL THE WOMAN AN INSECURE BLACK BITCH, FOR WHAT? BECAUSE SHE HURT YOUR FEELINGS?" she yelled.

"MA! I DON'T GIVE A FUCK ABOUT THAT HOE ASS BITCH!" Phoenix yelled into his mom's face.

SMACK! SMACK! SMACK!

She smacked him three times, and he didn't do a thing but hold his face.

"You better watch your fucking mouth son. Your mom is a thunderstorm, but I'm the hurricane. You get loud with your mom again, and I'm going to come over there. I know you don't want that!" Paxton said coolly.

"MA! Stop hitting me. She deserved it. She used me, and she never loved me. How the... how do you think I should react to that?"

"Well, you fucked her mom, and lied about everything else. You think she was telling the truth up there. Come on now! You know that girl up there better than anyone. When both of you calm down, you will apologize to her because you hit below the belt. You knew that she was insecure, and you used that against her. You were wrong, and you will apologize. Do you understand me?" Angela said to him.

He turned his head and shrugged.

I turned away from them and focused on Mr. Wilson's handsome black face.

"Um, I know you wanted to see your daughter, but I don't think it's best that you go up now. She's really upset right now, and I don't want her to be overwhelmed. I don't think she's going to have any visits for the rest of her stay here. Are you okay with that?" I asked him, trying not to focus on his very thick lips.

"I'm not okay with it, but you do have her best interest at heart. I can wait until she comes to stay with me, and we will talk then. Thank you for all you have done so far, Mrs. Bradshaw," he said.

"Oh, it's Ms, but thank you! I guess I will see you all again in a few days," I said.

"Bet," he said as his eyes roamed my body. When his eyes met mine again, I looked down.

I walked past him, and I could feel that his eyes were looking over my body. I was just ready to get to my parents' home and get in the fucking bed.

€

I was crying my eyes out under the covers of my sheet, when I heard a light knock on the door. I tried to clean my face up so whoever was behind the door wouldn't know I was crying.

"Pumpkin, I'm coming in," my dad said.

I'm forty-five years old, and my dad has always called me Pumpkin. He said that he doesn't care how old I am, he will forever call me that. When the door came open, I peeked from under the covers, and my dad had hot tea on a plate. Hot tea has always made me happy.

"Everything okay? You rushed in here and didn't even speak to your mom and me. I knew something was wrong. Is it that case that's been on TV for the last month?" he spoke.

"Yeah, Dad. It's so stressful because I have never worked on a case this complex before. We had visitations today, and it was just... a lot. This is the first time I've ever wanted to quit a case. Between this case and going through a divorce, it's taking a toll on me," I said, and sat up.

Oh, I wasn't just some forty-five-year-old who was still living with her parents. My soon-to-be ex-husband, Mario Bradshaw, was going through a mid-life crisis and decided that he wanted to kick me out the house that we have shared for the last twenty years, for a bitch twenty years younger than us. I wasn't out the house a good week before he had moved her and her three kids up in our house. It hurt my heart because Mario said he never wanted kids, but here he is catering to this bitch and her three kids. We have been going through this divorce over the last two months. I have signed my part of the deal, but he still won't sign, which is why this Lewis-Bailey case kind of hit home for me.

"God gives his battles to his toughest soldiers. This case is probably going to help you heal in more ways than one, trust, especially since it's something similar that you are going through," my dad said to me, while I was sipping the hot tea.

"Dad!" I burst into tears. "Mario and I have been together all my life. I'm forty-five. How can I find a man to be with me at this age? I always wanted a kid or two, but he never gave me one, and made me lose the one I was pregnant with five years ago. But he moved little miss Trinity up in our house with her three kids. I wasted twenty years of my life!" I cried so hard.

"Olivia Hill!" he called me by my maiden name. "I always kind of figured that it was him that made you lose your child. I wish you would have told me that then, and I probably would have killed him. I still want to, but he will have to live the rest of his life knowing what a good woman that he lost. Listen, you are very beautiful, and when I say beautiful, I mean, ANY man will be lucky to have you. Trust me, and what is for you. I'm a God-fearing man, and I believe that what's supposed to happen, will happen regardless. It's probably a blessing that you didn't have that nigga's kids. He probably would have been a piss poor dad, and you are not too old to have a child nor a man. Your mom and I had your baby sister at forty-five. God! I don't know what we were thinking, but we did it, and I would like to think that your sister turned out just fine... well sometimes, I worry about her."

"HEY! DAD! I heard that!" Olena said walking into the room with tattered, bloody clothes on."

Olena Hill was my baby sister. She was twenty years younger than me, and was the spitting image of me when I was her age. I have to agree with my dad on having this crazy girl at forty-five, because sometimes I feel like she is slightly off the rocker. I was the only child for twenty years, and got the shock of my life when they told me that they were pregnant.

I thought it was a sick joke, but sure enough, at forty-five my mom was sporting a baby bump. I hated that I let Mario knock me off my square like this, because Olena looked up to me, and I always preached to her about men, and not letting them cause you to lose focus.

"Big sissy! I hope you're not still in here crying over Mario's duck ass... my bad Dad, duck behind," she said snatching my tea cup out my hand, and taking a few sips, not even mentioning the fact that she had blood on her clothes.

"Olena, why are your clothes bloody?" my dad asked her.

"Well, I saw Mario and that bi... girl, Trinity out looking like a happy family, so I beat her up. He don't get to be happy when my sister is in here crying her eyes out. Like, Dad, how does he say he don't want kids, but is happily taking care of that girl's kids? He don't even know her. So, yeah, I beat her up, and got a few licks in on him too! She better be glad that I didn't slap them lil' tack head ass kids," Olena said.

This is what I'm talking about when I say that she is slightly off her rocker. She just spoke about beating up two people, and threatened the kids, like it was nothing. My parents definitely shouldn't have waited to get pregnant again. Just when I was getting ready to tell her what she did was wrong, my phone started ringing, and it was Mario.

"Put him on speakerphone," Olena said.

I answered and put it on speakerphone, and Mario was going off before I could even say hello.

"I NEVER THOUGHT YOU WOULD STOOP SO FUCKING LOW TO HAVE YOUR CRAZY ASS BABY SISTER COME JUMP ME AND TRINITY. SHE EVEN THREATENED TO BODY SLAM

THE KIDS. THAT'S HOW YOU DOING IT, OLIVIA?" Mario's voice boomed into the phone.

"First of all, are you going to sign the divorce papers?" I asked calmly.

"Fuck you!" he said, and hung up the phone.

"Olena, don't go nowhere near Mario and that girl again. I don't want you to go to jail, okay!" I said to her.

"But it was funnnnn beating her up. I'll probably beat her up two more times, and after that I swear I will leave her alone!"

"Olena!" my dad said her name in his authoritative voice.

"Okay, just one more time!" she said.

"Olena!" it was my time to call her name.

"Whatever!" she said drinking the last of my tea, and walking out the room.

My dad shook his head and followed her out the room. I'm sure he was going to give her a talking to. I needed that little laugh that Olena provided.

Now, back to this case! Phoenix and Kambridge belong together. After listening to him talk about her, and listening to her talk about him, they love each other. Will she be able to forgive him for sleeping with her mother, is a whole different story. I have to gather all this information and present it to the judge in a few weeks. I have to speak with Dr. Compton again, and make sure that he is a hundred percent sure that Kam's poisoning was not accidental, and to let him know that he will have to testify in court, if it makes it that far.

I honestly didn't want to take this case since it was so high-profile, but I had no choice. Believe me, this case has been taking my mind off this divorce with Mario, but what's going to happen when this case was over is what I'm afraid of. Listen, having reporters in my face every time they see me out, asking about this case, is exhausting. They know I can't say anything about this case, but they still insist on asking me about it.

"Yo!" my sister burst into my room and threw some clothes at me. "We are going out for a drink tonight. Worry about work on Monday. It's Friday! You're always working, and that's probably why you ain't notice that Mario was cheating on you with that bitch."

I held the dress up and my nose automatically wrinkled up at it. Olena knows I don't wear anything this revealing. I don't even think I wore anything this revealing before I met Mario.

"Does this dress come with a stripper pole or something? Because I'm not sure what's going to be covered and what's not!" I said while continuously surveying the dress.

"UGH! Olivia, don't be a fucking square. You have a banging ass body. Like, I pray my body is still as banging as yours when I get your age. Shit! You also need to find you a one night stand as well. You said Mario stopped fucking you like a year ago. Sis, come on! I still can't believe you thought shit was sweet. Damn! You did all you can do, and now you have to go out and have some fun. Fuck that nigga."

She was right. Mario and I hadn't had sex in a year, and honestly, I still didn't think he was cheating on me. I offered marriage counseling for us several times, but he insisted that if I didn't know what was wrong, he wasn't going to talk to a quack about it. I honestly didn't know what was wrong. One morning I walked downstairs, and he had mostly all my clothes in suitcases, telling me that we weren't working anymore. This nigga really tried to *Diary of a Mad Black Woman* me. Throw me out the house and shit, like I hadn't contributed to us getting that house. I left that house and hadn't looked back. I sent him the divorce papers three weeks after that, and this nigga still hadn't signed them, and that's been almost two months ago. I wonder if his little bitch knew that.

"Whatever, Olena. What time do I need to be ready?" I sighed in defeat.

"Damn, at least pretend you're happy to be spending time with your baby sister. Be ready in a few hours. We are about to help pay some tuition for some hoes tonight!" Olena said and bounced out the room.

∞

I stared at myself in the mirror in the little black dress that Olena gave me to wear, and I don't know why I was insecure, but I was. Well, honestly, I don't think that a woman my age should be wearing this. I had on some stilettos that I hadn't worn in ten years. I had my hair down from the usual ponytail that it's in. Olena touched my face up with a little of her make-up.

"Olena, I don't think a forty-five year old should wear this," I said to her, turning around, and looking at the bottom of my cheeks hanging out the dress.

"Olivia, we look like twins. Damn! Your body just a little thicker than mine. You not going to the strip club to find a husband anyway. Chill out."

I sighed and followed her out the door. Olena kept promising me a good time, so I was going to go with the flow. What's the worst that could happen?

Trent Wilson (Big Will)

*M*ane, strip clubs have changed since I've been locked up. I mean, I expected them to change, but not this much. You can touch these hoes now! Back in the day, you couldn't touch these hoes, and they couldn't get fully naked. Now, I'm watching this broad doing a headstand with her legs in a split, and a nigga rubbing money up and down her pussy. I came here with my brother and my godsons to let loose. I wanted to have a few nights of fun before my daughter came to my house, because after that, my focus would only be on her and getting to know her, before I have to go back to that hellhole for the rest of my life.

Mayhem left and went to go get us some of the baddest strippers, to come join us in our VIP section. I stared at Malice, and he was going through it. Ever since the visit with my daughter earlier, he's been on ten. He's been smoking blunt after blunt, talking about how he's going to strangle my daughter, and he ain't going to never let her be with no one else. I mean, he's my godson, and Kam's my daughter, so I'm going to try and stay out of it as much as I can, but if Malice puts his hands on my daughter in a harmful way, I'll have to beat his ass, respectfully. Korupt and I already came to that conclusion earlier. The only reason why he is as calm as he is now, is because the last blunt I rolled up for him, I crushed a Valium up in it.

Mayhem came back with four bad bitches, and they instantly started bending over, making their asses clap to Future. We were making it rain on their asses, until this caramel honey came and sat in my lap, bending over, giving me a full view of her fat ass pussy.

"Mane, slap that hoe ass! She like that shit!" Korupt encouraged me.

I smacked her ass, and the way her ass made all them waves let me know that ass was all natural. She straddled me, placing her titties in my face. She was making my dick hard as fuck, and if I was in the business of paying for pussy, I would have definitely took this broad in the back, and broke her off some real proper like. Don't get me wrong, I'm not hurting for pussy because I broke some of those women CO's off every other day. Them hoes even used to fight over me, and it was funny as fuck.

"Damn, Pa! That's all you? How old are you?" she asked as she grinded on me, making my dick even harder.

"Yeah, that's all me, and I'm fifty-five."

"Oh my god! Can you still work that big mothafucka? I promise you can take me in the back, and you won't have to pay me. I just want to feel this," she moaned in my ear and grabbed my dick.

"Nah, shorty! Maybe later."

"Shit, alright. I'll just bounce on your lap as if I was riding this dick!"

She turned back around and started bouncing on my lap to them young bucks, Migos. She bent over and started making her ass clap, while still bouncing. She almost made me change my mind about taking her ass to the back room. When the song was over, they gathered their money and left out the VIP section.

"Mane, that young girl almost gave me a heart attack," I said, and they started laughing.

I stood up to get a good view of the club, when I saw Ms. Bradshaw and a little replica of her, walking through the club. She looked dumb different from work, but I could tell that it was her. She even looked like she didn't belong in this environment. I started for the door.

"Where you going bro?" Korupt asked me.

"To talk to this baddie I see," I replied, and left out the door.

I caught up with her and her replica, and walked up behind her.

"Excuse me. What the fuck are—" she lost her words when she saw it was me.

"Ms. Bradshaw. You look different outside your work clothes. I like this look as well as the work look," I said. "Would you and—"

"Olena... My name is Olena, her baby sister, and yes is the answer to whatever you were about to ask," she cut me off.

"I was going to ask if you wanted to join me up in the VIP section with Korupt, Malice, and Mayhem."

"Mayhem... Mayhem Bailey? Yes, yes we want to join you," Olena said damn near jumping out of her high heels.

"I'm sorry, we don't want to impose on—" she started.

"Yes, yes we do want to impose! Come on, Olivia. What did I tell you in the car?"

She sighed and gave me a fake smile. I grabbed her hand and

111

started pulling her through the club, up to our section. All eyes fell on them when they walked into the room.

"Olivia? Damn! You look like a completely different person. I mean it's not a bad thing, but damn!" Korupt complimented her, making her blush.

I pulled her down on my lap while Olena sat next to Mayhem, but he was barely paying her any attention. That nigga's heart is cold as ice, and I don't know what bitch was going to be good enough to break through that ice.

"What you doing out here in this small ass dress? You applying for a job here or something?" I chuckled.

"This is Olena's dress. I knew it was too much. I told her that I was too old to be wearing the type of shit that she wears, but she said that I needed to get out. I haven't been to a club in years. I've just been focused on work. That could be the reason my soon-to-be ex-husband put me out," she said. "I'm sorry, I promised Olena that I wasn't going to talk about him."

"We can talk about that later. You want a drink?" I asked

"I'm sorry, Mr. Wilson, I don't drink," she said.

"Well, you do tonight! Have one drink to take edge off. I swear it seems like you want to jump off my lap. I'm not going to bite you unless you want me to. Do you like to be bitten?"

She blushed and shrugged her shoulders. Yeah, whoever her ex-husband is, is about to be a thing of the past for real, and he just don't know it yet.

"Olena, fix your sister and I a shot and a glass of Ciroc," I said to her.

She had a shocked look on her face, and then she smirked at me. She fixed the drinks and handed them to us.

"I'm going to take a shot with you," I said to her. "One...Two... Three," I counted, and we both threw back the shots.

"Whew! That was strong!" she said, rubbing her chest.

I laughed at her because Ciroc wasn't shit.

"Oh wait! Should you be drinking? You know you only have—"

"Olivia, stop worrying, and just let loose. Tonight is about fun, okay!" I said to her.

She slowly sipped on the glass of Ciroc while I watched her intensely. I could tell that she was watching me watch her, but I wasn't going to say nothing. Minutes later, she downed that glass and asked for another one, which shocked me, and apparently her sister as well.

A song by Trey Songz came on, and Olivia started grinding on me. Minutes later some strippers walked in the door, and she tried to get out of my lap.

"Where you going?" I whispered in her ear.

"I know you want a lap dance from somebody experienced. So, I'll move."

"If I wanted a lap dance from them, I would get one from them. I want one from you. Now straddle me, and show me how you ride a dick."

"I can't straddle you. My dress is too short for that, and I don't have on any panties. My dress will come up."

"Them niggas ain't paying attention to us. Trust me, and what I just tell you?"

"You said let loose!"

"Aight then! Do that! Now, straddle me!" I ordered her.

She straddled me, and just like she said, her dress started coming up. She was so worried about her dress coming up, so I held it down at the back, but the minute I looked down, I had an eyeful of caramel pussy, and my shit bricked up fast as hell. She stopped grinding on me and put her hand over her mouth.

"Ooooo! Um, is that you?" she giggled like a school girl.

"Yeah, that's me, but is that you?"

She followed my eyes down, and she tried to switch positions so I wouldn't see that shit, but it was already too late.

"Can you still fuck at your age, old man?"

"I can show you an old man, baby girl. You talking about me. You forty-five, do your pretty ass pussy still get wet on its own, or do I need a gallon of KY Jelly?"

She rolled her eyes and started back grinding on me. Beyoncé's song "Dance for You" came on, and I guess it was her favorite song, because she started grinding on me like she was truly applying for a job. She got up, turned around, and leaned back on me. Her back was on my chest, and for some odd reason, I felt compelled to nibble on her ear and kiss on her neck. She didn't stop me, so I decided to move in for the kill.

"You want to get out of here, Ms. Olivia? So I can show you how an old man gets down?"

She nodded her head, so I stood her up and pulled her dress down. I let my people know that I was leaving, and I'll hit them up later.

"Olennnaaa, don't wait up," she told her.

Olena was now being entertained by a stripper since I'm sure Mayhem wasn't saying too much to her. I had my arms wrapped around Olivia, and was walking extremely close behind her. I was kissing on her neck the whole way out the club, until I opened the door to my black Mercedes.

Once I got her situated in the car, I rushed around to the other side of the car and sped out of the parking lot. I turned on the radio and let the soft sounds of Babyface marinate in the car.

"Um, Mr. Wilson, please don't think that I have a habit of having one night stands or... sleeping with my clients' parents, well, most of my clients are old, and their parents are dead," she rambled on, and I could tell that she was very nervous.

"Olivia, what can I do right now to take the nerves away from you, that doesn't require alcohol or weed? I don't want you to be nervous. I want you to enjoy yourself."

"Um... um... I don't know. I have never done this before... had sex with someone other than my husband. Hell, I hadn't even had sex in a year. Oh my god! I'm talking too much again. Sorry, Mr. Wilson."

"Please call me Trent," I said.

I saw her nod her head really quickly. I took my right hand and started rubbing her thigh. She tensed up.

"Relax, ma! Let me relax you!"

I inched my hand further up her short ass dress, and found her fat ass pussy lips. I started thumbing her clit, and it immediately started poking out at me. I pushed my middle finger inside of her wet, inviting walls, while I continued to play with her bud with my thumb.

"Mmmhmmm," she moaned out.

"You like that, ma?"

She didn't answer, but the moaning told me everything that I needed to know. I kept my speed up, and she started bucking in the seat.

"Fuck! Fuck!" she groaned, and I felt her release on my finger.

I eased my finger out of her and put it in my mouth. She tasted exactly how I expected her to taste... good. Trying to focus my mind a hundred percent back on driving, and not stretching those walls out, was a task, but it is a good thing that I was only two blocks away from the house. I glanced back at her, and she had taken off like a rocket with her fingers between her legs. She laid the seat back, pulled her dress up, and started fingering herself fast as fuck.

"Shit, you need some help?" I asked her.

"Nah, you just keep... keep... keep fucking driving."

I whipped my car into the gate and into the garage. Baby was so focused on getting her orgasm off that she hadn't even noticed that we had stopped.

"Mr... Trent... do you like... squirters, uhhh?" she asked as she continued to finger fuck herself and play with her clit simultaneously.

"Hell yeah, I do. Get that shit off, because when we go in this house, you are only going to nut when I tell you to!" I ordered her.

Two seconds later, her thick ass squirted all over my fucking dashboard. I chuckled to myself and got out the car. I went around the other side and opened the door for her. I picked her up out of the seat and carried her in the house. I walked her upstairs and into my bedroom. After carefully placing her on the bed, I started to pull her dress over her head, stopping her from taking her heels off.

"Your body is so beautiful," I whispered, rubbing my hands over her smooth ass skin, before pushing her legs apart and getting on my knees.

"You sure you remember what you're doing old man?" she chuckled.

"I'm sure it's like riding a bike."

I haven't eaten pussy in so long, but she won't question how long it's been when I'm done with her. I ran my tongue up and down her wet slit a few times, while her body shivered under me. Sucking softly and tugging lightly on her clit, made her body start shaking. I pushed two fingers inside of her and she reached out and gripped my hair, something I've always loved for a woman to do. I finger fucked her fast and faster, until I felt her walls grip even tighter around my fingers.

"I'm about to cummmm!" she moaned out, pushing my head further into her pussy.

She came hard as fuck, and I continued to suck until she pushed herself into the middle of the bed. I stood up and got undressed. Her eyes were still closed when I straddled her. I played with my dick at her slippery opening.

Condom or no condom?! Condom or no condom?! I mentally toyed with myself.

"It's okay, Trent. I'm clean, but if you want to put on one then you can," she grinned.

"How did you know what I was thinking?"

"You seem like a decent man. So, I kind of knew what you were thinking, but please think fast before I start without you," she said, and placed her hand on her clit.

Without another word, I eased inside of her, and her eyes started getting bigger and bigger, the more I pushed inside of her. Her voice was caught in her throat. I wasn't by no means a small guy. I would like to think I was packing in that area.

"You're so wet," I whispered as I stroked her.

I eased out of her, and her pussy made a little popping sound. She was so wet and so tight.

"Trentttt, pleeassee fuck me! I need you to fuck me... hard."

Her wish was my fucking command. I pulled out of her and flipped her over on her knees, and rammed inside of her. I latched onto her thick ass waist and started giving her the business.

"How is that for an old man, huh?"

SMACK! SMACK! SMACK!

I smacked her big ass, and the ripples in her ass made my dick harder. She reached for my hand and placed it in her hair. I pushed her head down into the bed, and started pummeling her pussy. She started trying to push me back.

"Nahhhhh take this fucking dick! This how you fucking wanted it. Arch that fucking back, Olivia! Yeahhh, exactly like that!"

"I'm about to cummmmm!" she cried out.

"Me...fucking... too! Where you want this shit at?"

"Cum in meeee! Cum in meee!" she begged.

"Mmhmmm," I moaned as I could feel my dick getting ready to release.

She gripped her walls around me, and I painted her walls with my seeds. I didn't pull out of her until my dick was fucking empty. I fell on the side of her and stared at her.

"How was that for an old man?" I laughed.

"Trent... will you be my fuck buddy... until... you know!" she asked sleepily.

"Yeah, baby!" I said, and she fell asleep soon afterwards, with her ass in the air.

I put her under the cover and jumped in the shower. After I got out the shower, she was still sleeping, so I cuddled up behind her.

Something about this felt right. I don't know what, and I don't even know if it will last, but something about this at this very moment... felt right.

Judge Kason

The one thing that I thought I had a handle on was my personal life. I never thought for one second that my life would get this bad in just a matter of days. It all started because Kam wanted to kill her fucking self. I had been trying to look like a pillar of the community, but it was hard. I don't know where the fuck Kade, nor Kalena is. I went to Kade's job to try and talk to him, but it turns out that he had moved out the office. I even found out that he was only renting an office in that building, and not actually working for them people. One guy that worked there said that he only had one client, and it was Mr. Pryor Bailey, who goes by the alias Mayhem. I was pissed off because I don't know how the fuck he got that by me. I was losing control of my fucking life.

I went by Kalena's school to try and see her, to talk to her. I wanted to talk her into talking to her brother about coming home, but the school said that I couldn't talk to her without Kade's permission. The lady at the front called Kade, and he did not give his blessing. The woman told me that she would call the police on me if I didn't leave the property. I fucking pay fifty thousand dollars a semester, and I was pissed that she would try and call the fucking police on me.

I called Olivia to visit Kam, but she said that Kam didn't want any more visitors for the rest of the time that she is in the Psych Ward. So that was a no go! I knew for a fact that I couldn't sneak into the Psych Ward.

After a long morning, I took my lunch break to see what Elliot had for me, and the minute I walked outside, reporters were there waiting. I took a deep breath, and braced myself for the questions they were about to bombard me with.

"Judge Kason, why haven't you been to visit your daughter in the Psych Ward?" one reporter asked.

"How are your other kids taking this? Sources say that the kids are no longer in the house with you. Is that true?" another reporter asked.

"Ladies and gentlemen, as my lawyer and I stated a couple of weeks ago, my family and I are handling this in private. My other children are handling this matter just fine. We are just ready to have her home soon. Thank you!" I replied to them.

I brushed past them to Elliot's car, and as soon as I opened the door, one reporter had to go and ask about my stupid ass whore of a wife.

"Judge Kason, is it true that your wife was having an affair with your daughter's husband? Is it possible that your wife could have attempted murder of your daughter, well, step-daughter?"

I was getting ready to explode until Elliot pulled the edge of my blazer into the car. As soon as I got into the car, I yelled,

"WHEN WILL THIS FUCKING SHIT BE OVER?"

"It could be over soon!" Elliot said in his reassuring voice.

He placed a manila folder in my lap.

"What is this?" I asked opening the folder, seeing all the pictures of Dr. Compton with other women.

"The answer to your problems. We are about to go have a *talk* with the doctor!"

The whole way to the hospital the car was quiet. I was thinking that all my troubles were about to be over. After pulling into the hospital and parking the car, we got out and went inside the hospital. I approached the young lady at the front desk and read her name tag.

"Good morning, Ms. Sheila. Is there a way that I could speak to Dr. Compton?"

"Hold on for a second. Let me call him and see if he will talk to you. What are your names?"

"Elliot and Kason," I replied. "You can tell him that it is very important and can't wait."

She spoke into the phone, and then hung up. "You can go right down the hall to his office. He is expecting you."

I nodded my head to her, and we walked down to his office. We walked into his office, and he was just hanging up a phone call.

"Hello, young men. What can I do for you?" Dr. Compton stood up to greet us. "Have a seat!"

We took the seats in front of his desk and stared at each other for a moment.

"So, I have a proposition for you," I started. "If you tell Olivia and the police that the poisoning was accidental, I can make you a very rich man."

He looked at me with a funny look on his face. His eyebrows scrunched together as if he was thinking about it.

"Um, I took an oath to protect my clients, and I am already a very rich man. I'm here every day because I love what I do. I don't think I made myself clear last time, Kason, but this here," he waved his hands over his desk. "This is where I am the judge and the jury. If you didn't do anything that you didn't have any business doing, then you wouldn't have tried to pay me off. Point... Blank... Period. So, you and your janky ass lawyer can see your way out of here."

"I was hoping that I didn't even have to do this, Dr. Compton, but..." Elliot said.

He put the manila folder on the desk, and Dr. Compton opened it and flipped through the pictures, looking mortified. I could tell that he tried to swallow a lump in his throat.

"Dr. Compton, you wouldn't like for your wife to get wind of these pictures, now would you? Aren't these nurses that work around here? Don't these women have husbands of their own? Your wife will divorce you and take you for everything that you own, unless you forgot about your prenup," Elliot said.

"Well apparently, you should have done more research, because my wife and I are swingers. Maybe if either of you tried it, your lives wouldn't be such a shit show. Now, get the fuck out of my office. Thank you so very kindly, and I hope the both of you spend the rest of your natural born lives behind bars once this investigation is over," he smirked, and then winked.

"You're bluffing!" I snarled, not wanting to believe that this dude backed me, and one of the smartest men I know, into a corner.

"Hmph, well!" he smirked, and pressed a few buttons on his cell phone.

He placed the phone on speaker, and I could hear the phone ringing. Two rings later, a voice came over the phone.

"You better not be calling me to tell me that you have to work late, Phil. I'm so ready to see you fuck Amanda's brains out. My pussy is already wet thinking about it," the voice said into the speaker.

"No, honey, I was actually calling you to make sure that you picked up the strawberries. I can't wait to bury my face between both of y'alls legs tonight."

"Hmmm, I love you, Phil. I'm going to get them right now! See you tonight!" she said, and hung up the phone.

"You were saying?" he cocked his head to side.

The room got so quiet, and I swear I wanted to take that letter opener and stab him in his neck. If I hadn't checked in with the lady at the front, I definitely would have stabbed his bitch ass.

"Now, if you don't have any more pictures to show me, please leave my office. Thank you so very much!"

We left his office in a hurry. The minute we were back in the car, I was on Elliot's ass.

"Now what the fuck are we supposed to do?" I asked him.

"Okay, I'm going to ask you one last time, and I need you to be a thousand percent honest with me," he turned to look at me. "Did you poison Kambridge on purpose? Is there anything that I should know? This is your last time to tell me. The only way I can help you is that I know the truth."

Glaring at him with a stern look, "I promise to GOD! I did not poison, Kam! I didn't want to kill her, although I have threatened her several times. I...did...not...poison...Kam."

Elliot squinted his eyes at me as if he was trying to search my eyes for the truth, or if I was lying.

"Okay, then!" he said. "That's the end of it, and the last time I ask you."

He dropped me back off at work, and I walked inside the crowded courthouse. When I made it to my office, the attorney general was sitting in my chair. I guess he could see the baffling look on my face, wondering how he got in my locked office.

"Um, I got the master key from the janitor, I hope you don't mind," he said standing up.

"Attorney General Stanton, how can I... how can I help you?"

I was stuttering because any time you are a judge, or any elected official, the LAST person you want to see in your office for a non-scheduled visit, is the attorney general. I'm not sure what he is going to say, so my nerves instantly started bouncing around in my head.

"Judge Kason, have a seat, please."

Uh-oh, I thought to myself.

"My office has been getting calls ever since you and your wife were arrested for the attempted murder of your daughter. Voicemail after voicemail has been calling for me to fire you, but I kind of like you. So, here is what I'm going to do. How about you take paid administrative leave... just until the investigation is over?" he said.

"People will think that's kind of an admission—"

"That's really the only thing that I can offer you at this moment to be honest, Kason. Take it, or be fired. What do you think people will think if I fire you? Kason, I can't have people filling up my voicemail and picketing outside my office and this courthouse, because you tried to kill your daughter."

"I didn't try to kill my daughter, Stanton."

"Sure. Well, please have your things out of here by the end of business today. Thanks. When all of this blows over, you will have your cozy office and your seat on the judge's table back, I promise," he said, and walked out of my office.

€

It took me three hours to pack up my damn office. Three whole hours. I had to take the walk of shame with all my boxes on the cart. I rolled the cart out the back of the courthouse, and what do you know? Reporters were waiting for me there too. It was like they sniffed that something was going on. I ignored each and every question they were asking as I placed my boxes in the trunk of my car. I didn't even take the cart back in the building; I left it right on the sidewalk.

Looking at the silver lining in this, I thought about maybe starting to meet with connects that are not working with Korupt's ass so I could get my drug business off the ground. I could take a much-needed vacation that I haven't taken in years. I could work on having a relationship with Kalena and Kade, because I know that Kambridge and I having a relationship will never happen. I could go visit my parents' graves, which I hadn't done in years, and I'm for sure they would be pissed at me if they knew what I had become. I pulled my burner phone out of my arm rest and sent out a text.

Me: Need to meet. Warehouse. 2AM.

C: Bet.

I pulled into the garage and saw that Tracey's hoe ass was at home. We had been sleeping in separate rooms and not saying one word to each other, but when we made appearances, we looked like a happy couple. Come to think of it, I probably should have been beating her ass instead of Kam's ass, because she was innocent in this whole thing.

Walking down the hallway to my home office, I had to pass by the guest room that Tracey was sleeping in. I heard moaning in her room, and I just knew that this bitch didn't have another nigga in my house. I put my ear to the door so I could hear clearly.

"Fuuckk, Malice! You feel so good!" she moaned out.

"Damn! I'm so glad I married your ass," I heard that fuck nigga Malice say.

I turned the knob, but the door was locked. I took a few steps back and got in position to kick the door down.

BOOM!

I kicked the door down and only saw Tracey laying on top of the bed, staring at her phone with her hand between her legs. She looked at me like she had seen a ghost. I quickly snatched the phone away from her, and I couldn't believe my fucking eyes. There was a fucking video of Malice and Kam fucking.

"How did you get this, you fucking weirdo?" I asked her.

She jumped up and tried to fight me over the phone, but she must have forgotten that I am damn near a foot taller than her, and I weigh a smooth hundred pounds more than her. I mushed her back down on the bed, and she came for the phone again.

POW!

I reared back and punched her in her eye, and I knew that it was going to be black in just a matter of minutes.

"Get the fuck up again, and I'mma dot you in that other one," I ordered her.

I looked back at the video of Kam and Malice. I shook my head, disgusted at the way he was fucking my baby girl like she was a fucking slut. I exited out the video and saw other videos of them fucking. In another place, I saw Kam's messages, and I realized that I was in Kam's iCloud.

"You stupid bitch! You hacked into Kam's iCloud?"

She looked like she was scared to answer me, so I walked closer to her, towering over her as she was laying on the bed.

"You better answer me before I beat you to a fucking pulp. Did you hack into Kam's phone? Is this how you found out that she was married?"

She nodded her head quickly.

"Why would you do this, Tracey? Did you fall in love with a male escort?" I asked softly.

I was pissed off. Pissed beyond anyone could ever imagine. You don't want the only woman you ever loved to have fallen in love with someone else. No matter how lumpy the road has gotten.

She nodded her slowly.

"Did he give you any indication that he felt anything more for you than sex? Or did you just make shit up in your head? You better fucking talk, Tracey."

"It wasn't like that at first. It was just sex. I pay him, we fuck, and then bam, I leave. We never talked about anything more than sex. Before I knew that he was the guy that Kam was fooling around with, she had this glow about her. She was truly happy with him. Sometimes I would just randomly catch her biting her lip, or with a smile from ear to ear. I wanted that. You stopped loving me Kason, and you can admit that."

"What are you talking about, Tracey?"

"After I found out that Malice was the source of Kam's happiness, I became jealous. Jealous of my own daughter, and I knew I shouldn't have been, but damn. I wasn't getting any of that from you, Kason, and you know it. You can admit that after I fucked Trent, you started hating me. You only gave me Kalena, so you could shut me up about you hating me. You tried to prove that you loved me, but you didn't. You should have just divorced me. I know you sent Trent to jail because of me," she whispered that last part.

"I sent Trent to jail because he was a drug dealing murderer. Did you know that?" I asked her. "How dare you say I didn't love you. I gave you the best life. You didn't have to work if you didn't want to, you chose that. You could have all the diamonds you wanted. You think Trent could have given you what I did?

"I knew everything about him, and I didn't look at him any different. At least he lived his truth. You don't! You're no worse nor better than Trent, nor Paxton. I know you used to run with them. Yes! Yes, Trent could have given me everything I wanted. You must have forgotten that the news said how much money you got from him when you seized all his accounts. How much was it? Close to fifty million dollars, and he wasn't even thirty-five yet. Come on. That didn't even include his investments that he put in our daughter's name, and other aliases. Trent is very smart, unlike you!" she snapped.

"Tracey. Tracey. Tracey," I called her name, shaking my head from side to side.

"Don't call my name. You act like I don't know all your dirty little secrets. Mr. Grim Reaper. Mr. I dropped Korupt's gun to get him sent to jail for five years. Mr. I stole all Korupt's gold, and hid it. Please, spare me, Kason. You are the worst type of man there is. Trying to pretend to be something that you are not."

"I tried to give you everything..." my voice cracked.

"THAT IS THE POINT! KASON, I NEVER WANTED EVERYTHING! I WANTED YOU... I WANTED OUR FAMILY... I WANTED FAMILY VACATIONS IN THE ISLANDS. I WANTED LOVE... HAPPINESS. I DIDN'T GIVE A SHIT ABOUT THE MERCEDES. I DIDN'T GIVE A SHIT ABOUT THIS HUGE ASS HOUSE. I DIDN'T GIVE A SHIT ABOUT ALL THE DIAMONDS.

I... JUST... WANTED... US," Tracey screamed at me.

"YOU PUT EVERYTHING BEFORE US. EVERYTHING. THE ONLY REASON I CHEATED WITH TRENT IS BECAUSE YOU WERE NEVER HOME! EVER! EVER! EVER, KASON! YOU STOPPED TAKING ME ON DATES. YOU STOPPED BEING THE NICE MAN I MET! YOU TURNED INTO SOMEONE THAT I PROMISED MY PARENTS THAT YOU WOULD NEVER TURN INTO."

The tears were falling down her face at a rapid pace, but I wasn't moved by those tears. Fuck her, if I'm being honest.

"Excuse me," I said. "What about your parents?"

She slid off the bed and got in my face. She stood on her tiptoes just so she could be even closer to my face.

"My mom knew. My mom said this as soon as you started running for your little campaign. My mom said that you didn't need to win because power would change you... for the worse. I told her that she was lying. Why you think we didn't talk for the last couple years of her life? I never wanted to hear her say anything bad about you. KASON... I CHOSE YOU OVER MY PARENTS! YOU!" she pointed her index finger into my chest.

"Nobody fucking asked you to do that, especially not me. Since your mom was Miss Cleo, did she see that you were going to try to murder your own flesh and blood, over a man that never wanted you. Did she see that you would try to ruin everything that *your* daughter worked so hard for? I know it was you who ruined Kam's shop. I'm putting two and two together, now."

She stared at me with her chest heaving up and down, not refuting anything that I just claimed. This was always a thought, but I shook it away after she said that she would never do anything to hurt her daughter. I thought about all the times she would save her from my wrath. After that, I thought she was a good mom, but a whore of a person.

"Tracey, respond to what the fuck I just said," I said.

Her chest heaved harder, and she just started crying even harder, even dropping down to her knees which confirmed everything that I said.

I picked her up by her scrawny little throat and threw her on the bed. I clenched my hands tight around her throat, trying to pop her eyes out of her head.

"So, you tried to kill your own daughter? How about I kill you, huh? You already know more than you were supposed to know regarding my damn business. Who else did you tell?" I grilled her as she clawed at my hands.

I eased up just to get a response out of her.

"Don't worry about who I told, you stupid bitch! Kill me. Kill me. Kill me, and everyone will know your secrets. I know everything, Kason. I... know... everything," she chuckled, and clenched back down on her throat.

My chest heaved up and down as I continued to choke my piece of shit wife out. She kept clawing at my hands, until they started to get slower, and slower, and slower, until she took her last breath. I kept my hands around her throat until I was sure there was nothing left in her body. I started to breath normally, and chuckled after I realized what I had done.

"Kason, I heard about—" Elliot burst into the room, and then paused. "Kason, what did you do?" he said rushing over to me and my wife's lifeless body.

"She... she admitted to... poisoning Kam because of that little boy toy Malice. She also admitted to wrecking Kam's shop. I couldn't stop myself," I whispered.

"Kason, fuuucckkkk, you make my fucking job so fucking hard. Damn. Damn. Damn. Damn," Elliot said, pacing the floor and rubbing his temples, while I continued to straddle my wife's dead body.

"Look at this," I said, opening her phone back up and pushing the phone in Elliot's face. "This is what I walked in on her watching. She hacked my baby girl's iCloud, and was watching... watching their sex tapes. She was very obsessed with Malice."

He stared at the phone and kept staring at the phone, like he was going into a trance.

"Damn, nigga!" I said snatching the phone out of his face. "Tell me what the fuck I am supposed to do. Damn! I'm not going to jail for this," I said.

"Of course not. You got the best damn lawyer in the state. You know I wouldn't let you go to jail for this. I got an idea."

He was rubbing his hand under his chin, and then smiled at me, making me mirror his smile. Whenever Elliot smiled like that, he had just found a loop hole.

∞

In the middle of the night, we drove an hour and a half away from Chicago, to Lake Michigan. My eye was jumping, and my hands were shaking. I don't know if it was because of the adrenaline running through my veins because I was getting ready to cover up my wife's murder, or if it was because I was scared. Elliot and I were dressed in all black, masked up with gloves that wouldn't leave any type of fingerprints. We were pulling Tracey's body inside of her car, on the back of the truck.

After we made it down the dock, we took the car off the hook. Elliot carefully used Tracey's hand to turn the car on. He let the window all the way down, so the creatures in the lake can be able to get in there and destroy her body. So by the time they find her body, it would be nothing left.

"Come help me push!" he whispered loudly.

I walked over and placed my hands on the back of the car. He placed her foot on the gas, and it damn near kicked dirt up on me. We pushed the car as fast as we could, in the water. We stood there for an extra thirty minutes watching the car sink.

After the car was under the water, we hopped in the truck and left. I blinked my eyes a few times, and a few tears fell from my eyes.

"You're crying?" he asked.

"Yeah, just trying to see if I can cry on sight when I get in front of those cameras, once we go to the police with the letter you forged," I said to him.

My phone vibrated in my back pocket.

C: Where you at? We been waiting on you for twenty minutes.

Me: Something came up. My bad. I'll reschedule later.

C: You not acting like a nigga who trying to take over. Damn. I'm done fucking with you.

Fuck! I thought to myself.

Fuck Chow! I'll find some more lil' niggas who are ready to make some money.

The whole way back to my house, the truck was silent. Elliot has been my lawyer ever since I've been a judge, so I know that he will ride for me to the very end. At least I hope so. I kept cutting my eyes at him, wondering if I could really trust him. Only time will tell, but if I have to take another life, I will not hesitate.

Cat Jenson

I been smoking cigarette after cigarette because my nerves are on ten. I haven't talked to Malice in what seems like forever. I know it was fucked up for what I sent to him about that stupid bitch, but it was true, and it was definitely how I felt at the time. I've been watching the news to get an update on that bitch's progress. I swear I wished that she would have died, so maybe I could have gotten Malice back.

As soon as my phone lit up with a notification from CNN, I instantly had an idea. I was going to go see Kam, to make sure that she was not thinking about getting back with him. I looked in my closet to find the most expensive, sexiest outfit that I had. I jumped in the shower and washed my body good. When I got out the shower, I put some mousse in my hair just to make sure that my blonde hair was curly. After applying my flawless make-up, I gave myself a once over in the mirror, and smiled at how I looked to be my age.

I called Susan at the bank and told her that someone was probably going to call her, and the only thing that she needed to say was yes. She agreed, and I was off to the hospital. Most people may call me crazy, and it's true, but love makes you do crazy ass shit. Trust me. I've only been in love twice... my deceased husband, and now Malice. It seems like I'm going to have to let Malice know what happened to the last man that crossed me. That is the one thing that I had never told him.

He knew everything about me, except that.

When I got out the car, I made sure to put my shades on, so the cameras couldn't get a good look at my face. When I walked in the hospital, I kept my head turned away from the cameras until I made it to the elevator. I kept my head down because I know there are cameras on the elevator. When I reached the Psych Ward, I got off the elevator, and went to the front desk.

"How can I help you? Please take your shades off," the lady said.

I slid my shades off and looked the lady in her eyes.

"I'm here to see Kambridge Bailey," I cringed at calling her by my future last name.

"I cannot confirm or deny that a patient by that name is here. I'm sorry, ma'am."

I closed my eyes, trying not to get an attitude with the young lady. She was only doing her job.

"I understand that you are doing your job, but I am her lawyer. We have several things to discuss."

"I'm sorry, but Kambridge is not supposed to have visitors without her case worker Ms. Bradshaw."

"Lydia," I said after reading her name tag. "I got permission from Ms. Bradshaw to come see her. I can show you my credentials. I even have Ms. Bradshaw's office number, and you can call her."

I pulled out my IDs, and then gave her the number of Susan at the bank. She looked at my ID and then looked back at me. She raised her eyebrow and then picked up the phone. I pray that Susan didn't forget and answered the phone the way that she is supposed to answer the phone. She spoke into the phone for about two minutes and then got off the phone.

"Sorry about that Ms. Jenson, but Mrs. Bailey is such a high-profile client, and we want to do everything to make sure that she is protected. So many people have come up here pretending to be a family member of hers, trying to get pictures of her. We just want to keep her protected."

"Thank you, Lydia."

She told me what table to go sit at, and Kambridge would be out momentarily. I pulled my compact mirror out my pocket to make sure that my lipstick was straight, and no lipstick was on my teeth. As soon as I closed the mirror, I was staring in Kambridge's dark eyes. Kambridge is beautiful, and god, I wish I could deny that. It pained me because I instantly knew why Malice would fall in love with her. She doesn't look like anyone who has been in the hospital for a month, and that's what made me hate her even more. Her skin was glowing, and her thick hair was braided into two big braids down her back. She even smirked at me, making me want to flip the table over on her.

"Um, have a seat, Kam," I said to her.

"I would much rather stand," she said. "What are you doing here, Catherine? Haven't you done enough?" she asked cocking her head to the side.

I took a deep breath before opening my mouth to respond to her.

"He wasn't going to ever tell you, honey. I thought that as a woman—" I started.

"Spare me the *woman to woman* hoopla, Catherine. Had you really been on some *woman to woman* type shit, then you would have told me the first day you stepped your pale ass into my store. If you were on some *woman to woman* type shit, you would have told me, instead of trying to embarrass me. So, nothing you did was on some *woman to woman* type shit. You were on some hoe ass '*I want your man*' type shit, and the *only* reason why I'm not dragging you by your thin blond hair, and punching you in your pale wrinkly face, is because I am trying to get out of here in a timely manner, but rest assured, Ms. Cat. Your time is coming!"

"Whatever," I waved her off. "I was just coming to tell you that Malice and I are going to get together. He didn't have the balls to come and tell you himself," I said and stood up.

"Hmm, I see! I also saw my name tatted across his collar bone when he came in to see me, and that was just a few days ago. Even after telling him that I was using him for my father, and I never loved him, he said that he was not signing the divorce papers. So, good luck with that relationship. Good day, Ms. Jenson," she said, and walked away.

I was pissed because I came here to shake her up, but she ended up shaking me up. She said everything with a sinister smile on her face, which let me know that she probably would beat my ass. I gathered my feelings and left the hospital in tears.

€

Walking the aisles in the cold grocery store, I decided to get some of Malice's favorite foods and try to entice him to come over for dinner, so we could talk. I know he is a seafood man, so I got some mussels, crab legs, crawfish, and even some oysters from the deli. I planned on filling his stomach up and fucking him good. Before I knew it, Kam was going to be a thing of the past.

"Kam loves all food, and she is willing to try anything, but she really loves crab legs. So, we can get her all things seafood," I heard from behind me.

I slightly turned around, and there was Malice, standing there along with his family, Trent, and her caseworker. I immediately felt my heart rate rise. Kam wasn't lying. He wasn't going to leave her alone, no matter what she did. So, I felt obligated to say something. I walked up to him, and his brother instantly grabbed his wrist, so I felt bold. I knew that Malice and his family hated the cops, so there was no way that he was going to attack me in public. A white woman at that.

"Oh, you wouldn't hit me in public, now would you, Malice? After everything that I've done for you, this is how you repay me, huh? I gave you twelve years of my life. Fucking and sucking you good, and you leave me for a broad who can't do nothing for you. You left me for a bitch, who was USING YOU! USING YOU! You ain't have shit, Malice. Shit! Everything you got, I paid for it, directly or indirectly. I put you on! I made sure you never had to clock into no one else's job, while your parents were sitting across town in their castle, watching you struggle. You—"

Before I could finish my rant, Malice caught me by my throat with his other hand, and squeezed so hard. He was biting his bottom lip like he always does when he is pissed off about something.

"Phoenix, honey! Put her down!" I cut my eyes at his mom, who was putting her hair up in a ponytail.

Phoenix slowly let me down. I fixed my shirt and tried to walk away.

"Cat... is it?" I heard from behind me.

I turned around and looked into his mom's face.

"Yeah, that's my name, why?" I said with an attitude.

"I'm going to give you five seconds to put your hands up to defend yourself, but first I'm going to let you know why I'm going to beat your ass. First, you took advantage of my sixteen-year-old son, and basically pimped him out. Second, you tried to ruin his life with his wife, and third, because you a weak ass, hating ass hoe."

POW!

Before I could even reply, Angela punched me in my fucking nose, and I could feel the blood rushing from my nose. After that first punch, she started raining blows on my body, eventually knocking me to the ground. I couldn't get one lick in. The licks she was delivering were so fast and so hard, I swear it was like Malice was sneaking a few licks in with her. She stood up, and I thought she was done. She started kicking me in my side. I could feel my ribs cracking as she delivered the swift and hard kicks to my side. I covered my face so she wouldn't kick me in it.

"Stupid bitch! Come near my family again, and you will fucking regret it!" she seethed. "Look at me!"

I slowly uncovered my face and placed my hands down to my side. At this point, it hurt to breathe. I slowly looked at her, and her husband was holding her back.

"Catherine. Do you understand me?" she asked me with her a smile on her face, like she didn't just beat my ass to a bloody pulp.

I nodded my head slowly.

"Okay! Now, don't get up to fast; you might pass out."

They walked away, leaving me on the cold floor of the grocery store. I looked around as much as I could, and people were literally ignoring me on the ground bleeding. Is this family really that damn powerful where no one will fuck with them? I picked myself up off the ground and hobbled to my car. I looked at all the wounds that I had, and realized that I needed to get to an emergency room. I sped back to the hospital I had just left, and I had to crawl out the car. Eventually, I passed out, right in the emergency room doorway.

Kambridge

I stood with Olivia at the door before we got ready to walk out of it. She said she and Trent rode together to come and pick me up, but he had gone around the corner to get some gas, because he ain't know how long it would take to get me discharged from this place... once and for all. I inhaled and exhaled twice.

"Today I begin a new life; for I am the master of my abilities, and today is going to be a great and beautiful day," I said, imitating Jody from the movie *Baby Boy* that I had watched while I was in the joint.

I called the Psych Ward the joint, because I swear you were treated just like prisoners. Had to be told when to eat, and when to sleep. You had mandatory classes, and therapy you had to take. You could only talk on the phone at certain times of the day. The food was bad, and I am sure that I have lost at least like ten pounds since I have been in the hospital. I was already skinny, now I look like a toothpick.

"Kambridge, you are sooo extra, and I think it is the funniest thing in the world," Olivia said laughing so hard. "*Baby Boy* is a classic, and I cannot believe that you had never seen it before."

"Well, growing up, my da... Kason, didn't let us watch certain things in his house, and since I've been grown, I just never had a desire to watch it. Now, I wouldn't call it classic. It's just about a man playing two women that he has kids with, and still living with his mom. That's a tragedy to be honest. Yuck."

Olivia had to hold her stomach because she was laughing so hard, but I was telling the truth. I could see a sleek black Mercedes pull up in front.

"That's your father right there. You're ready. Don't answer any questions, ok? Don't say anything. Matter of fact, put these ear buds in."

She handed me her phone, and I placed the earbuds in my ear. I pressed play, and Jennifer Hudson's "If This Isn't Love" started playing. When he opened both the passenger side door and the back door, Olivia and I made our way outside, and through the sea of reporters. She was trying to shield me from the pictures, but I'm sure she was doing a horrible job. The minute I was in the back seat of the car, I turned the music up as loud as it could go so I couldn't hear Trent talking to me.

I'm calling his phone up

Just to tell him how much

I really love him 'cause

He's everything I want

He listens to me, he cares for me

So I truly believe

God sent me an angel

Up from above

That's gonna love me for life

Might as well be perfect only because

It's the only way I can describe

I tried to hide the tears slowly falling down my face. Those words hit me hard because I thought what Malice and I had was perfect. I mean, I knew it was early in the relationship to be getting married, but I felt it was right. I felt that he really had my best interest at heart. I never want to see him again. I really wanted to take the out of sight, out of mind approach to get over him, but Michelle said that wasn't the right way to do that.

After Malice left the joint, after our heated conversation, I had a nervous breakdown. I couldn't breathe. I knew the only way to get Malice to leave me alone was to lie. I knew that he was going to hate me as much as I hated him after I told him about my dad's plan, and Connor. I will never touch Connor again, not even if he was on fire. After Michelle was able to get me under control, I broke down and told her everything about me. From as far back as I could remember. I told her. She was very empathetic as I showed her my scars that my... Kason left on me.

Michelle told me that Malice and I moved too fast, and I was blinded by love. She even tried to be on his raggedy side talking about he would have eventually told me, and he wouldn't have married me if he didn't feel anything for me, but... she said but, that's a secret that he should have told me before we said I do, so she agreed with me somehow. She also told me to try and see things from his side, and she suggested that we talk, and after the talk, if we can't work things out, then we divorce, but little did Miss Michelle know, I ain't talking to him about shit. I'm filing those papers as soon as I can.

I continued to wipe my eyes. I looked up to see Trent cutting his eyes at me in the rearview mirror, and paying attention to the road. The more I look at him, the more I can see myself in him. Our hair, the dark eyes, and the rich dark skin. He's really a handsome man. The music lowered, and I felt her phone vibrate. Being nosey, I looked at her phone and read the notification. It was a message from Olena, her sister. She told me about her during one of our conversations.

Olena: *That man been had you cooped up in that house for days. I know you are pregnant by now. Are you coming home tonight since his daughter is getting out the crazy house today? You sure you comfortable being around her?*

I yanked the ear buds out of my ear, and threw her phone in the front seat at her.

"You supposed to be my fucking friend, but you are fucking him. Is this some sick joke? And you can tell Olena that you are safe to be around me... for now." I snapped on her.

"Kambridge LeeAnn, I understand that you are upset, but you will not disrespect your elders? Do you understand me?" Mr. Wilson said as he pulled into the yard of a huge house.

I would have been able to enjoy the beauty of it, if I wasn't pissed off.

"Kambridge, I'm sorr⊠" Olivia started, but Mr. Wilson held his hand up.

"You will not apologize to a disrespectful child," Mr. Wilson said.

"Fuck off!" I snapped, and got out the car, making sure to slam the door as hard as I could.

I stomped up to the house, and luckily the door was open. I slammed the door, and locked them both out. The minute my foot hit the first stair in the house,

"SURPRISSEE!" I heard people yell out, but I kept going up the stairs.

When I was at the top of the stairs, the welcome home banner was a dead giveaway that it was my room. I went into the room and slammed the door. I slid down to the floor and started to cry. I pulled my knees up to my chest and wrapped my arms around them.

Knock! Knock!

I reached behind me and locked the door, so whoever was knocking, they couldn't come in. A couple minutes later, I heard someone playing around with the lock, and then I heard it click. Whoever picked the lock slowly slid the door open, while scooting me away from the door. I turned my head hoping whoever would just leave.

"Kambridge, what's going on? Why did you come up here? We're throwing you a welcome home party, and you up here crying. What's going on?" Kade said, and squatted down in front of me.

I shrugged my shoulders.

"For real? So you up here crying for no reason."

"For starters, I never asked for a welcome home party."

"Kam, Michelle recommended that you be surrounded by love and support. That's what the people downstairs are trying to do for you. That's all. You don't even have a reason to be crying right now."

"Olivia is fucking Mr. Wilson."

"Wait, so you're crying because two consenting adults are doing what adults do? Trent was in jail for twenty-two years. Would you rather him fuck with a bitch who he don't know, or a woman who actually has your best interests at heart?"

I shrugged my shoulders.

"I don't know why I got so mad. I guess I just felt like I don't even have a chance to get to know him before some woman will be taking all his time away from me. I only got like five months left with him. He will be trying to split that between me and her, and I guess that's why I flipped. I don't know too much of anything anymore. My whole life has been a lie. The people who I thought loved me didn't, and it's just⊠"

First, I love you. Your sister loves you. Your father loves you. Shelly loves you. He has a very crazy way of showing it, but Malice loves you."

"Don't speak his name around me. Fuck him. I don't give a damn if he loves me or not."

"Sorry, I don't want to upset you. Get cleaned up, and come downstairs. Ok."

I nodded my head. Kade kissed me on my forehead and walked out of my room. I stood up and looked around, and it was so nice. Hardwood floors, huge TV on the wall, purple décor, and a desk for my computer from Kason's house. There was even a phone box on the desk as well. A plush purple carpet in the middle of the floor. It was really nice in here. I walked into my huge closet, and every piece of clothing and shoe I owned was placed nicely in the closet. I knew someone had to take their time putting this room together, so I guess I could be grateful. I opened my drawers and my clothes and underwear were in there. I grabbed some leggings and a crop top so I could change out these clothes.

I walked into my bathroom, and this was every girl's dream. My make-up stand was just like it was at my house with Tracey and Kason. It had the perfect lighting, and all I could think about was how perfect my beat face was going to be. I had already took a shower this morning before I was discharged from the joint, so I changed clothes really fast, so I could have some extra minutes to do my make-up. The first stroke of my brush on my skin almost made me have an orgasm. I can't even remember the last time I had put on make-up. After I admired myself in the mirror, turning from side to side, I realized that I needed to switch my look up, and that is the first thing I plan on doing once I get all these people out the house.

I took a deep breath before I made it to the bottom of the staircase. I walked into the living room, and it was filled with a couple of my friends, and the rest was family. Shelly ran over to me and gave me the biggest hug in the world.

"I missed your chocolate ass!" Shelly squealed. "The store has been doing great, and your work Facebook page has been booming girl. Now, it's time for you to make a personal Facebook, and all that other stuff. Girl, some girl even started a GoFundMe for you as if you needed the money. They raised over fifty thousand dollars for you, and I got it, and spruced up the shop. So, when you see it, you are going to love it!" Shelly pulled me in for another tight hug.

"Damn, you can't get all the damn hugs," Aiysha said, politely moving Shelly out of the way. "Come in tomorrow right away; I can feel your hair sticking me. Might have to use a whole pot of wax on you. You know how hairy you get."

I rolled my eyes at her and started making my way around the room. I approached Kalena. Laying eyes on her made me feel bad because I know that she was really hurt when she heard about the dumb stuff that I did.

"Kalena, I'm sorry—"

"Don't worry about it. I'm just glad that you are okay, but if you ever try that again, I'll probably cut your throat and kill you myself," Kalena said pulling me into a tight embrace.

I looked around the room, and I spotted *him*. The *him* that knew my body better than I knew it myself. The *him* that could make me laugh and cry. The *him* that I loved more than life itself, but too bad that I hated his bitch ass. I really wanted him out of here. Don't even know why he came here to begin with. Not to be rude, I walked over to the Bailey family and hugged Mayhem first.

"Damn, lil' sis! Was they even feeding your ass in there? You tiny as fuck now."

"Whatever. I'm about to get on this protein so I can thicken up. Please, call me Kam."

"You tweakin'. You are going to always be my lil' sis, no matter what you and my brother got going on."

I shook my head and hugged Mr. Bailey. He told me that everything was going to be okay. His mom pulled me in and told me that if I ever needed to talk, to dial her number. Malice was sitting a chair down from his mom, but I ignored him.

"What? No love for your husband?" Malice said, and stood up.

"I ain't got no fucking husband," I snapped, and the room got dead silent.

"You got a husband as long as those papers at the courthouse say we married."

"Obviously, those papers don't mean shit. Stop fucking talking to me anyway. Shouldn't you be with your white bitch!"

I folded my arms across my chest and rolled my neck.

"Shit, I ain't got no bitch! The only bitch I got is your black ass. If you want to get technical with the shit."

"Phoenix. Mind your damn mouth when you're speaking to your fucking wife," his mom hissed.

"You a mothafuckin' lie! Didn't you say that a man of your caliber would never fall in love with a... what was it? An insecure black bitch. Those were your words. Get the fuck away from me, and make sure you don't go too far, so the server can serve those papers quick. Let's just dissolve this. You stay the fuck away from me, and I will gladly stay away from you."

"Kam, shut the fuck up. You know I ain't fucking mean that shit. You threw a jab, so I threw an uppercut. End of story. Let's just talk like adults when the party is over."

"FUCK THAT! FUCK YOU! Your little white bitch came by yesterday and told me that you two were getting back together. So why are you here?"

"Huh? Wait. No one was supposed to see you without me. Kam, what is going on?" Olivia asked.

"I didn't ask. All I know is, she came up to the joint and basically told me that I needed to stay away from Malice, but little does she know, I am going to be the least of her worries. I don't want him no more. Period," I replied to Olivia.

Malice started taking small steps towards me, and I started taking small steps back. I know him, and if he gets close to me, he will grab me.

"See, Kambridge LeeAnn Bailey, I don't think you understood our vows when we stood in front of that Justice of the Peace. It said in sickness and in health, for rich or for poor, for better or for worse. Did you hear that Kam? For better or for worse!" he took the last few steps so fast, that I didn't even realize it until his strong hand was around my neck, pulling me to him.

His mom tried to pry his hands away from my neck, but he wasn't budging.

"Mom, I'm not hurting her. In fact, she likes it," he said looking at his mom, and then looking back at me. "Don't you like it, Kambridge? You are always begging me to choke you. What's different now?"

I closed my eyes trying not to think of the time when Malice choked me until I almost passed out, giving me one of the best orgasms he has ever given me. I felt my clit throbbing. My body betraying me. He wasn't just holding me in one place. He was slightly rocking me. My eyes were getting low, and my body was getting ready to cum, until he started speaking.

"Kam, at the end of our vows, we both said until death do we part. I think I told you that once you took my last name, you belonged to me forever. Forever. For...ever. Now, who you belong to?"

"Y... y...you," I stuttered.

"That's what the fuck I thought. Now, when you get finished being mad, we are going to sit down and talk like adults. Do you understand me?" he asked.

I nodded my head quickly. A smirk went across his face before he leaned in to whisper in my ear.

"I know that pussy is soaking wet right now because I smell her. I'm not going to make you nut, but just know...another nigga will never make you wet like I can."

When he let me go, I reared back and punched him right in those deadly ass lips.

"DAMNNNNN!" the whole room said at the same time.

"Don't fucking touch me again!" I snapped, and walked away from him.

The rest of the party went off without a hitch! I talked to everyone at the party except for my husband. Well, he couldn't talk because he had to keep holding that wet towel wrapped around an ice pack up to his lips. I got a glimpse of his swollen lips when he was talking to his mom, and I noticed that I got a good lick in on him. I promise that I will never try that when we are by ourselves.

After the party was over, Mr. Wilson had encouraged everyone to leave, and that he will handle the cleanup. The only people left were me, Olivia, and Mr. Wilson. We were tackling the kitchen and the living room together. No one was saying anything to me, but Olivia and Mr. Wilson were making small conversation. Every now and then, I would look at them in the kitchen, and they would be looking at me. I put my pride to the side and went and sat at the bar while they washed the dishes together.

"So, you're really my dad?" I asked breaking the ice.

He nodded his head slowly. Olivia dried her last dish and was getting ready to walk away.

"Olivia, you don't have to leave," I said. "I'm sorry for overreacting earlier. It's just that I have had so much to happen in my life within the last month, and I don't know who I can trust. Then I figured that I would have to share⊠"

"Kambridge, I will never try to take your dad away from you. I can assure you that he loves you very much, and you are the most important thing to him. We are truly just friends that⊠"

"Friends with benefits," I clarified, and she blushed really hard.

"Kambridge, you are the most important thing to me. You always have been since the day that you were conceived. I know exactly where we were when you were conceived. We were in a bathroom restaurant, while she was a on a date with Kason. I know... I know... I loved your mom with all my heart. We fell in love... well or what I thought was love, quick. The minute she told me that she was pregnant, she said that she had to leave me alone because she hadn't planned on leaving Kason's bitch ass. I was hurt. The only way I could see her is if I threatened to go to the media regarding her being pregnant with you. She even wanted to abort you, Kam! I couldn't let her do that, and she knew that she couldn't do anything to jeopardize Kason's campaign. The day you were born, I went to the hospital, and I got in a heated altercation with Kason. Shortly after that, Kason had me pulled over and arrested. The last picture I got of you from Tracey was this baby picture of you."

He reached into his pocket and pulled out a picture of me at my one year birthday party. The tears started falling down my face.

"Why don't you have a wallet?" I asked through my tears.

That was the only dumb ass thing I could think of to say, because my mind was so blown after hearing this information.

"Well, when you've been in jail for twenty-two years... you kind of get used to not having things," he replied.

"So, do I call you Dad, now. Or Father?" I asked him.

"You can call me whatever you want. Just don't curse at me again like you did earlier. You kind of hurt my feelings when you did that."

"I'm sorry again, but Mr. Wilson, can you tell me why Kason has it out for you and Mr. Bailey? I know it's more to it than you just fu... having sex with Tracey and getting her pregnant."

"Um, maybe this is something that we all should sit down and talk to you about. I don't want you to hate us... or even hate your father-in-law."

"Oh. Okay. Set a dinner date for us tomorrow. Olivia, can you cook? I can. I'm sure you want to know about Mr. Wilson's past just as much as I want to. Tomorrow at seven. Just us. Mr. Bailey, Angela, you two, and me. That's it. Please tell Malice not to bring his ass over here because I'm done with him."

"Oh sweetie! No, you're not. The way he had you in front of everybody, I could tell that—"

"Her father is in the room, Ms. Bradshaw. Save whatever you have to say until it's just you two," he chuckled.

"I'm going to go get ready for bed. I guess I'll see you two in the morning, or whatever. I don't know if you're staying or not. Olivia, you're safe to be around me. I'm not a killa... but don't push me. I learned that from the rapper Tupac in the joint."

Olivia put her hand over her mouth and started to laugh hard.

"Kam, you had never heard of Tupac?"

I shrugged and kind of shook my head. I didn't know Tupac until I had watched that movie *Above the Rim* in the joint. I learned a lot just from being in there for a week. I had watched movies that were forbidden in my house, and even listened to music that I hadn't even heard of before.

"Dear God! What was going on in that house?" Mr. Wilson asked with a serious look.

"I gave you the gist of it in the emails we were sending. The details. You don't wanna know, but you rescued me. I can tell you that much," I said, and headed for the stairs.

"Kam, I'll be up to tuck you in, in a few," he said.

"Mr. Wilson, I'm not five. You don't have to tuck me in."

I walked upstairs to my room and shut the door. Moments later there was a knock on the door, and Olivia slid into the door.

"Hey! I kinda wanted to talk to you. I know you're not five anymore, but let your dad tuck you in. He has never had a chance to do that. Let him feel like he hasn't missed out on anything, okay? Can you do that for me?"

"Okay! I will. Also, can we go shopping for some things in the morning? I think I want to switch up my looks a little bit."

She nodded her head, before replying, "Anything for you."

She quietly closed the door.

I hopped up to get my computer and phone. I needed to get connected to my business. I needed to see my accounts. The minute I turned on my computer there was a note that was already on the screen.

My Dearest Wife...

Kambridge, I decided to take a break from setting up your room and write a letter to you. I don't know how else to get to you, and I hope that you will read this letter in its entirety. I wanted to let you know that I love you so fucking much, and I want you to know that I am very sorry for how you found out about my male escorting services. I know I'm a piece of shit for not telling you, but I can promise you, I never ever ever ever cheated on you after I gave you my last name. I love you. You changed my whole life. You changed my life for the better. I am truly a better person because of you. I'm truly sorry for causing you to almost kill yourself, and I feel so bad for causing you to lose our child. I was really looking forward to being a father. I pray we get the chance to make another baby. I really feel like we should talk like two adults, even if it doesn't end in us getting back together. Kam, if I don't hear from you within twenty-four hours of you reading this letter, I will leave you alone and let you live your life.

Your husband,

Phoenix Allen Bailey, Sr. (I'm sure our kid was going to be a boy)

I rolled my eyes so hard at everything in this letter. I closed the laptop and went into the bathroom to free my skin of the make-up. I slid in the bed and waited twenty minutes for Mr. Wilson to come in and tuck me in, but he didn't. I left my room and went to tap on his door.

"Yes," he said, sticking his head out his door.

"I thought you said that you were going to tuck me in."

"Okay! I'm coming!"

He followed me into the bedroom, and I got in the bed. He pulled the covers over me, and then rubbed his fingers through my hair.

"I never thought that I would ever have a moment like this. At one point, I stopped praying for a miracle, but then the moment I saw you walk into the jail cell, I knew my life was going to get better. I mean, I hate that's the way it happened, but I'm glad it happened."

"I feel like I robbed you of a chance to be a grandfather. Are you mad at me?" I started to burst out into tears.

"No, baby girl. No. I'm not mad at you. I just want you healthy, and I promise that you are going to be a mother one day. You're going to give me some beautiful grandbabies. I hate that they would have to get to know me from behind bars, but I'm willing to do whatever I have to do to help you out. I love you so much, Kambridge."

"I love you back."

He left my room, and not long after he left, I got some of the best sleep that I had gotten in a long time.

Paxton 'Korupt' Bailey

"*P*ow! Right in the kisser," I laughed as I imitated how my daughter-in-law knocked Malice in his mouth. His shit had swollen up like two watermelons.

"Ha ha ha ha he he he," Malice fake laughed behind the ice pack that he was holding against his lips, while Mayhem was snickering.

"Paxton, leave my baby alone," my wife said, and laid Malice's head on her shoulder and rubbed her hands through his hair.

"Mane, that nigga ain't no baby. Stop babying him. His wife told him to leave her alone, and I guess he thought that she was playing. Pow! Right in the kisser!" I imitated Kam again.

Malice waved me off.

"In all seriousness, Malice, how much do you know about that Cat lady?" I asked him.

After my wife had to beat her ass in the store the other day, I looked more into her. I wanted to know what he knew, and I was going to tell him what I found out about her.

"Actually, we hardly talked about her past. All I know about her past is that she had a husband who died in a car accident. That's all I know. She used to be a lawyer, but now she teaches other students for the bar exam. She sold her husband's law firm, and that's why she got all the money that she has now, and he had a healthy life insurance policy. So, she's doing well regarding money. Why what's up?"

"Well, after your mom tossed her up in the store, I looked into her background. All of what you said is true, but did you know that she takes psych meds? And there were rumors that she killed her husband because he had a black mistress. Also, she paid detectives, and other people, to say it was just a car accident, but really the tires were loosened on the car. So, it concerns me that she will try to harm you son. You will have security with you every time you leave your house. Starting today. I don't want to take any chances. Understand me?"

"Harm me how? Like, kill me? Dad, I'm not worried about that woman. The most she will do is throw out some empty threats, and honestly Dad, she loves me too much to kill me. Trust me. All she wants is some of this monster, and she will calm down. If my wife don't get her act together, I'mma have to hit her up for some top."

SMACK! SMACK!

My wife slapped him upside his head twice, and then grabbed his chin, making him look at her.

"Phoenix, promise me that you won't mess around with that woman anymore. She is a woman first. You know what types of feelings she has for you, and she ain't right in the head. Love will make you do some crazy things. Please leave her alone."

"Aight, ma! You need to keep your hands to yourself too ma, dang! You been hitting me a lot lately."

"Because you been doing stupid shit lately. Now, move! Me, your father, and your brother have a dinner engagement that I need to get ready for."

"Wow! Why am I not invited?"

"Well, because your wife invited us for dinner at her house."

"Well, put in a good word for me. I ain't going to be begging her too much longer, to be honest. I mean, I know I was wrong for not telling her about my life, but I never cheated on her when we got married. I wrote her a note on her computer telling her if I ain't hear from her within twenty-four hours of her reading that note, then I was going to leave her alone, and by the time y'all get back, it will have been twenty-four hours."

"Do what you feel is best, son, but you know you ain't gon' be done with that girl," I let him know.

"Just put in a good word for me, Dad. You know how good you are with the ladies," Malice said with a serious voice.

∞

"Damn, you looking good in that dress, woman!" I admired my wife's ass as she walked in front of me into the truck.

"Thank you, Daddy! I can't wait for you to take it off me tonight."

"Ugh, Ma! Kill the visual. Y'all way too old to be having sex. Yuck!" Mayhem said shaking his head.

"Boy, fuck you! You just need to find you some pussy that you want to be in until you're past fifty. Mind ya' business," I said to him.

"You got it, Pops!" Mayhem said.

Once we were seated into the truck, we headed towards Big Will's house. I was going to make sure that my bro lived his best life for the time that he was going to be out that hellhole. I took him to the strip club to have some fun, and he ended up with Kam's case worker. I knew she wasn't no bitch he was just hitting, because the only thing he said when I asked about her was 'she was cool.' I knew that meant that it was more than just a fuck, and I found out that she hadn't left that house since he took her there a few nights ago. I told him that his old ass better not fuck around and get her ass pregnant. She's forty-five, and he's fifty-five. They asses are too old to be trying to raise a kid, although he said that Olivia wanted kids, but her soon-to-be ex-husband told her no. He said that she also said that she fell in love with Kam when they first started talking. Olivia said that Kam reminded her so much of herself. So, in my opinion, she would be a good step-mom.

"What's on your mind Daddy? You got that look in your eyes when you're thinking about something," Angela asked me.

"Nothing, really. Just hoping that Olivia is as cool as Big Will says she is. I don't want him stressed out about this broad while he's out. I want him stress free and living his best life for the time being. Kam should be his only focus, not a broad."

"Shut up Pax, and stop hating. He is living his best life, and I think Trent knows if a woman is playing him or not. Kambridge is the most important thing in his life. Even though he has never had a conversation with her until a little while back, she has never left his heart. You know that."

"Yeah, woman I know that. It's just—"

"Just nothing. You just wanted him to fuck different bitches, and he don't want to do that. If he wants to focus on Kam and Olivia, then he... ohhh, I get it. You just mad that he won't have time for you," she chuckled. "My big baby mad because he has to split his time between three people. Awwwee," she spoke in a baby voice while pinching my cheek.

"Watch out, man!" I said trying not to laugh at her.

"Dad it sound like you hating to be honest," Mayhem interjected.

I was getting ready to respond to him, but the driver interrupted us.

"Mr. Bailey, I don't want to alarm you, but I think that we are being followed," Charles said.

Our windows were tinted dark as fuck, so I could turn around and look. Me and Mayhem pulled our guns from our waists, and Angela pulled hers from her purse.

"Hit a sharp left, Charles," I commanded.

"Baby, I think there are multiple people in that truck. They are going to fire us up," Angela spoke while looking out the back of the window.

"Charles, make a sharp right."

He made a sharp right, and I could see good into the car. It was like three niggas in the car, and it was going to end bad for them. I could feel it in my soul. My adrenaline was rushing. I hadn't been in a shootout in decades, but today is my lucky day.

"Baby, when I tell Charles to make a sharp left. See if you can shoot out both tires. Okay?"

My wife screwed her silencer on, and let the window down a little bit. I waited until she was in a very good position, and I told Charles to hit the sharp left. He did, and my wife executed the shots perfectly, making the car topple over twice.

"See if I can shoot out both tires. Nigga I was born for this. Don't you ever try me," my wife said unscrewing her silencer.

Luckily, this road was empty as fuck, which was not normal, but God be working in my favor sometimes. Charles did exactly what I wanted him to do without asking. He doubled back around quickly, and pulled up behind the truck that had landed back on its tires.

I told Angela to stay in the car, and me and Mayhem crept up behind the truck. You could hear the grunts and groans from their mouths. They were hurt badly. Mayhem trained his gun on the guy in the front seat, and I trained mine on the guy in the back seat.

"Who sent you?" I asked him.

He spit out a mouth full of blood, before replying, "Fuck you! You're going to kill me anyway."

"You're right!" I said.

POW!

I gave him a clean shot to the head. I scooted to the guy in the front seat, and placed my gun to his forehead.

"Now, who sent you idiots? I only ask once."

"Fuck—"

"Wrong answer!"

POW!

I realized there was a hole in the windshield, meaning we were missing one. In front of the truck was a body. A limp body, but he was alive. I know the 'play dead' role when I see it. I have done it a few times. I squatted and tapped the back of his calf muscle with my gun.

"Hey. Get up. I'm not going to kill you, but who sent you?"

"Ka... Ka..." he started to choke on his own blood.

His phone started to ring in his pocket, and I grabbed it. I answered it.

"Is it done?" the guy's voice came through the phone.

"Kason, now you know me better than that. Tell your next set of boys better luck next time," I said into the phone.

The phone hung up, and I smirked to myself. I don't know why Kason keep playing with me. My wife told me to leave him alone, but he keeps fucking pushing it. When we got back to the truck, Angela was eagerly waiting for the information.

"Did you get some answers before you shot them?" Angela asked.

"You know I always get answers. It was Kason's bitch ass."

"We have to kill that bitch, and we are going to have to tell our daughter-in-law that tonight. It's lights out for that sack of shit."

My wife knows how to get me turned on. When she gets amped up and starts talking that gangsta shit, my dick gets hard as fuck.

"We are going to get him, bae. Calm down before I show our son how he got here," I chuckled.

The rest of the ride to Trent's house was cool, but we kept looking out to making sure no one was following us. The moment we got out the car, we could smell the food. It was smelling good too. As soon as Mayhem knocked on the door, it came open, and there stood my beautiful daughter-in-law, who now had a new look. She had orange hair. Looking like a black Jessica Rabbit.

"Uh, am I at the right house?" Mayhem jokingly asked her.

"Yes, you are. Come right in guys!" she said.

She peeked her head out around us before she shut the door and locked all the locks.

"Who you looking for?" I asked her.

"I just wanted to make sure that you were alone, and y'all didn't bring any uninvited guests. Make sure no one was hiding in the bushes or something like that."

I chuckled at her as we walked in the kitchen, to see Olivia, and my bro kissing all over each other by the bar.

"Damn, my nigga! Make sure you ain't dropped no damn slob in the food while y'all over there sucking each other lips off and shit."

"Whatever, Mr. Bailey," Olivia said grinning like a school girl.

I knew then that her ass was feeling my brother, and the way he stole glances at her, let me know that he was feeling her too. We sat at the table and waited for Kam and Olivia to serve us. My wife wanted to help, but Kam insisted that she stay seated. After we prayed over the food, it was quiet for a moment, before Kam started to speak. I knew what we were here for, but I just didn't expect her to dive right off into the conversation like that.

"So, I have to ask. What is the relationship that you and Mr. Wilson have with Kason? I mean, I know all y'alls problems didn't start the day I was born, so what happened, and I want the truth. I can take it."

"Aight. I was cool with Kason back when we were teens. Kason never was a bad boy so I don't even know why he's pretending to be one now, but we will get into that later in the conversation. Long story short, he was about to get his ass beat over a pair of his new school shoes, and me and your father saved his ass. Once I let the block know that he was cool, people never bothered him again. He started coming around wanting to get in the game, but I knew he was a yogurt cup, so we only let him deliver packages."

"I don't mean to interrupt, but... yogurt cup?"

"Soft. Kason was soft. Never ever ever ever even held a gun before. All that changed when he said that he was ready to join the big boys. He said that he wanted to rob someone. Let the nigga hold my gun to stick up the store, and he dropped my shit. I ended up going to jail for a few years for that. Well before that, I had robbed my connect and stole the gold that he had stolen from someone. Don't worry, it will all make sense in a minute. So, in jail, I told Kason about my gold so he could move it for me, but this nigga ended up stealing it all, but used some of it to pay for school."

She twisted her lips up like she wanted to say something, but she didn't.

"I know you are probably wondering why am I mad about that, and you're absolutely right. I wanted Kason to have a better life, because like I said before, he's a yogurt cup. He wasn't built for this type of world like your father and me. It wasn't so much that he stole it, it was the fact that he lied about it, and didn't even give me the rest of it. So, I went around trying to force people to tell me if they knew about my shit, but they didn't. I ran up on his parents for some reinforcement, but that was a bust, and... at their funerals was the last time I saw Kason."

"Reinforcement? Funeral? Are you saying that you killed my grandparents, Mr. Bailey?"

The room got really quiet, and I felt like you could hear Kam hold her breath waiting for the answer.

"Yes, Kambridge, I killed your grandparents, but that's a part of the game. If Kason doesn't know anything else, he knows how the game goes. So, ever since he has become judge, he has been trying to get back at me by locking up all of my family and friends, starting with your father. He set him up. Kambridge... I have several people in my pocket. Trust me. Your father had never been to jail, and for what he had in his car, at best, he should have gotten fifteen to twenty years. Your father doesn't get life in jail for what he had, Kambridge."

"I understand. The game is the game," she whispered quietly.

"I think that's enough for tonight," Trent said.

"I'm fine, Mr. Wilson," she said to him. "Mr. Bailey, did you have Malice use me for that... to try and get your gold back?"

I paused for a moment before answering, "Yes, I did, but it didn't work. He fell in love with you, and I didn't want him to at first, for the sole purpose of a moment like this. Secrets coming out and hurting the people that care most about you."

"I want to be mad, but I really can't, Mr. Bailey. My dad... Kason, wanted me to set up Malice, but I ended up falling in love with his dog ass too. He kept saying that you, him, and Mayhem are drug dealing murderers, but I never got that vibe from either of you. I never told Kason anything regarding y'all, because I never knew anything about y'all until we went to St. Maarten. He never told me, and unfortunately, he had a listening device in my suitcase, so he heard everything. He said that I was going to have to testify against you, or something like that," she said and looked up at me with the brightest eyes.

At that very moment, I felt like a piece of shit that I had partook in using this very innocent girl for something so selfish, and caused all of this in her life.

"I have to be honest with you. After this stunt tonight, Kason sending three men to kill me and my family, I'm going to kill him. I just wanted to make that clear to you," I said to her.

"WHAT!" Trent said and looked at me crazy.

"Yeah, man. I'll catch you up on that later."

"Mrs. Bailey, can I ask you a question? If Mr. Bailey slept with your mom, what would you do? Would you forgive him?"

Her eyes welled up with tears, and I could tell that she was truly in love with my son. I don't even see them surviving without each other. It seems like their love is like a virus, and it's going to eat at them both until it kills them, or until they get back together.

"Um, I honestly don't know what I would do because I have never ever been put in a situation like that before, but my husband has cheated on me before, several times. I stayed with my husband because I loved him, and we had very hard times in our relationship where we loved each other, but didn't quite like each other. It caused us both to start doing things to try to see who could hurt each other the worst, and then all of a sudden it stopped. Like out of nowhere... stopped. We sat down, talked, and realized that what we were doing was stupid as fuck. He didn't want to lose me, and I didn't want to lose him. Does that help?"

"I don't know. I guess," she solemnly said. "Guys, thanks for coming. I'm going to excuse myself and go get ready for bed. Mr. Wilson, can you come tuck me in when our company leaves?"

"Yes, I will be right up," he said.

My man was happy. This was the life that we were supposed to have; having dinner with our families and kids.

He watched her until she was out of the dining room, and then he looked at me with his eyebrow raised.

"Mane, that nigga had three fucking amateurs trying to ambush us, and we took 'em all out. That nigga is going to have to see us, man. Not like he would ever get that much firepower to ever go against us, but it's the principal."

"I want a piece of that nigga alive. I wanna beat that nigga the way he would beat my baby girl. A nigga broke down and cried after seeing all those scars he put on her. Like she showed me a few before, but to see them, and to rub on them had me infuriated. I'mma beat that nigga with a belt, and see how he likes that shit," Trent said.

"Well, I got word that he ain't a judge no more. Well, they benched him until the investigation with lil' mama is over with," Mayhem said.

"About that, how is that case going?" Angela asked Olivia.

"Well, I did have to add a protection detail to the doctor. I'm not supposed to be telling you all this, but Kason and his lawyer tried to shake down Dr. Compton and tell him that the poisoning was accidental, but Dr. Compton told them to get the hell out of his office. So, the minute that we can get a hearing, we will know if it's going to trial. After Kason flaunted his power in front of me and my officers, I requested for another judge to come in and do the hearing. I want to make sure my client gets a fair trial, and she won't get that from a judge here in this city," Olivia said.

We laughed and talked for the next hour or so before Trent said that he was going to tuck his baby girl in. Olivia thanked us for coming, and escorted us out of the door. I don't know about Kason, but for me, life was good, and was going to get better.

Kambridge

The minute my alarm went off, I jumped up quickly, and recited my new mantra from *Baby Boy*. *Today I begin a new life; for I am the master of my abilities, and today is going to be a great and beautiful day.* I am going to say that every morning. I was so excited to go back to work that I couldn't contain it. I hadn't pressed a shirt in four weeks. Four whole weeks. I jumped in the shower and took care of my hygiene. I looked in the mirror at my orange hair, and laughed. I didn't mean to get it this dark, but I got to laughing and talking with Olivia, and left the shit on my hair too long, and now I look like a black ass Jessica Rabbit. I had my hair straight with a few bumps at the ends, so I pulled it up into a top knot on my head. I put on a black Adidas hoodie and pants, paired with some Rihanna Creepers. You know I had to do my make-up.

I looked around for my keys, but then I remembered that I didn't have my keys to my car. I went, and knocked on my dad's door, and he told me to come in. When I walked in, he was standing in his mirror in a black Jordan flight suit. My mouth gaped open at how he was dressed like me.

"Um, Mr. Man, where are you going this morning?" I asked.

"Well, I hope you don't mind an old man tagging along. I just wanted to see what you did for a living. I don't have to go if you don't want me to go."

"It's fine. You can come with me if you want. I came to your room to ask how I was going to get to work since I don't have my car," I said to him.

"Oh, we actually had your car from Kason's house, but then we got rid of it. I didn't want him to track your car here, so we got you a new one," he said to me, and then threw me a set of keys.

"I meant to ask you, how did you get this house? Do you have money? I have money in my savings account, and if—"

"Baby girl, I have money. I'm fine."

When we got to the garage, I saw my car. It was the same car that I said that I was going to get once I turned twenty-five. It was a white Mercedes AMG. I wanted to cry, but I didn't want to mess up my make-up. I walked around the car and saw that my car tag had 'MB Wife'. I rolled my eyes because I knew that Malice had purchased it. I turned the alarm off and got in the car. When I slid into the seats, it felt the same as when I had slid into the seats of Malice's black Mercedes AMG. Mr. Wilson slid into the car, chuckling at how I was admiring the car. Attached to the steering wheel was an envelope. I snatched it off, opened it, and read it aloud for myself, and Mr. Wilson.

"To my wife: I love you more than life itself, and it makes me happy to see you happy. This is a gift to show my love and appreciation for you. I hope you squirmed and screeched when you slid into the seats of your car, like you did when you slid into the seats of mine. My heart beats for you woman, and I pray that you find it in your heart to forgive me for keeping that part of my life away from you. We can start all the way over if you want... as friends, and then work our way back up to our marriage. I'll go to counseling. I'll do whatever you need me to do, if it leads me back to you. Happy Riding. Phoenix, Sr."

I chuckled at him calling himself Phoenix, Sr, and stuffed the envelope in the arm rest.

"Phoenix, Sr?" Mr. Wilson asked.

"He believes that our child was a boy, so he named himself senior. I don't know how you do that, but whatever makes him happy," I said.

I backed out of the garage, and the ride to my store was very quiet until my dad spoke.

"I don't want to tell you how to live your life, but don't be so headstrong that you miss out on love. Don't look at me with those big eyes. Don't be so hard on him. Maybe have a conversation with him, and then after that, you guys can go your separate ways."

I let out a huge sigh, because I don't see why we need to have a conversation, because my mind is already made up. I figured the conversation that we had back at the joint was enough for us.

"So, you and Olivia are getting pretty serious, huh?" I asked, changing the subject, hopeful that he would leave me alone about talking to Malice.

"I wouldn't say serious because you know, I have to go back into that place, but we are getting more and more cozy. Don't want her to get her feelings hurt when I have to go back to prison."

Thinking about him having to go back into prison made me get real quiet. I didn't want to have to talk to him in that environment after getting time with him on the outside. We pulled up to my store, and it was a long line coming out the door next to my shop. Reporters were outside as well, and I was hoping that they were out there for this new place that opened. There wasn't a sign on top of the store, and the window was covered up by patrons, so I don't know what's going on inside the store.

"What the...?"

The minute I put the car in park and jumped out, the reporters rushed over to me and Mr. Wilson. They were asking me question after question after question. Mr. Wilson shielded me until I walked into my store. Shelly was standing behind the counter, showing customers some of our shirts. I took a minute to look around the store, and the updates that Shelly had made to my store were perfect. There were flowers everywhere, and at first I thought that they were from Malice, but they weren't. They were from people that were sending me well wishes after everything that I had been through.

After the customers that Shelly was helping left out of the store, me and Mr. Wilson approached the front, and she came around and embraced me in a tight hug.

"Girl, I ain't know who you were walking in here with his orange hair," she laughed pulling at my orange top knot. "Hey, Mr. Wilson. How are you? Y'all came in here looking like twins. You like your daughter's place of business?" she addressed him, and hugged him at the same time.

"Yes, I like it. This is nice baby girl," he said looking around, and then kissing me on my forehead.

That made me so happy, because Kason had never been in here

to tell me that he even liked the place. I knew that Kason was toxic because of the way that he would beat my ass, but I thought that he at least loved me a little. Mr. Wilson has been so attentive to me, that it's like he's almost smothering me with love. I never felt anything like this before from neither Tracey, nor Kason. It's so refreshing.

"Do we have some orders, Shelly?" I asked her, because I wanted to show Mr. Wilson how to do my job.

"Yes, we do. I'm actually about to start on an order right now, but since you are here, you can work on one, and I can work on the other one," she said.

"Shelly, I want to thank you so much for holding down the fort while I was out of commission. We have to go on a vacation soon. Is that okay with you?"

"Girl! I was so happy to take over. I was starting to think that I could start helping you full time. Be your manager or something."

"Oh girl! You know I can use the help sometimes," I said following her to the back with Mr. Wilson in tow. "Mr. Wilson, this is where all the magic happens. I also have to thank Mayhem for replacing all my machines with bigger and better machines. My store was vandalized, and I still don't know who did it. I believe it was either Cat, or could have been Tracey, you never know these days."

"Oh, girl! I also added an embroidery machine. I know that you had been wanting to learn how to do that. It took me a while to get the hang of it. I'll show you how to do it," Shelly offered.

"Oh my god! Thank you, Shelly Shell! You are really a god send!" I hugged her again.

For the next two hours, Shelly and I both tag teamed with showing Mr. Wilson how to work the machines, and he was getting the hang of it quickly. I was listening to him entertain Shelly with some of his prison stories. She was just as intrigued as I was when he was first telling me. I just so happened to look up and see Kason on the TV screen, along with Elliot.

"Quick! Turn that up!" I told Shelly, who was closer to the TV.

I miss her so much. When I first read the letter, I immediately started combing the streets, and asking people if they had seen her, since you had to wait to report a missing person to the proper authorities. Tracey, if there is any chance that you are listening to this, can you please come home? We can fix this, and get you the help that you need. Please come home.

After Kason got finished speaking on the camera, a missing person flier of my mama, and her vehicle, came on the TV screen with the news lady talking in the background.

Judge Kason came home to a Dear John letter from his wife Tracey, admitting to intentionally trying to kill their middle daughter, Kambridge, after a steamy love affair between Tracey, and a Mr. Phoenix Bailey, Kambridge's husband. In the note, Tracey also admitted to vandalizing her daughter Kambridge's store. She stated, and I quote, 'I can't live with myself after knowing what I did to my daughter. I didn't mean for any of this to happen. By the time you read this, I'll be long gone. Please don't come looking for me. Please apologize to my daughter for me. Love always, Tracey.' If any of you spot this car, or this lady, please contact the authorities.

The camera cut back to Kason and Elliot standing on a podium next to a blown-up poster of the missing person flier, and him crying. I stared at his ass in disgust.

"The devil doesn't cry," I spoke thoughts aloud. "She's not missing. He killed her," I said, as if I was talking about a random person in Chicago being killed, instead of my own mom.

Mr. Wilson and Shelly both looked at me like I had sprouted two heads out of my neck.

"Why are y'all looking at me like that? I might have been born at night, but not last night. That's a fake cry if I ever saw one. Plus, he's always said that he would kill her if she ever left him, and that he would get away with it. He's threatened us plenty of times. Trust me. I don't know how he did it, but I'll bet you any dollar in my pocket that he had something to do with it, and that creepy lawyer helped him as well."

"Kam, how are you feeling? Like... do you need to go talk to your counselor?" Shelly asked.

I shrugged my shoulders because I ain't know what to feel about anything anymore.

"I'm not a danger to myself anymore, Shelly. I just... I don't know how to feel about any of this, really. I don't know for sure that Tracey is dead, but I can just bet you that she is, and at the hand of Kason. Do I care? Yeah, in a sense, she did birth me, but does she deserve any tears from me? No. She could have saved me from beatings. She could have saved me from my first big heartbreak, but did she? No. So, I'm good. I can't change that. Michelle told me to give my focus to things that I can change. Tracey and Kason are just two people that didn't deserve to have kids," I said, and started back pressing the shirts that I was working on, no longer wanting to talk about Tracey and Kason.

My phone went off, letting me know that I had a text message.

Kade: Please tell me that you saw the news just now. Mom is missing. Do you think...

Me: Yes, I'm back at work. You know Kason. We don't have to think. We already know. The only question we have now, is if her body will ever resurface, and how are we going to get Kason to admit to having something to do with it.

Kade: Our lives are going to be one big shit show until this shit is all over with. You know they benched him from being a judge.

Me: Our lives? At least you don't have a wife that's in the news for fucking with your dad. Yeah, Mayhem told me that last night. Did you know that Mr. Bailey killed our grandparents? Kason's parents. Apparently, Kason stole from Mr. Bailey, and he said it was a part of the game or some shit. Kade, I just feel like I'm living in one big nightmare. Do we tell Kalena that mom is more than likely dead, or do we just go along until the body is found?

Kade: Kalena is smart. She's seen Kason in his worst form. I'm sure she won't put anything past him anymore. However, don't text anything like that again. Delete that last text message out of the thread.

Me: Okay. I love you. Gotta get back to work.

Kade: Love you back.

"Shelly, what's up with that new place next door, and why were there so many people lined up?"

"Oh, there is this new hip-hop dance studio, or something like that. The choreographer worked with Beyoncé, Usher, and Breezy before, so everybody is trying to get classes with him. I haven't seen him yet."

"Oh. Sounds great. I'll probably go introduce myself after work is over. Maybe we can work a deal or something regarding outfits for his team, or make-up."

"Like father, like daughter. Business minded," Mr. Wilson chuckled.

***

The work day went by quickly because we were busy the whole time. When Shelly left to take all the boxes to the post office, me and Mr. Wilson cleaned up and locked up. Walking outside, I could see that the lights were on in the studio, and the music was blasting. The window was frosted, so you couldn't really see inside.

"You can wait in the car. I'm going to stop in here, and introduce myself to the owner," I said to Mr. Wilson.

He looked like he wanted to protest, but he didn't. He walked to the car, and I walked inside of the studio. The guy was in the mirror dancing his ass off, looking like Chris Brown. I was intrigued. He saw me standing at the door, winked, and kept dancing until the song went off. He turned and walked towards me. He had on a pair of black joggers with a white tee shirt, and it was soaked. He had his hair in the popular hair cut that the boys are wearing now; shaved sides with a pony tail on top of his head. The way his was curled, you could automatically tell that he was mixed with something.

"Dontay James, Jr, Tay, or DJ," he said with his sweaty hand held out.

Black. He's mixed with black. I thought to myself. I stared at his sweaty hand, and he chuckled, and wiped it on his sweaty pants like that would make me shake his hand.

"I just wanted to introduce myself. My name is—"

"Kambridge. Kambridge Bailey. You are allllll the news has been talking about for the last month. I feel like I know you already."

"It'll be back Lewis, soon. I wanted to come introduce myself since I work right next door. We'll probably be seeing each other a lot. What was the line for today?"

"Oh, great! It'll be nice to work next to a very beautiful woman," he said and smiled.

His teeth were very straight and white. Looking at his facial features, he looked like he could be Chris Brown's distant cousin. He had a sandy red beard and a thin mustache with a pair of full, pink lips enclosed in the middle of it. His eyes were dark gray, and I must say that he is very fine.

"The line was because I was auditioning for a hip-hop recital that I will be putting on in three months, and it seems like there are a lot of dancers in this area. Would you like to try out?"

"Oh no, no. I have two left feet, Dontay. I'll trip over there, and fall and crack my head wide open to the fat meat shows," I chuckled.

"I can help you. Dancing relieves stress, which I'm sure you are under with everything that is going on, ya' know! Come on, let me show you an eight count right quick."

"I can't dance, Dontay! I don't want you making fun of me."

"Come on," he urged. "Let me see. You ain't gotta be scared, and you can't look worse than what I have seen today. Trust me."

He walked over to the stereo and pressed play, and Beyoncé's song "Partition" came on, and he waved me over to him.

"Watch me... in the mirror," he commanded.

He tapped his foot four times, and then bust into some damn moves that looked complicated for Michael Jackson.

"Wait a minute, that was eight moves? It looked like thirty-two," I whined.

"Watch me again."

He did the eight count like five more times, and I was still standing there looking stupid.

"Let's try. Just follow me."

We did the first four counts like three times, before I concluded that dancing is not for me, and I need to quit while I'm already behind.

"You're getting it; I'm not going to let you give up. You're getting the hang of it, but clean your moves up. Make it look crisp. Stop flapping like you're a fish out of water. You have to move like you're in the military. Like if one of you are off, you all are off."

"Okkayy," I groaned.

"Also, don't think too much about it. You can tell from your face that you are thinking about the moves. Almost as if you are forcing yourself to do the moves. Just dance. Don't think about it."

Before we could get back to the moves, Mr. Wilson had stepped in the door with his gun at his side, and Dontay damn near jumped out of his skin.

"Don't worry, that's my dad," I whispered to him.

"Oh!" he blew out a sigh of relief. "I thought that he had come to rob me or something. My Glock over there in my bag. He looks different than the way they showed him on TV."

"Well, they only showed his mugshot," I said to Dontay. "Sorry, Mr. Wilson. I'm coming. My bad for keeping you waiting," I said looking at the clock on the wall, noticing that I had him waiting for almost thirty minutes.

"Don't worry. Finish what you're doing."

"Don't worry about it. Just go over that eight count I taught you, and we can work some more whenever you get a chance. Also, take my card. All my information is on there. We can do private lessons if you don't want to practice with everyone else," he said, and flashed me that million dollar smile.

Dontay followed me over to Mr. Wilson and fist bumped him, and we left out the studio.

"You're going to get that young man hurt really bad, girl," Mr. Wilson said as soon as we were in the car.

"Please don't say by Malice, because I am truly not worried about him. I'm going to the courthouse first thing in the morning. I don't want to talk about this anymore. Our marriage is over, and there is nothing for us to fix. It won't work," I said, basically answering every question that he was going to ask.

My only hope is that he lets me go, and signs everything quick. We don't have anything but those bank accounts, and we can just take what we both put in, and that will be the end of that. I shouldn't be thankful for this, but I'm kind of glad the baby didn't survive, because I literally don't want nothing left of Malice, but I'm keeping this damn car. He knew this was my favorite car.

Malice

I was damn near pacing a hole in the cement waiting for Kam to pull into the garage. I timed it, and she should have been here at least forty-five minutes ago. She couldn't have read the letter that I left on her computer, because I told her that if she didn't contact me in twenty-four hours, then I would leave her alone. Surely that is not what she wants. How could she want that when she had secrets too? I had just finished my fifth blunt for today, when the garage started to raise.

I could see from here that she had rolled her eyes. When she stepped out, my eyes bucked out of my head when I saw what she had done to her hair. I loved it. She looked like a black Jessica Rabbit.

"What's up, Unc?" I greeted and dapped him up, while Kam tried to slip into the house, but I grabbed her by her wrist, pulling her to me. I waited until my uncle walked in the house to speak to Kam.

"Kam, why are you treating me like this? You know I love you. I get it, I fucked up, but what can I do to make it up to you?"

She folded her arms across her chest, and started tapping her foot against the pavement. She stared at me with watery eyes, and in my heart, I knew that she was getting ready to say something that I didn't want to hear.

"There is nothing... well, there is something that you can do. Just sign the papers when they are delivered to you. Malice, this marriage cannot be fixed. You lied to me. You married me with all those lies in your heart. Our shit was built on a lie."

Cocking my head to the side and squinting my eyes, I glared at her.

"Kam, you acting like you ain't have secrets in your heart! You acting like you wasn't trying to set me and my family up for your wacky ass step-daddy. You acting like you came in this thang innocent. Don't do that!" I snapped.

"Oh please, I wasn't a prostitute. My secret was nothing compared to yours!" she hissed.

"WHAT? YOUR SECRET COULD HAVE GOTTEN ME AND MY FAMILY ARRESTED FOR THE REST OF OUR LIVES. KAM, I TRUSTED YOU!" my voice elevated.

"BUT OBVIOUSLY NOT ENOUGH TO TELL ME THAT YOU FUCK FOR MONEY! OBVIOUSLY NOT ENOUGH TO TELL ME THAT YOU FUCKED MY MOM. WHAT KIND OF TRUST IS THAT?"

I closed my eyes for a moment so I could get myself together. I didn't want to get too upset, because we wouldn't get anything done this way.

"Kam, that was my life before I met you, but when I married you, I ceased all that shit. I never cheated on you."

She rubbed her temples like I was getting on her nerves. Her chest started to rise and fall quickly.

"MALICE, YOU DON'T FUCKING GET IT! STOP TRYING

TO MAKE IT SEEM LIKE MY SECRET IS WORSE THAN YOURS! YOU FUCKING LIED! YOU KNEW FROM JUMP STREET... THE DAY YOU FUCKING SAW THAT HOE IN THE RESTAURANT, THAT YOU FUCKED HER. YOU LOOKED ME DEAD IN MY FUCKING EYES, AND TOLD ME THAT YOU DO NOT KNOW THAT WOMAN," she yelled at the top of her lungs. "DEAD IN MY EYES, MALICE!" the waterworks started, and it was making me feel bad as fuck. She started punching me in my chest, and I stood there and took them licks like a man. "YOU HAD EVERY OPPORTUNITY TO TELL ME, BUT NOOO! YOU WENT AHEAD AND MARRIED ME. EVERYTHING BAD HAPPENING IN MY LIFE IS BECAUSE OF YOU."

"Hol' up! Everything bad happening in your life is because of me?" I pointed to myself. "You never had no good times while you were with me, huh Kam?" I asked her and stepped closer to her, making sure she barely had room to breathe. "You never knew what real love was until I stepped into your life. You can't tell me that our love can't overcome this shit."

"The whole world... nigga, I don't know if you saw the news today, but Tracey is missing, and they have our pictures plastered all over the fucking news like we are—"

"Oh, I get it. You're embarrassed. You can't be no more embarrassed than me right now, Kam. My family is being painted as if they are bad people because I had to fuck women for money. You scared to make this shit work because the world is going to talk shit about you staying with the man who fucked your mom, before he knew she was your mom. Is that what it is?"

She shook her head no, but I knew that she was lying. She is the worst liar. I dropped down to my knees and latched on to her waist. Before I knew it, my tears were slowly sliding down my eyes. She was trying her best not to look at me.

"Kam, look at me! Are you sure there is nothing that I can do to make us work? Do you love me? No, Kam, look at me. Do you love me? Look me dead in my eyes, and tell me that you don't love me, and you don't want to work this out, and I promise you that I will leave you alone. You will never hear a word from me again."

"Malice, I don't want to work this out. I married you so I will always have love for you, but I don't want to be with you anymore."

I buried my head into her stomach and bawled like a baby. This is the most vulnerable that I have ever been, and it was killing me. I felt like I couldn't breathe. She was trying to pry my arms away from around her, but I just couldn't dare let her go. She was mine.

"Kam, I'm sorry," I sobbed. "I'm sorry for making you harm yourself. I'm sorry for making you lose my son. I can't live without you, Mama! We can make this marriage work. I'll go to counseling. I'll do whatever you want, just please don't divorce me, please."

"Malice, there is nothing more to discuss. Please let me go," she begged.

Feeling defeated, I let her go. She walked in the door and slammed it. I could hear the locks click. I sat there on my knees until I heard the locks click again, and the door open. I didn't look to see who it was.

"Son, get up! Give her some time," I felt my uncle place his hand on my shoulder.

"I'm good, Unc. I did all I can do. If she can hold that over my head, then I don't need her. I just got on my knees and begged this woman to be with me. The only woman that I have ever felt this way about, and she shit on me as if her shit was smelling like roses. I'm good, Unc. I'll let myself out," I said, standing up and wiping my eyes.

I let the garage up with my spare clicker and walked out.

"Malice, don't do anything stupid and that you will regret, son!" my uncle said to my back, but I kept walking.

When I got in my car, I sped to the nearest bar. I needed a drink so bad. Something to drown my problems away. I valeted my car and walked inside the bar. I knew I would be left alone in here, because this is where the rich white people be. The live band was playing music, and it is also what I needed. Hopefully, the band can play louder than my thoughts.

"Hello, is it just you tonight?" the lady at the podium asked.

I nodded my head.

"If you want to sit at the bar, you can just grab a seat. They are first come first serve," she cheerfully said, and I offered her a weak smile.

I took the last seat at the bar that was kind of in the corner, so I could lean against the wall and get a good view of the whole bar.

"Hey, my name is Taryn B, and I will be your bartender. Is there anything that I could get you?" she asked, while placing a napkin in front of me.

"Just get me two of the strongest drinks you got back there," I said to her.

I watched her walk away, and my eyes automatically went to her ass. She was tall, slim thick, and chocolate. Moments later, she walked back over with two glasses of dark liquor. I don't even want to know what it is, I just wanted it to burn these damn thoughts away. I took one big gulp of it, and I knew it was Crown Royal. I kept drinking until it was all gone, and immediately started on the second glass.

"Hey, do you want to add some wings or something with those drinks?" Taryn asked me.

"Nah, I'm good shorty. You can bring me two more of these though."

I was just finishing off the second drink when she brought me the other two, and sat them in front of me. I caught her hand, and she started to blush.

"What time you get off?"

"At twelve. Why you ask? You trying to have some fun?"

"Yeah. I'm going to get me a room right over there, and I'm going to leave you a key at the front desk. If I'm not in there when you get there, just shower, and wait for me. Can you do that for me?"

She nodded her head and was blushing hard. I could tell, even though she was chocolate as hell.

"What's your name?"

I looked up at the TV that was behind her head, and yep, they were running that fucking story a-fucking-gain, making me angry as fuck. I pointed at the screen, and she turned around. She slowly looked back at me with a solemn look.

"Don't feel sorry for me, ma! It's a part of life."

"I knew you kind of looked familiar, but I ain't want to say anything. I have to get to my other customers. Those drinks are on the house. I'll meet you later," she said and walked away.

After sipping on my fourth drink, I actually started to pay attention to the band, and they were playing Alicia Keys', "Doesn't Mean Anything." I knew the words by heart, because that was the first song that would pop on when I turned on my New Edition station.

All at once, I had it all

But it doesn't mean anything, now that you're gone

From above, it seems I had it all

But it doesn't mean anything since you're gone.

I hummed the part of the song that made me think of my stupid ass wife. I got up and left two one hundred dollar bills on the counter under the cup. I walked over to the hotel, and got a room. As promised, I left a room key with the lady at the front desk. When I made it to the room, I pulled my phone out, and my finger hovered over my wife's name, but I decided not to call her.

I left the room and took the elevator all the way down to the garage to go outside, because I didn't want no one to see me leave. The crisp night air was making it chilly. I pulled my phone out and scrolled my phone book. My thumb shook as I held it over her name. I pressed her name and held it to my ear.

"Hello," she answered on the first ring.

"Um, you love... me?" I asked her.

"What the hell kind of question is that? You know I love you. You sound drunk. Do you need me to come get you?" she replied.

"Yeah... yeah, I do. I'm standing on this... corner. I'mma send you my location."

I hung up the phone before she could respond. I sat down on the curb. I felt like shit. My wife hated me, and she was really my life line. Like, I haven't been to school since this shit went down, and I just don't feel like it. I feel depressed. Kam had ruined me, and I would never give a girl my heart ever again.

Twenty minutes later, I saw her car coming to a stop. I stood up and got in the car.

"You are sloppy drunk. Where did you come from? Where is your car?" she blurted out question after question.

"Just drive, Cat. I don't have a destination in mind. Just drive, please," I said, and let the seat back.

After ten minutes of driving, the car was silent as hell.

"Cat, why you do me like that? I would have never did you like that. You ruined my life, ma. You bought the building, crushing my dreams, but why did you have to send that package to my wife? Huh? I lost my kid. I lost her. Everything is just gone. I been depressed. If you really loved me, why you do that to me?" I sniffed.

She didn't reply until she pulled into this run-down park. She turned the headlights off. There was no streetlight over here. She turned the light on in the car, and stared at me while I was crying. Her face started to turn red. I had never felt this weak in my life. Crying in front of women and shit.

"Malice. We could have worked out. You never even gave us a chance, and then she waltzed in, and took you away from me. How you think I felt? I never did anything to you, but be a good woman to you," she cried. "And look at you. You in here crying over this girl, and y'all ain't even been together a year. HOW YOU THINK THAT MAKES ME FEEL? I NEVER FELT YOUR LIPS ON ME. I NEVER FELT YOU INSIDE OF ME, AND YOU'VE KNOWN ME FOR YEARS," she screamed.

Ignoring her screams, I asked, "Cat, you wanna know why I never got in the game?"

"If you wanna tell me, I'll listen."

"I'm a hothead. I don't forget when people cross me. If I got in the game, the murder rate in Chicago would be higher than it already is. When I was fifteen, I snapped this boy neck, and killed him when he tried to rob my family. I promised myself that I would never mention that again to anyone. I pushed it so far back in my mind that it's like I never done it. I don't think about it. The only people that know that is you and my family. I never even told my wife about it. Do you feel special now?" I looked at her, and she had a smirk on her face like she had won the lottery. "Now, tell me something about you, baby."

I grabbed her hand and kissed it. I damn near gagged at the smell of the cigarettes all over her hand.

"I'm a murderer too," she whispered. "I killed my ex-husband and his mistress. She was black, and for a long time, I hated black people, until I met you. You were so nice and respectful. My intentions weren't to fall in love with you, Malice, but you were just too good of a man. The statement 'once you go black, you never go back' is true. You were nothing like my ex-husband. He became blatantly disrespectful with her. Going on work trips for weeks at a time. Stopped including me in shit, so one night, I followed him and his bitch! I loosened the tires on his car, and I can only assume that he was taking her to the cabin that WE bought, and the car flipped over, killing them both. I really love you, and I promise you that I wouldn't ever hurt you. I'm sorry for everything I did to you, and I never meant anything I said to you regarding losing your child. I was just upset," she explained.

I nodded my head, and at the thought of my child that would never see the light of day, I wept. I grabbed her by the collar of her shirt and pulled her close to me. I licked my lips as if I was getting ready to kiss her. Our noses were touching, and I stared into her teary blue eyes. She wiped my tears away.

"Cat, you know... you can say sorry all you want, but it won't change the fact that because of you, I have nothing," I spoke through gritted teeth.

I grabbed my gun from side, placed the gun under her chin, and pulled the trigger before she could even breathe another word. I let her go, and her lifeless body fell back against the door. Blood splatter got all over the ceiling of the car, and a little bit got on me. I pulled my phone out of my pocket and dialed my life saver, while I placed my gun back on my side.

"Yeah, nigga," he answered the phone.

"5455," I said into the phone and hung up.

The number 5455 is a code for 'kill'. I sent him my location.

I looked over at Cat's body. I chuckled at the fact that her blue eyes were still trained on me, and her mouth was shaped into an 'O'. I pulled out the blunt and lit it. I let the seat back and started pulling on it.

"You know Cat, you were cool as fuck to be honest. Like, you were cool as fuck. I don't know where shit went wrong with us. I thought you understood this shit was only temporary. If you had just kept your mouth closed, you wouldn't be sitting over there with your damn brains leaking out your head. You had this coming though. You had to know it. You walked in my woman's shop, got a shirt made, and showed up at our dinner with the shit on. Then you send her a video of us fucking! Not only did you do that, you had to send her the picture of me leaving the hotel with her mom. Then you told me that you hoped both her and my child died. What kind of shit is that? You had to know your time was coming, mane!" I spoke to her as if she could respond.

"Now, look at you," I flicked the ashes from my blunt on her. "You was fine too. Body right. You could have had any nigga you wanted. Tsk. Tsk. Tsk." I shook my head.

Twenty minutes later, I saw two trucks, a tow truck, and a van pull in, and kill their headlights. Dressed in all black, they got out, and made their way over to the car. The driver's side of Cat's door opened, and her body dropped out like a mannequin.

"What the fuck yo?" Mayhem jumped back and whispered loud as fuck. "What you do?"

"Is that rhetorical?"

My door opened, and it was my dad.

"Son, are you drunk? What happened?"

"Is that rhetorical?"

He snatched me out the car so fast, and started undressing me like I was a kid. He put my gun in his waist band. My dad started spraying me with a special solution that rids my skin of gun powder, or anything that could be picked up from a DNA swab. I looked over at Mayhem and his guys, who were getting ready to make this area look like we had never been here. Standing out in the chilly air with nothing but briefs on sobered me up real fast.

"Son, you reek of alcohol. What is going on? How did you end up with her? I need step by step."

"Well, I went over to my uncle house so I can try and get my wife back, but she turned me down. So, fuck her. I went to the bar, went in and had four drinks back to back, walked to the hotel across the street, checked in, left, and called her. We came here, and boom, I killed her. Oh yeah, she admitted to killing her husband after I admitted to... you know... that thing I did when I was fifteen."

"When we finish here, I'm going to go back to her house, and make sure she ain't leave no crazy shit laying around the house that could lead back to you," Mayhem said to no one in particular. "Malice, you aight?" he asked me.

I looked at him and shrugged my shoulders. No, I'm not alright, but I just ain't feel like talking about it. His team got the car up on the tow truck and covered it with tarp. I don't know what they were going to do, but I know that no one would ever see her car or her body again.

When my dad was done with me, he gave me a pair of blue jeans and a black polo shirt to put on, along with a black hoodie.

"Oh, I need a ride back to the hotel. This girl is going to be there waiting for me."

My dad shook his head, and I followed him to his truck, leaving Mayhem and his team to do their job. On the way back to the hotel, the truck was quiet as a mouse, until my dad spoke.

"Malice, do you want to talk about it?" he asked me.

"Nah, Dad. I don't want to talk about this ever again. I'll store this in the back of my mind along with the other one. It's all good."

"You're not going to harm your wife, are you?"

"Nah, Dad. I'm not going to hurt her. I love her, but I am going to leave her alone. I don't know what else to do. If she wants to continue to be mad over that shit, then what am I to do? I'm just going to move on."

My dad didn't reply, and we both stayed silent until we pulled into the garage of the hotel. I used my key to get on the elevator, and my dad blew his horn, letting me know he was leaving. I walked back up to my room and stood on the outside for a minute. I took a deep breath before I stuck my key in the door, and walked in. When I walked in the room, Taryn was laying on the bed butt naked, and my dick instantly got hard.

"Fuck, you sexy as shit!" I groaned.

SMACK!

I smacked her on her thick ass, and that shit rippled like a mothafucka.

"I was wondering when you were going to make it back. Everything okay?" she asked me, looking me up and down.

"Yeah, it is now. Taryn, to be honest, I came here with the intention of fucking you until you could barely walk, but I just don't have the energy right now. Can we just lay here and chill? You can stay naked, and I'll rub on that ass. Your skin soft as hell."

Grinning, she replied, "Yes. We can chill."

I got undressed, pulled the covers back, and we got cozy under the covers. We didn't even talk because the minute I was comfortable, I fell into a very deep sleep.

€

2 weeks later...

It had been two weeks since I saw my wife physically, but apparently, she made her some personal social media accounts on Snapchat, Facebook, and Instagram, which prompted me to make some just so I could see her. From her social media accounts, it looked she was happy without me, and it was killing me inside. The minute the world got wind of her social media accounts, her follower count went through the roof. I found myself combing through her comments, looking at all the men trying to spit game at her. My heart skipped a beat when she checked a girl in the comments for saying that I was a bad person. Kam told her that I wasn't a bad person, but I made bad decisions.

I had been watching the news to see if someone would report Cat missing, but nothing came up yet. I don't know what Mayhem did with her car or her body, and I didn't even care. I'm just glad that she was gone out of my life for good this time. Mayhem said nothing was in her house but cameras. He watched all the news feeds, and saw that Cat had even fucked that white boy Connor, Kam's ex, which made me even happier that I popped her bitch ass.

While watching Kam's video on Snapchat, a phone call came through, and it was Taryn. We had been getting to know each other over the last couple of weeks. She said that she wasn't going to try and force anything, because I was still married, and she knows how I feel about Kam. Taryn is the same age as me, twenty-eight years old, and she was born and raised here. She is the only child. She's very friendly, and I think that's what I need right now. A friend.

"Hello," I answered.

"Hey, you! You want to come down here and sit with me on my lunch break?"

"Yeah, I ain't doing shit else. I'll be down there," I said and hung up the phone.

I haven't see her since we left the hotel two weeks ago. I ain't been nowhere really, because I been trying to duck the process server, and plus I been depressed. I know I said I was going to leave Kam alone, but I still didn't want to be served. It'll just make things too real for me. I wanted to be her husband just for a little while longer, in case she changes her mind.

I was headed to the door when I saw Mayhem sitting in the kitchen, glued to his phone.

"So, you not going to school no more, Malice? You giving up on the dream you had before you even met Kam because shit not going the way you want it to? So, all that fucking that old ass pussy is in vain, because you are quitting school. You—"

"Mayhem, stay the fuck out of my business, bro. I got this."

"Apparently, you don't nigga. You ain't left this house in two weeks, and school started a month ago. You ain't doing your work online because your laptop ain't left the living room table, because you been cooped up in that room stalking that girl online. Take your ass back to school. I ain't going to tell you to get over your wife. You need to truly let your wife go," Mayhem advised.

"What the fuck do you know about love? You ain't never been in love, nigga. You don't know what I fucking feel inside. I feel empty, nigga. Kam was my other half, and now I feel like I don't have a soul. Sometimes, I don't have the energy to even get up, bro. This shit is painful. I can't eat. I can't sleep. Do you see these bags under my eyes? And then I spend hours just staring at the phone, hoping... wishing... that she would call, and say, Malice... come home... I miss you. We can make this work," I said, and my bottom lip started to quiver, knowing I was about to tear up again. "This shit hurt. I don't have time to be trying to overwork my brain, trying to listen to a professor."

"Have a seat, bro. Don't look at me like that."

I walked over to the table, pulled the chair out, and took a seat in front of him.

"First things first, I have a bitch doing your work for you, so you're not behind. I had your classes switched over to online, not even having to explain what was going on, because your shit is all over the news. Second, you need to take accountability for your actions and the consequences of them. Don't look at me like that. I am on your side. I will always be on your side, but I told you the moment you realized that Tracey was her mom, you should have told Kambridge. Everything is your fault. Take accountability. Third, leave...that...girl... alone. If it's meant for you all to be together, then you will be together, because that's just the way the world works. Fourth, Kam loves you. Just give her space. She doesn't need you adding to her stress. She has a lot going on, including finding out the man that raised her is not her father, her mother trashing her store, her mother trying to poison her, having to get a new kidney because of her mother, and her father killing her mother. You see how much she got going on. She doesn't have time for a relationship now. When you are served, sign the papers and free her."

"Damn, when you put it like that... damn. I feel like I was only thinking about myself and not everything else that she had going on. Thanks for putting it in perspective for me, bro."

I dapped him up and left the house. I sped to the bar and saw Taryn wave me over to a booth.

"Everything okay? You still not getting any sleep?" she asked as I pulled her soft ass into a tight embrace.

"Nah, I ain't. I'll be fine. Is everything okay with you? Is work going okay?"

"Yeah, it's pretty slow right now. Um, I think you are about to be served. There is a man walking this way that I have never seen in here before."

I turned around, and before I could make a dash, the man blocked me.

"Phoenix Bailey, you have been served," he said, throwing the envelope into my lap, and rushing away.

I tried to act like I wasn't fazed by it, but I was. I guess I was just going to have to take my brother's advice, and set her free.

Kason

*B*eing alone in this house has made it seem so much bigger than it was. The only person I had been in contact with, is Elliot. Kade and Kalena have gotten their numbers changed, and I wouldn't dare try to get in contact with Kam, although I have thought about it plenty of times. Neither one of them contacted me regarding their mother being 'missing,' and I could almost sense that they knew I was full of shit.

I was pissed as fuck that those niggas didn't even get one shot off at the fucking Baileys. I knew it was a suicide mission when I sent them, but I also thought that they would at least get one shot off. But when Korupt picked up that phone, I knew for a fact that he had murdered them niggas. The news only confirmed what I already knew.

I laid my head back in the chair, thinking about when I first met Tracey. She was the baddest thing in high school, and no one had even touched her. I was the first person to break her in, and our life was great, well to me. We went to the same college, and we were everyone's favorite couple. Tracey was oblivious to my crimes I committed while I was fucking with Korupt, or so I thought. I don't know how she knew, and now I will never find out.

As much bad shit as I have done, I never would have thought that me murdering Tracey would make me have nightmares. I have been doing my best trying not to sleep, but the minute I fall into a deep sleep, I have a dream that she is standing over me with a knife, and I swear that when I wake up, I see an outline of a figure disappear. At this rate, I'll never sleep. It'll probably be better once everything has blown over. News stations are still talking about this shit. You would think that we were those fucking Kardashian bitches or something. Every fucking news station I turn on, they are talking about my wife having an affair with my daughter's husband. The news just recently caught Kambridge coming out of the courthouse, and they were asking her if she had filed for divorce I was just ready to put all this shit behind me.

My phone rang, and it was Elliot.

"Yeah, this is Kason," I answered the phone.

"Um, I got good news and bad news. Which do you want first?"

"Shit, I guess I'll take the bad news first."

"Well, the bad news is that they found a judge, and you will have to attend the hearing to see if they are going to take Kam's case to trial, but the good news is that the case will never make it to trial, since we already have the note that Tracey left. I'm going to move that the case be dropped because Tracey is missing, and she admitted to everything in the letter," he said with extreme glee in his voice.

"That sounds good, I guess."

"Why you sounding all slumber like that? This is good news. You won't get charged for something that you didn't do. Have a drink or something."

"It's not about that. This big ass house just seems so empty without my family here. I was not supposed to be living like this. You know what I mean, but life happens. How are my kids doing?"

205

"Well, I know you can see from the news that Kam is now looking like Jessica... Jessica Rabbit, and uhhh, Kade took Kalena out of school because she was being teased. I think she is now being homeschooled by some woman that Korupt's wife hired. Kade is still working for Mr. Pryor Bailey, and Kam filed for divorce, and I think that her uhhh husband is now seeing another woman... a Ms. Taryn Bledsoe. Oh, Trent has been fucking Kam's case worker."

"Damn! Can we use that against her in court at the hearing?"

"Dude, did you forget how to be a lawyer? You know that we cannot use that against them. You not thinking straight man. You need to get your head in the fucking game if you plan on getting this case dismissed."

"You know Elliot! I don't know how I forgot about this shit! I have cameras in here! Damn I am fucking tripping. Come over right away," I said and hung up the phone.

I started doing a little dance in my seat, because I knew that this case was going to get dismissed, because for the simple fact that I'm sure Tracey is on camera doing whatever she did in that room to make Kam sick.

∞

After scrolling for hours through recordings, Elliot was shaking his head, but wasn't saying anything. Of course, on the recordings, we saw where Tracey was taking her dumb ass into Kambridge's room, and wiping her room down with whatever she was wiping it down with, to make her get mercury poisoning. I saw her taking it to the garage. The very day the doctor spoke to us about her condition, Tracey moved whatever she had from the garage, got in her car, and left. So, we will never truly know what the fuck was making Kam sick, but we all knew that she ended up with mercury poisoning.

"Elliot, why the fuck you keep looking like that? Can we use that or not?" I asked him.

He cut his eyes at me like I had grown another head out of my neck or something. He started tapping me on my forehead.

"You know why we can't fucking use that. You know EXACTLY why we can't use that. Why the fuck were you putting your hands on her like that though, Kason? That's your fucking daughter. Also, are you using your fucking brain?" he asked me while tapping on my forehead. "If you fucking try to send that in for evidence, then you will be subpoenaed for the whole fucking tape. They will see you beating the living daylights out of that girl, and you can still be prosecuted as an accomplice, Kason. Come on now, you have been doing this for twenty years."

"Fuck!" I slammed my fist down on my desk. "So, what do we do now?"

"Shit! All we have is that letter, and hope that we can get the case dismissed, because if this case goes to trial, Kason, this is going to be hard. You are making my job hard as hell right now."

"I know. I need a fucking drink, and I need some personal contact before I lose my mind. I can't go out my door without the people all in my damn face asking questions. It's like those fucking people don't have families or some shit."

"Well, that's what happens when your life becomes high-profile.

Maybe you should go to church or something. You need to be seen out and looking like you are grieving or something. Don't stay stuck in this house; you might go crazy or something. Understand me?"

"Yeah, I got it."

When Elliot walked out the door, I slammed my computer shut out of sheer frustration. I grabbed my coat, keys, and headed out to my car. I was going to have me a drink and I needed to get out the house. I didn't even call my security team, because I was feeling like I didn't care what happened to me. When I pulled out of my gate, reporters were still there taking pictures, and I swear it pissed me off that these people really ain't got no fucking lives.

After thirty minutes of driving in silence, I pulled into a bar that I frequented, and took a seat out of view from everyone. I ordered two shots of Jack Daniels, and the bartender brought them to me quickly, and I instantly chugged them down. I asked for a glass of Hennessey, and while I waited for my glass, I pulled out my phone. At times like this, I wish that I was cheating on my wife, and had some hoes I could call to get this nut off. I hadn't had sex in I don't know how long. I thought about calling the secretary who had been flirting with me, because I really needed to be inside of something.

"Are these seats taken?" I heard a voice ask me when both chairs on both sides of me slid from under the bar. I squinted my eyes and tried not to show my fear, but with both niggas sitting at my sides, I was damn near ready to piss myself.

"Aye, miss, we'll have whatever he's having, on him," Korupt said to the bartender.

Without looking at me, he said, "So, you thought it would be cool to have some lil' niggas come and try to murk me? What made you think that you would be successful in that?"

Trent pressed the gun into my side, and to the people sitting across the bar, you would think that we were just three people having a conversation.

"You wouldn't kill me in front of everybody in this bar," I taunted.

"You're right. You're right. Unlike you, I have a little tact about myself. I just wanted you to know that you are easy to get to whenever I want to get to you. Also, my wife told me to leave you alone, but you started back fucking with me, and that is unacceptable, so I'll be seeing you."

"If you kill me, you won't get none of your shit back."

Lucky for you, I don't want it anymore. From the looks of how this case is going to go, you're going to need it more than me. Hopefully, your lawyer will be able to keep money on your books when you go to jail."

"Go to jail for what? I didn't try to kill my daughter. I'm sure you've been watching the news."

"Correction: You didn't try to kill *my* daughter," Trent said from the other side of me.

"Tomato... Tomato. Your seed, I raised her. Her last name Lewis. All the same," I shrugged and took a sip of my drink.

I felt the sharp pain in my side, and I looked down to see that I was bleeding. Trent had stabbed me. I wanted to scream out in pain, but he stopped me. I felt him move the gun away from my side, but I ain't know that he was going to stab me.

"You clearly forgot who the fuck I am, Kason. One more smart remark, and I'm going to forget that we in this bar, and put something hot in your side, instead of this knife. Stop acting as if I stabbed you deep enough to kill you."

"Well, we are going to leave you to your drinks. Don't get too drunk now," Korupt said, and tapped me on my shoulder.

They both got up and left me there at the bar. I needed to leave so I can go nurse this knife wound, but I ain't want to step outside until I knew for sure that those two nutcases were out of the area.

Kambridge

$\mathcal{I}$ limped into work this morning because my body was in pain. For the last two weeks, I had been working with Dontay on my dance moves, and soon, I was going to be good as fuck at dancing, and might even participate in the Hip-Hop Dance recital that he is putting on in a few months. It's been taking my mind off Malice, and his stupid ass bullshit. Instead of his dumb ass just signing the fucking divorce papers, he contested it. I'm like nigga, we don't even have anything together. All we have is those bank accounts. All he has to do is take what he put in, out, and I'll do the same, but noooo, he wanted to make the shit difficult.

While I had been working with Dontay after work, I had been getting to know him. He was twenty-five, and had moved from Los Angeles to Chicago to help his mom care for his grandmother. She had been diagnosed with cancer, and opted to do in-home hospice. He had moved to LA with his uncle when he graduated from high school, so he had only been there for seven years. I was very impressed when he said that he worked with people like Chris Brown and Omarion. He showed me pictures of them together, and videos of him dancing on stage alongside of them. I felt like I knew someone famous. He hadn't asked for my number or anything like that, but we have exchanged social media, and his social media was way more popping than mine.

"Good morning, baby girl. How are you feeling? Did you soak in the Epsom salt like I told you to?" Shelly asked me.

"Girl, yes. I feel better than I did yesterday, but my thighs are still burning," I chuckled.

"Okay, that's good. So, I see that Malice has been talking to some girl. She was all on his Snapchat laying up under him," Shelly said, and I could feel my cheeks start getting hot. I didn't expect him to have a new bitch this fast. Damn! The nigga didn't even beg me as long as I thought he would have, but whatever.

"Girl, you ain't got to tell me. I don't follow him on Snap, but somehow the snap 'accidently' came to me. You know my page is public so people can send me snaps. I didn't even snap him back, and then he snapped again like two minutes later, and told me that it was accident. I instantly got annoyed by it, but I wouldn't give him the satisfaction," I said.

"You know mami, if you were white, your face would be very flushed. You love him, and you miss him, and you're jealous. I'm your best friend. I know you. Just give the man another chance. Both of y'all started with very messy slates, and I think that you guys should start over with a clean slate."

"Whatever, I'm over him. I just want to divorce him and never look back. I don't ever have to deal with him again."

"Oh, bullshit, Kambridge. Your dad and his dad are brothers. There is no way that you will never see him again. Chill. As if you never wanted to see him again anyway. You want him to beg you, so stop it. And the type of man that Malice is, he loves you, but he definitely ain't going to beg you."

"Whatever, Shelly. I hate him," I said, as the bell dinged and Dontay walked in.

"Hey ladies," he said, and embraced me.

He smelled so good, and I almost wanted to keep hugging him until Shelly cleared her throat.

"Hello, Dontay, how are you doing?" Shelly spoke to him.

"I'm doing good. Do you ladies want to go out for lunch around twelve?"

"Nah, I can't! I have something to take care of at the courthouse," I informed him.

"Damn, you ain't divorced that nigga yet? I'm trying to get a fucking date, and I'm trying to be respectful," he backed me against the counter and stared me down, making me swallow hard. "Soon, I won't be able to be respectful anymore," he bit down on his bottom lip, and I had to turn around. I couldn't stand to look at him anymore.

"Um, I'll still see you after work, if that's okay?" I said to him without looking at him.

"Yeah, that's okay," he replied.

He grabbed me by my waist and pulled me backwards on his body. There was literally no room in between us. He kissed the back of my neck.

"I'm ready whenever you are," he whispered in my ear, and then walked out the store.

I looked up at Shelly who was looking at me with a weird look on her face, but I had to explain myself.

"Look there is nothing going on between us. I don't even know why he did that, but I'm not ready to date anyone now. I have too much going on."

"Sure, tell me anything. You ain't got to lie to me to kick it," Shelly laughed.

I waved her off and went to the back to start working on the online orders that we had. I needed to keep my mind off this court appearance that was coming up, and I was trying to keep my mind off Dontay, and him wanting to date me.

∞

"I don't even know why I'm here," I said to myself as I pulled into the courthouse parking lot.

We had only been married for four months now, and here we are going through this shit. All he had to do was sign the papers, and let this thing be over. Olivia and Mr. Wilson were waiting for me in the front. They asked me if I wanted to hire a lawyer, but there is no need for a lawyer.

"Hey, baby!" Mr. Wilson spoke, and hugged me.

I hugged Olivia, and we walked inside. When we made it to the waiting area, Malice was there along with Mayhem and his parents. I rolled my eyes at him, as I sat across from him. I was so mad, but I couldn't keep quiet.

"All you had to do was sign the papers, you idiot," I said to him.

"Sign the papers for what? You want the divorce, I don't. Fuck outta here," he said waving me off.

"But—" I started.

"Lewis case," a lady came out of the door, and said.

He and his family had to walk by me to walk in the door. As soon as he walked by me, he stopped, sniffed, and yoked me up.

"Why the fuck you smell like another nigga, huh?"

"Get your hands off me before I punch you in your mouth again," I snapped at him, and he let me go, only because Mayhem snatched me off him.

We took a seat at the tables that were in front of the judge, and our families sat behind us. I really cannot believe we were in a courtroom.

"All rise! This court is now in session. The Honorable Judge Gaines is now presiding. You may be seated," the bailiff said.

This was so fucking weird. I don't even know why we were in here to begin with. I feel like there should have been cameras in here to record us like we were on Divorce Court. It's really not this serious. I feel like Ashton Kutcher is about to jump out on me, talking about 'I have been pranked'.

"So, I've reviewed your papers, and you guys have only been married four months. Is there a reason why you guys are wanting to call it quits after only four months?" Judge Gaines asked.

"Ma'am, he had sex with my mom. I think that is good enough reason to get a divorce," I said.

"Before I married you," Malice sniped at me.

"You knew before you married me that you had sex with my

215

mom. Had I known, I would have never married you," I rolled my neck at him.

"Mane—" Malice started.

Bang! Bang! Bang!

The judge banged her gavel.

"From now on, only speak to me, and not each other. Thank you," she spoke like she had an attitude. She was middle-aged and white, hell, Malice probably hit her ass. That's probably why she got an attitude sitting up there.

"Mr. Bailey, is there anything that you would like to say?"

"I don't want to get a divorce because I think that this can be worked out," he said to her.

"Well you thought wrong," I replied to him.

Bang! Bang! Bang!

"ONLY SPEAK TO ME! DO... NOT... SPEAK... TO... EACH... OTHER!" she shouted.

I bit my bottom lip to keep myself from shouting out something very nasty to her. I kept looking down at the desk because I ain't want to look in her face.

"Do you guys think that counseling will work?"

"NO! YES!" Me and Malice both answered her at the same time.

"Your honor, he has a girlfriend already! I don't know why he's trying to sit over there and pretend like he's so dang heartbroken over me. He's been flaunting her around on his social media. WE ain't got no assets, so I don't see why this can't end right here," I said to her.

I don't have a girlfriend," he smirked at me.

"YES YOU DO!" I screamed.

"I didn't know you cared so much, Kambridge," he said, keeping his cool.

"I don't! Stop *accidently* sending me snaps before I block you. I'm letting you stalk me in peace, so tell your little girlfriend to chill before I block you from—"

BANG! BANG! BANG!

She banged her gavel hard as hell, which low-key kind of scared me.

"Okay, I tell you both what, since neither of you can listen to what I am saying, maybe you can listen to what a marriage counselor is saying. You both are going to counseling separately once a week, and together once a week, for three months. If one of you skips ONE counseling session, then you both will be held in contempt of court, and you will be placed in jail. Now, get out of my courtroom, and I don't want to see you two again until three months from now, or if Mr. Bailey agrees that he no longer wants the marriage to work. Good day, ladies and gentlemen."

She banged her gavel and left us sitting there with stupid looks on our faces. I was pissed. I was so mad that I started crying. I rushed out of the courtroom with Olivia and Trent on my heels. I didn't stop until I got on the steps of the courtroom. I grabbed the railing so I wouldn't pass out. Two minutes later, Malice and his family walked out.

"You must have fucked her. There is no way that she would have made that ridiculous judgement, if you didn't have a hand in it. You fucked her didn't you," I said to him as he kept going down the steps. He turned around and looked at me.

"Trust me, if she was paying, then I definitely would have jumped in it," he said grabbing his crotch. "She seems like my type, right?" he asked cocking his head to the side.

I don't know where the extra adrenaline came from, but I leaped on him, and we both tumbled down the rest of the stairs. I landed on top of him, and I started wailing licks on him, but he was blocking them. He ended up grabbing my fists, containing me.

"Yeahh, that's what I like Kam! Try to hit me again," he laughed, and flipped us over, making him land on top of me. He pressed my hands above my head, making me immobile. "What are you going to do now, huh?"

"I hate you!" I spoke through gritted teeth.

Mr. Wilson and Mr. Bailey ended up yanking Malice off me. I jumped up and wanted to get at him again, but Mayhem restrained me.

"I hate you, Phoenix Bailey. I regret the day I ever laid eyes on you. I wish I would have taken off that day, and never run into you. I hate you! I hate you! I hate you! I hate you! I'm so glad I lost our child, because I never want to deal with you again," I spoke through my tears.

He looked at me, and his face softened up tremendously. I could tell that I hit a nerve when I said something about our dead child.

"For real, Kam? You wanna go low like that? Fuck you! See your dumb ass in counseling. Keep fucking with me, we'll be married for the next thirty years," he said, snatching away from our fathers and walking away.

I snatched away from Mayhem and walked away. I rushed to my car, not wanting to speak to anyone but my friends. I sent out a group text to Aiysha, Shiana, and Shelly, telling them to meet me at the bar. I hadn't had a strong drink before, but I needed one...bad.

∞

I had just downed my Sangria after telling Aiysha, Shelly, and Shiana about the fiasco that went down in court. They were staring at me, speechless. I needed them to say something.

"Kam, did you really jump on him like that? Like superwoman... and y'all tumbled down the stairs? Seriously?" Shelly asked, trying not to laugh.

"Shelly, it's not funny. I promise you it's not. I scuffed up my damn knee. I can feel that shit, now that I'm sitting here and have calmed down a lot."

"Kam, when y'all go to counseling, please take it seriously, ok. I think that if you two don't get back together, you maybe can become friends. You two have been through something very traumatic," Shiana said.

"Fuck that! Go through the motions, and divorce his ass," Aiysha said. "That nigga embarrassed you, and now the whole damn world knows that he was a male escort."

I raised my eyebrows to that statement and glanced at the door to see Connor and Holly come in the door, hand in hand.

"As if this day couldn't get any worse. Don't look now, but here comes Connor and Holly," I said, and rolled my eyes so hard.

The minute he noticed me, his hand slipped out of hers. She realized why he did, and she clutched his arm. Holly needed to know that Connor Wiles was the least of my worries.

"Hey, Kambridge, can I talk to you for a second... in private?" he asked me.

"Nah, I'm good. I heard how you tried to play me. Talking about we were going on a date, and you know that was far from the truth. I don't want to speak to you in private because last time we were speaking in private, you threatened me," I reminded him.

"Kam... just come here for one damn second," he growled, yanking me up by my arm, leaving Holly standing there looking stupid, and pulling me outside. Once we were outside, he pushed me against the wall, and I tried to get away, but he held on to me tighter.

"Connor, let me go, damn!"

"I ain't letting you go. I just need to talk to you for a second. Please, I'm not going to hurt you. I was just talking. Kam, you have my heart--"

"Don't you dare tell that fucking lie, Connor Wiles. If I had your heart, we wouldn't be apart, so miss me with that. We would not be in the condition that we are in now. It was you who fucked around on me," I said to him.

"Nah, *ma*. Ain't that what your *husband* calls you?" he asked. "You told me you ain't like no thug dudes, but you married one. Come on. Are you that fucking naïve, Kambridge? You really thought that dude was for you, huh? Now look at you," he antagonized me.

"Look at me, Connor. I found someone who loved me for who I

was. I never had to cover up for him, ever. He kissed all over my scars, and didn't care one way or the other if I wore make-up for him. If you want me to take it further, he is the one that bet me not to wear make-up, nor cover my arms up, attempting to help me love myself more, when you walked your greasy hair ass in my store, and told me that I should cover. Go back in there and talk to Holly, because that's who you wanted first," I snapped at him.

"Kam, please, you don't love him. You don't fall in love with nobody you met after two months, and you damn sure don't marry them. You are tripping."

"Connor, let me go before I—"

"Before you what, huh? You think that because you're married to a thug, that you can kick my ass," he laughed, pushing me against the wall harder. I could feel the wall imprinting into my skin.

Click!

We both looked towards the sound, and it was Malice, holding the hand of his girlfriend. He was pointing a gun at Connor.

"Nope, it's because she has a husband that will kick your ass. Let my wife go, and go tend to your bitch, before I splatter the concrete with your brain matter," he spat.

Connor's hands went up in the air, and he backed away from me, slowly. I looked at the ground because I didn't want to see Malice holding this girl's hand in front of me.

"Man, you got it. I'm done with her whore ass anyway," Connor said, and tried to brush by him, but Malice popped him in the back of the head with the butt of the gun. I jumped at the sound of Connor's jaw crushing against the pavement. I tried to brush by Malice, but he grabbed onto my arm. I tried to snatch away, but he held a pretty tight grip on me.

"Kambridge, I want you to—"

"Malice, I know you are not about to try and introduce me to this bitch you fucking. You better let me the fuck go, my nigga. I'm over you," I said snatching away from him.

"Bitch? I don't know you, and you don't know me," the girl said.

"Taryn, you need to chill," I could hear him tell her when I was walking back into the doors of the bar.

"How about Malice showed up, hand in hand with that bitch, and he fucking tried to introduce me to her," I said to the girls.

"I called him. I'm sorry," Shelly said, with her face turning red.

"From now on... don't call him for nothing. I don't care if my car had turned over in the streets, and I started to burn alive, and he was the only person that could put me out... don't call him. Let me burn to death. Do y'all understand me?"

All of their mouths fell open, with their eyes bucked. They looked like they wanted to laugh, but I was dead ass serious.

"Shelly, I'll meet you back at the store. I got to get away from here."

I threw my money on the table for my drinks, and headed towards the door, walking past Malice, who was sitting there entertaining *her*. I guess she was a bartender here. You can mark this off as a bar that I will never attend again.

Back at the store, I didn't have any customers or online orders, so I wandered into Dontay's studio, and he was in there working with a group of eager girls, who could dance fifty times better than me.

"Everybody work on those sets of twenty-four," Dontay spoke to the group, and then walked over to me with a goofy smile on his face. "What's shaking, Mama?" he asked me as we both took a seat on the bench. "You look mad irritated right now."

"Yes, I am," I sighed in frustration. "Court was a disaster. Instead of the old hag sitting up there looking at us granting us the divorce, she court ordered us to marriage counseling, and if we don't go, we will be sentenced to jail... to... jail. To... jail, Dontay. Not only that, we got into it really bad after court, and got into a fight. A physical fight, well on my end. He didn't hit me. He laughed at me. To make matters worse, my ex-boyfriend showed up at the bar where I was, with the girl he was cheating on me with, and then he tried to rough me up, until Malice showed up, and threatened him, with the GIRL on his social media. You know this nigga tried to introduce me to her?" I vented quickly.

"Wow! That really was a lot. Kambridge, I think that you are very beautiful, and if he is able to date, then I think that you should be able to date as well. Let me take you out tonight. Let's skip dance rehearsal and go out for a bite to eat or something, so we can talk more. I have to get back to these girls. Is that okay with you?"

"Yes, that is fine with me," I smiled at him.

He kissed me on my cheek, and then wiped it away. I walked out of his studio, happy that I was going to be getting out with someone that wasn't family or a friend.

Dontay James, Jr.

*K*ambridge was fucking beautiful, ok. The pictures of her on the internet and TV and shit, didn't do her any justice. Her big, beautiful ass lips, and her big, beautiful ass eyes. Her little ass body. Everything about her was beautiful, and I swear that I had already low-key become obsessed with her. Working with her over the last two weeks allowed me to get to know her personally, and not what the TV has been saying about her.

The TV has been saying that she was a psychopath, and had mental problems because she tried to kill herself, but after everything that she has been through, who wouldn't have tried to kill themselves. I mean, finding out about her husband and her mom, who wouldn't want to kill themselves after that? She had been through a lot. The only person they were making to look innocent in this was Kason, and even I could see from a mile away that he was lying about something. The news was saying that his kids turned their backs on him when he needed them the most, especially with his wife missing. The note that his wife left admitted to everything that she had done, and it's funny because Kam didn't even seem sad that her mom was missing.

I was so ready to take Kam to dinner, because I wanted to look her in her face because she was just that sexy to me. It was like time was going by slow because I was ready for this work day to be over. As

I was teaching the girls, I thought about my grandma, the reason that I came back to the city. She is sick, and I don't want my mom to have to take care of her by herself. I was hurt knowing that the doctor gave her six months to live, but she was in good spirits. When her energy permitted, she would sit up in bed and laugh with me and my mom while we watched TV, and there were days where she would barely open her eyes. Sometimes, I wish that God would just take her away from all the pain, because I know that she is in pain.

The moment that the girls left, I cleaned and locked up. Kam was waiting by her car outside. She looked up at me and smiled, making me smile back at her.

"Where do you want to go?" I asked her.

"You choose a spot," she said.

"I know this spot over on the other side we can check out," I said to her. "Do you want to follow me, or how are we going to do this?"

"I can follow you over there, so you won't have to do too much driving."

I would have been willing to do anything for her, but if she insisted on following me over there, then we could do that. She got in her car, and I got in mine. She followed me for thirty minutes to the other side of town, and found this nice little mom and pop restaurant that stays open late. This is one of the most neutral restaurants where people of all gangs and shit can come here. Basically, this place is safe. There has never been a fight or anything here, so we would be safe here.

We parked next to each other and got out. I grabbed her small hand and kissed it, making her smile. Her hands were so soft, that I couldn't help but to caress it a little.

"Seat yourselves," the woman said when we walked into the restaurant.

We took a seat, and we stared at each other momentarily. She looked around like she was kind of scared to be here.

"You are safe here, Kam. I know you told me that you don't come on this side of town often, but I can guarantee you that you are safe here. I know that you could use some good soul food."

"I don't know how you could read my mind. I have only been over here three times. So, I'm kind of nervous," she looked up and smiled at me.

The waitress walked to give us our menus, and to take our drink orders. When she walked away, we scanned our menus in silence. I looked up at her, and I could see her mouth twisting up, like she was thinking.

"I know there is a lot to choose from, but the deep-fried chicken and macaroni is very good. You can also get the pork chops and collard greens. What do you have a taste for?"

"Everything, I am starving."

"Just get the chicken platter. It's right up there in the corner."

"Yummmm, I can already taste it, right now," she smiled, and licked her lips.

The waitress came back with our drinks and took our orders.

"So, I never asked you, but what made you become a choreographer? Did people around here think you were gay for it?"

"Well, honestly, I have always loved dancing. It started with watching Michael Jackson, James Brown, and New Edition. Their moves were dope as fuck. So, I did their moves up until middle school when Usher came out. He changed the game for me. I mimicked all of his moves, and in high school, I became the drum major. Honestly, no one really thought I was gay. Hell, being the drum major got me all the girls," I laughed, but it was the truth.

"Oh my GOD! You were in band? Well, my school didn't have a band, but I had violin recitals back in school. I love playing the violin. That's one of the many things that kept me sane. I haven't played in what feels like ages."

"I got an idea. How about at the Hip-Hop Recital, you have your own opening, playing your violin? Then we turn that mothafucka out because I want you dancing, Kambridge. You have gotten better and better. You don't even look like a stiff frog anymore."

"Oh my god! That would be nice, but the type of people that will be there, might not listen to someone playing a violin."

"Yes, they will. I can assure you that they will. It's going to pop it off in a major way. What's your favorite song to play on the violin?"

"My favorite song to play is—"

She paused when the waitress sat our food in front of us. She took in the smell, and I could tell that the smell had literally made love to her nose.

"It is Halo by Beyoncé," she finished her sentence.

"You might as well box that shit up. Ma'am, she could use a few to-go boxes," I looked up to see Malice walking towards us, along with his brother Mayhem.

"Malice, what are you doing here?" she groaned like she was in pain.

"Nah, the real question is, what the fuck are *you* doing here, and with this nigga? You know this nigga?" he questioned her like I wasn't even sitting here.

"We on a date, and if you don't mind—" I started.

"I do mind that you are on a date with my wife. Kambridge, get your ass up before I toss your mothafuckin' ass up," he snapped.

"You have Taryn, and I'm currently dating. Please leave me alone so I can eat."

He got quiet, and our waitress showed back up with the to-go boxes. He sat the boxes down and started emptying her plate into the containers. She shook her head and watched as Malice emptied her plate. I could tell in her face that she was pissed.

"I'm really sorry about this, Dontay," she said, as Malice snatched her up from her seat.

"Don't fucking apologize to that nigga, and my man, if I catch you around my wife again, I'mma bust a cap in your ass. Have a good evening," he tipped his hat to me, and walked out with Kam close to him.

She looked back at me and gave me a half smile. I knew that getting close to her was going to be hard, but she was going to be worth it. People may think I'm a pussy for not standing up to them, but everybody knows that Mayhem is quiet, but deadly, and Malice is a hothead, no matter how hard he tried to hide it. When I was younger, word around town was that he had snapped a nigga's neck for trying to rob him. Ain't no telling what he would do to me, but like I said before, she would be totally worth it.

Malice

My feelings were hurt when I had to drag my wife out of that restaurant a few days ago. I mean she was on the side of town with a nigga that she doesn't even fucking know. That nigga could have easily gotten her ass killed or something like that. I can't believe she went out on a date with another nigga after our court session, after I saved her life from that white ex of hers. I know shit looked crazy how I walked up holding hands with Taryn, but I wanted to let Kam know that me and her were just friends. That's it. I mean, I send her snaps of us to make her jealous, but that shit doesn't work. I honestly don't know what else to do. I hoped that this counseling shit worked out for us because I really want to be with her. I know I keep saying I'mma leave her alone, but I just can't.

This waiting room was cold as I waited for Kam to show up for our first marriage counseling session. I don't know if she has had her personal session yet, but I'm going to have mine tomorrow. I kept looking at the time, and Kam still hadn't shown up. I pulled my phone out and was getting ready to call her, when she walked through the damn door. She had her hair pulled up into a tight bun on top of her head. She didn't have on any make-up... just the way I liked her. She had on a sweat suit with the Chanel bag purse across her body. She ignored me as she went to go check in. She didn't even sit next to me, but the petty in me made me get up and go sit next to her.

"Did you break both of Connor's arms?" she asked me as soon as I sat down.

"Maybe, or maybe not. At least he won't put his hands on you again, and he won't come near you again. Isn't that what you wanted?" I replied to her.

She sighed heavily and shook her head. We waited for five more minutes.

"Mr. and Mrs. Bailey," a woman I assumed to be our counselor, called our names from the door. She was a very beautiful black woman with long silk hair, and she had a smile that was going to light up the room.

"Good afternoon, my name is Rachel Simpson, and I will be your marriage counselor today. So, can you tell me why you two are here today?" she asked.

Before I could even speak, Kam took off like a rocket.

"You know why we are here. You have our case files all over your little desk. You have been watching the news. You know that I tried to kill myself. You know that my husband and my mom had an affair."

"We didn't have an affair," I stressed.

Rachel held her hand up so I could let Kam finish talking.

"You know that I had to have a kidney transplant because according to Kason, my mom tried to kill me. You know that we are court ordered to be here, and if we don't, we will go to jail. You know all of that, but you are still asking us why we are here. I don't know why I just couldn't keep my same counselor, Michelle," Kam said, and rolled her big eyes.

"Kambridge, Michelle is not a marriage counselor. She is a Psych Therapist. You can still see her if you would like, but not about your marriage. However, counseling only works—"

"If you work it... yeah, yeah, yeah, I know. I don't plan on working things out with him. This is his fault that we are sitting here," she said.

"Why is this his fault? Is everything Mr. Bailey's fault, Kambridge? Look at me when you speak please," she spoke so eloquently.

"Yes, it is. He could have told me that he is a male eso—"

"Was!" I corrected her.

Rachel held her hand up again to stop me from talking.

"Would you be less upset if you had known that he was a male escort, or if he hadn't had sex with your mom? You can only choose one. Which are you more upset about?"

"It ain't no which. I'm upset about them both. He could have told me that."

"I'm asking you to choose a which... now choose. Are you upset about him being a male escort, or upset about him having sex with your mother?"

"How would you feel?" Kam asked her.

"This session is not about how I feel, but how you feel," Rachel retorted.

This exchange between the two of them was getting me excited. Not that way, but she was breaking Kambridge down, and she was getting upset. I had never heard Kambridge talk this slick to nobody but me. I hated this change in her, but I liked it as well.

"I don't know which one I'm mad about. I'm mad about them both. How could our marriage possibly work when every time he slides in me, I will think about him sliding inside of my mother? It'll make my fucking skin crawl thinking about it. Kissing him in his mouth, I have to think about him kissing my mother."

"Hol up! I ain't never kissed no broad, but you. Besides a peck on the lips when I turned thirteen. You are the only person that I have ever gave this tongue girl. Let's get that straight. You don't remember how hesitant I was to kiss you? I was scared that I wouldn't kiss you right. Kambridge, look at me," she looked at me with tears in her eyes, and mine welled up as well.

"I hate that you make me feel vulnerable and weak. Got me crying and shit in front of other women. Kambridge, I promise, on my life, on our deceased kid, that I have never ever ever kissed another woman the way that I have kissed you. When I put my face in between a woman's legs, I had dental dam! I have always strapped up. You're the first girl that I have had unprotected sex with. I have never slipped up. Kambridge, I just need you to understand that."

I tried to wipe her tears away, but she smacked my hands away.

"Kambridge, how do you feel about what Mr. Bailey told you?"

She shrugged her shoulders, while wiping her tears away.

She looked up to the ceiling and sighed really hard, "I just don't understand why you had to be a male escort. You could have been anything. You are so smart, Phoenix. You could have been an accountant. A banker. A—"

"Drug dealer. I could have been a drug dealer. That's kind of the only option that my dad gave me. Kam, I'm not the type of person who wants to clock into someone's job. Do you know how long I would have had to work if I wanted to save up just for the down payment on that building I wanted? Do you know how long it would have taken me to buy the equipment that I wanted and needed for that building, huh? So, I found a way to get the money, without hurting anyone at all. That's it. I never knew about Tracey being your mom, and I know it doesn't make things better, but Kam, if you could just give us a chance to try and make this work, I believe that we can."

"Kambridge?" Rachel called her name.

"I think that we need some time apart. I mean, really apart. I love him, and I will never stop loving him, but we should take a break. I have been through so much, and a relationship... a marriage, is just something that I can't focus on at the moment. My mental health is shaky. I lost a child, my kidneys, a mom, a dad, but gained my real one, who has to go back to prison in a few months. I basically have to start all the way over, and I can't do that being pressured to stay married. I'm going to have to be a mom to my teenage sister, and imagine how that is going to be. You were a teenager before. I just want my life to go back to being normal," she spoke, and she basically said the same thing that Mayhem was telling me.

"Mr. Bailey, have you heard what your wife said?" Rachel asked me.

I nodded my head slowly.

"Here's what's going to happen. I'm going to sign off on your marriage counseling sessions, but I would like for you to keep your individual sessions to come see me. Your fathers are very close knit, and I want you guys to be able to co-exist in the same room. Is that okay?"

We both nodded our heads slowly.

After the session, we walked out of the office together. My heart was hurting, but I knew that I had to do what was best for her... for us. Luckily, we were parked right next to each other, and it looked like we had his and her cars.

"Kam," I called out to her.

She turned around with an attitude. I walked up on her and got really close to her. Her breath became hitched. She didn't know what I was going to do, and I didn't know what I was going to do. I was just happy to be close to her without her swinging on me.

"So, where do we go from here?" I asked her.

"I don't know. I need some time," she whispered.

"Kam, I'll always be here for you, aight? Just know no woman will ever mean as much to me as you do. You're the love of my life, and I'll always be here to protect you. I'm happy that we had a chance to connect on so many different levels. You're smart. You're beautiful, and have the kindest heart that any man could ever ask for. Kam, I hate the thought of you possibly being with another nigga, but make sure that nigga knows that you have a crazy ass ex-husband, who will still lay a nigga down over you. Feel me?"

She chuckled and then flashed me a smile. The smile that I fell in love with. Cupping her chin, I raised her head up and placed my lips on hers. Our tongues danced around in each other's mouths, and I felt my body getting hot. The way she was breathing as she kissed me, let me know that she was feeling the very same way that I was feeling. She grabbed the back of my neck and pulled me as close to her as she could. My dick was getting ready to burst from needing to bust a nut.

I pulled back because I didn't want to start nothing that we couldn't finish.

"We should stop," I whispered.

"Yes, maybe we should. Just bring me the papers whenever you get a chance okay," she said, wiping my lips off.

I opened her car door for her, helped her in, and watched her drive off. Leaving her alone was going to be easier said than done. If her ass still loved me, there was a strong chance that we would get back together.

Kambridge

The last two weeks have been...interesting. I hadn't heard from Malice. The 'accidental' snaps stopped, but I found myself following him. I could see that he and Taryn were getting closer, but I couldn't be mad, because this is exactly what I wanted. Dontay and I were still working together on the Hip-Hop Recital. He hasn't mentioned what happened at the restaurant, and neither have I. I'm assuming that he won't try to date me again until I'm officially divorced. I had been waiting for Malice to take the papers to the courthouse, or at least bring them to me, but he hasn't. I don't know what the holdup is this time. If we don't go to jail, then I'm fine.

I had just finished doing my make-up, when Mr. Wilson came and stood in the doorway of my bathroom. He was dressed like a 'dad'. You know those annoying dads who wear those silk two-piece suits. He looked handsome. He had his hair in two big, thick braids like he always has it.

"How are you feeling about seeing him today?" he asked.

Today was the day of the hearing. Honestly, I wish that we wouldn't have a trial, because I don't want to see Kason no more than I have to. I want to get this thing over with today and pray I never see him again.

"Um, I don't know. I haven't seen him in two months. So, I think

I will be okay. How are you feeling? I feel like time is going by so fast. You only have four months left with me. I feel like I'm missing you already, and you haven't even left yet."

"Hey. Don't you worry about me, or tomorrow. This is the best gift that I have ever gotten in my life. Being able to spend time with you and get to know my daughter. I have something for you that you were supposed to get on your twenty-fifth birthday, but I want to give it to you today. That's if you don't mind."

"No, I don't mind. I love gifts."

We mirrored each other's smile.

"Are you ready? Olivia and your lawyer are waiting for you down at the courthouse. Don't give me that look with those big bright eyes. For these types of things, you need a lawyer. You couldn't handle a mothafucka like Elliot by yourself. His name is Jackson Murphy, and he is really the best in the business. Trust me. He did everything he could for me, but Kason just had much more firepower than me at the time."

"Okay. Let's go," I said to him.

He helped me into the passenger seat and made sure I was all the way in before he shut the door. I was looking out the window the whole drive.

"What's on your mind, Princess?"

Just him calling me Princess put a gigantic smile on my face, because Kason had never called me that. Even though the first month I was being an asshole towards him, he never changed. Even though I was giving him one word answers, he never stopped asking me questions. He never stopped talking to me, even though I'm sure I gave him a hundred reasons to not talk to me.

"I'm just wondering how my life would be if you had never gotten arrested. If you were there for me from day one, I wonder what my life would be like. The way you call me Princess. The way you treat me is how I would want my man to treat me. I can finally say that I want a man like my dad, and not like my brother."

"Damn. I feel like I want to shed a few tears or something. Kambridge, if I had never gotten arrested, your mother and I would be together, married, raising you and our other kids. I loved your mother, but she was too scared of Kason, like I couldn't have protected her from him. Kambridge, if I had never gotten arrested, you would have had the best life that I could give you. All of this wouldn't have been happening right now. You would have gone to a school with people like you, and wouldn't have to worry about no white person picking on you because of the color of your skin. If I had never gotten arrested..." he paused. "We don't have to continue talking about that because I am out now. I know I can't make up for twenty-two years in four months, but I'll do my best. Just know that I am your best friend. I mean... I'll cringe when you talk about lil' niggas, but I'll listen. I mean, even when I walk back up in that bitch, I'll still be able to protect you from behind there. Do you believe me?"

"Yes, Dad. I believe you," I whispered.

I don't know what made me finally call him Dad, but I felt that this was the perfect moment for it. Trent is my dad.

"Aww, Princess. You don't know how good that felt to hear you call me that," he smiled.

We pulled into the parking lot, and there were reporters all over the fucking place.

"Oh my god! Once this is all over, remind me to never get famous. This shit is fucking annoying. My bad for cursing, but damn. I feel like I can't do shit in peace," I snapped.

Five black men in suits rushed our car. I realized one of them as being Korupt's security, and I was happy that those reporters weren't going to be in my face, asking me stupid ass questions. The security guards opened the doors for us and ushered us through the chaos outside the courtroom.

The moment we got inside the courtroom, I could feel my anxiety go through the roof. I wanted to turn around and run out into the barrage of reporters. No one was in the courtroom but family. I didn't look around, but I could sense that my husband was in the room. I could see Kason and Elliot sitting at the front, and I felt like my chest was getting tight. I eased to the front where Olivia stood with a well-dressed man, who I assumed was Mr. Murphy. They stood to greet me, as I took a seat in between them.

"How are you feeling?" Olivia asked.

"I just want this thing to be over. Can we get this thing over right now? I can't look at him," my eyes watered.

"It's going to be okay, baby. I hope that we can get this thing over today too. I haven't been feeling well over the last couple of weeks," Olivia said.

I squinted my eyes at her, and she looked back at me with a weird look. I was getting ready to ask her if she could be pregnant, but the judge walked in. I'm so sick of standing up in front of judges, to the point where if I never saw a courtroom again, it would be too soon. His name was Judge Joe Gill. Judge Gill was an old, stubby white man with a bald head, that wore gold circle glasses, and he looked like he was mean as hell.

"Where is the District Attorney?" his voice boomed.

The door burst open, and in walked a very beautiful black woman. She was thin, and she looked very frustrated. I had never seen this woman before.

"I'm here, Judge Gill. Sorry for my tardiness. My desk was clu—"

"Save the excuses. You should have been on time. Let's get started," he said cutting her off.

"Well, the case of Kambridge Lewis-Bailey and Kason Lewis, and presumed missing, Tracey Lewis," she fumbled through her papers.

"District Attorney Krystle, are you prepared for this hearing?"

"Yes, I am, Judge Gill," she said taking a deep breath.

It seems like she is new at this thing.

"On August 4th, Kambridge Lewis-Bailey swallowed a significant amount of sleeping pills. Her brother, Kade Lewis, found her and rushed her to the hospital. Dr. Compton was able to save her life. She was five weeks pregnant at the time. After testing her blood, he found substantial amounts of mercury poisoning in her system, which caused her kidneys to shut down, in turn making her have to have a kidney transplant. Surgery was successful because her father Trent

Wilson, donated one of his kidneys. Dr. Compton called the police, and we picked up the case. The case is against Kason and Tracey Lewis. However, Tracey left a note admitting to poisoning Kambridge.

When Kambridge woke up, I couldn't question her because her caseworker, Olivia Bradshaw, stated that her mental health was not in shape to be questioned regarding this subject. One statement I got from Olivia regarding Kambridge was, 'Kason and Tracey are still subjects that she didn't want to talk about, but she knows for a fact that one of them tried to kill her.'"

"Okay, Murphy, present your case," Judge Gill spoke to him.

My lawyer stood up and started talking.

"Judge Gill, my client's step-father will use that letter that his wife left to say that this case should be dismissed because there was an admission in it, but he may or may not have played a part in it as well. Kambridge had a good and hard life growing up in the Lewis household. She was a grade A student, but when she came home, she had to fight a different fight... with her step-father. Notice, I keep calling Mr. Lewis her step-father. Her real father is sitting in the back of the room, Trent Wilson, who had been sentenced to life in prison, because Mr. Wilson had an affair with Tracey."

"Objection... Relevance?" Elliot stood and said.

"Make your point, Murphy," Judge Gill spoke.

"Kason Lewis may not be innocent in this whole thing. Tracey and Kason could have conspired together. Tracey could have wanted her daughter dead because she fell in love with her ex-husband, and Kason could have wanted Kambridge dead because she was getting closer to finding out who her real father was." Murphy sat down and gave me a reassuring look.

Elliot stood up, unbuttoned his blazer, and started talking.

"Judge Gill, I move for this case to be dismissed. The letter that Tracey Lewis left admitted that it was her who tried to kill her own daughter. That is one of the reasons why she left, because I am sure that she didn't want to answer for her crimes. How Kason disciplined his daughter has nothing to do with this particular case."

"District Attorney?" Judge Gill called her.

"I would like to call Kambridge to the stand," she said.

I looked from Mr. Murphy to Olivia, and was shaking my head profusely. I didn't want to go up on the stand. I didn't want to look Kason in his face.

"Judge Gill, my client is not able to take the stand," Mr. Murphy stated.

"If she doesn't take the stand, I will be forced to dismiss this case," Judge Gill said.

A part of me wanted exactly that to happen, but I had been through too much for Kason to get away with still being the golden boy. I watched the news last night, and they really tried to make it seem like Kason was a great husband, and Tracey was a bad wife. Tracey was a bad wife and a bad mom, but Kason was not innocent either. I have watched a few episodes of *Law and Order,* so I think I can mentally prepare myself in the couple minutes it's going to take me to walk to the stand.

I stood up, watching my feet as I walked towards the stand. This was going to be hard for me. I was going to try and keep my eyes on the District Attorney, so I wouldn't look at Kason, nor my people. The seat was cold through my slacks, which helped with how hot my body was.

"Mrs. Bailey, is it?" she asked.

I looked up to see Malice glaring at me with that bitch Taryn right by his side, and I instantly got mad. He was sitting away from his family. They were sitting on the last row, and Kade was now sitting with Trent. He must have come in after I got seated.

"No, you can call Kambridge. Please call me Kambridge or Kam," I emphasized.

"How are you feeling today?"

"I feel well. Some days are better than others, but I'm making it. Trying to get back into my normal life as much as I can."

"Good. Can you walk me through the last thing you remember before you woke up in the hospital," she asked me.

I glanced up at Kason, and he was looking at me with a look that I had never seen before. I got scared. I kept looking down, but no matter how hard I tried to keep looking down, my eyes kept going back to Kason's. His jawline was flexing hard. It was like he was telling me that he would kill me if I said anything that could get him locked up.

"Um... I had. I was... I went in..." I stopped, and took a deep breath. "When I woke up that morning, I didn't feel well. I had a headache, and I threw up. My mom tried to give me some breakfast, but I didn't want any. I was too excited to eat. I knew that I was pregnant by my husband. That's what we had been working on ever since we tied the knot in

St. Maarten. When I made it to work, I had my best friend go get me several pregnancy tests from the store. When she came back from the store, I was getting ready to go into the bathroom when my mailman had come in the door. I went to go take the pregnancy tests, and when I came back, my best friend had opened the package for me, and it was my husband... um," my eyes watered, and I looked back at Malice. "My husband was on video having sex with other women, women that included my mother. I went to go confront him, and things got... very ugly."

"When you say things got ugly? Did he physically abuse you?" the District Attorney asked.

"No. He didn't. He never put his hands on me. I tore up his things, which I really feel bad about now. After that, I drove to a gun store, because I was tired. Tired of living. Tired of feeling like nobody loved me, but the guy at the gun store wouldn't sell me a gun."

"When you say, 'tired of living' and 'tired of feeling like nobody loved you' what does that mean?"

I got real quiet, and I stared at Kason, and it was like I couldn't keep my eyes off him. Kade looked just like him, and if he wasn't such a mean-spirited person, Kason would be so handsome. He cocked his head to the side, almost as if he was trying to hypnotize me into not saying anything.

"Objection, Your Honor, Intimidation. Kason is looking at my client trying to intimidate her," Mr. Murphy stood and said.

"Kam, are you okay to continue?" Krystle spoke.

I looked back at my dad, and he nodded his head. He mouthed to me 'I love you' and I gave him a weak smile.

"Yes, I am ok to continue. I felt like no one loved me because of the way that my parents treated me. Kason was abusive... very. My mom ignored it. The closest I had to peace was when I went to work, and when I was in the arms of my husband. Long story short, either one of them could have tried to kill me."

"Objection, Your Honor, Speculation," Elliot stood and said.

"No further questions. Kam, you may step down."

I walked back over to my seat, and Kade winked at me.

"Your Honor, one last thing before you retire to your office. I have evidence that Kason may have been involved with this, and that the case does not need to be dismissed," Jackson stood and spoke.

"Your honor, that evidence cannot be used as me and my client were not briefed on this," Elliot stood and said.

It looked like they both were getting ready to go at it.

"Murphy, you know better than that. Let it play," the judge sighed.

My lawyer walked around the desk to the tape player that was next to the woman typing on a type writer. He put the tape into the player, and then pressed play.

Um, Shaw, can I call you back in just a moment, please? A disrespectful child just walked into my office... without knocking.

I remember this moment. This happened right after I came back from St. Maarten and found out that Kason had placed a listening device inside of my suitcase.

You could hear scuffling, and then glass breaking.

Now, you listen to me you lil' bitch. I have let you disrespect me enough. You come home when you feel like it. You stay over at that nigga's house when you feel like it. It seems like you forgot what I was capable of doing to your ugly black ass.

The next thing you heard was my screams filling the courtroom. You could hear the exact moment my skin tore open from the licks that Kason was putting on my body.

See, Kam, you make me fucking do this to you.

Listening to Kason's voice, you could tell that he had no remorse for his licks.

It's time for you to dead that relationship anyway. ... I got everything I needed from that little tape. Are you going to dead that relationship?

When I screamed out for my brother, I instantly put my hand over my ears. I started crying so hard because I started remembering every time he attacked me like I was an animal. I couldn't hear any more of it. I turned around, and Kade was standing up reaching for me. I stood up, and he pulled me into his arms, where I always felt safest after one of my dad's attacks on me.

"It's okay, sis. He will never hurt you again. Calm down, ok. Calm down. I'm here. Your real dad's here. You got us. Ok," he whispered in my ear as he continued to embrace me.

"Turn it off! That's all I needed to hear," the judge said, banging his gavel. "Kambridge, I need you to come back to your seat, please."

I walked back to my seat, and when I sat down, Olivia put her arm around me.

"I don't need time to go to the corridors. This case is going to trial. Your lawyers will be contacted with a court date," the judge said.

He ended court and left the seat. I kept my head down until Kason and Elliot were out of the courtroom. Moments after the doors closed, we all heard commotion outside the courtroom. I turned around, and no one remained in the courtroom, but me, Olivia, and Murphy. I ran outside to see Mayhem and Korupt trying to hold my dad back, and Elliot and a police officer holding Kason back.

"YOU A STUPID MOTHAFUCKA! YOU HATED MY DAUGHTER THAT BAD THAT YOU WOULD BEAT HER LIKE SHE WAS A FUCKING MAN! COME FIGHT A REAL MAN, YOU FUCKING PUSSY!" my dad shouted.

"FUCK YOU, TRENT! TAKE YOUR ASS BACK TO PRISON, GAY BOY!" Kason shouted back.

My dad tried to rush him again, but they managed to usher him out of the courtroom, and outside. I rushed outside and managed to squeeze past the reporters. When I made it to the parking lot, Trent was pacing behind the car. As soon as he spotted me, he ran to me and wrapped his arms around me.

"Baby, I am so sorry. I wish I was there to protect you. This is all my fault. I am so sorry. I'mma kill that nigga. I swear to God, you will never have to worry about that pussy ass nigga again," my dad uttered quickly.

"I'm fine, Dad. I promise. Please don't get in trouble and get taken away from me sooner than you have to. Okay?"

"Princess, I can't make any promises. Hearing your screams just woke up the sleeping beast that I thought died a long time ago," he said, and kissed my forehead.

My dad opened the car door for me, and before I could get in, Malice approached me with a sympathetic look on his face.

"No. Don't feel sorry for me. I haven't spoken to you in a couple of weeks, but text me later, ok. Thanks."

I got in the car and shut the door. My dad stayed outside and talked to Mr. Bailey for a few minutes longer before he got in the car, and we drove off. I text my girls to let them know about court, and to see if the lingerie party was still happening. They were the only ones who truly kept me sane for the last several weeks.

Me: Hey y'all. Court was a bust. We have to go to trial. Is the lingerie party still happening?

Aiysha: Oh man! I'm sorry. Yes, but if you need some time, you don't have to come.

Shelly: Yes, the party is happening. Aiysha, she is coming. We didn't pick out that sexy ass set for nothing.

Shiana: I'll be there.

Me: Malice brought his bitch here today too. The nerve of him, and he hadn't brought me the fucking divorce papers. LOL. Y'all, I am so over him. He tried to talk to me and fight Kason after the hearing.

Aiysha: Girl, fuck him. He needs to bring you those papers, so you can move on to that sexy ass Dontay. Plus, you need some dick, and I'm #TeamDontay

Shiana: LOL! Aiysha girl, shutup. She needs to get her some dick from her husband. #TeamMalice

Shelly: *I am with Shiana. #TeamMalice*

Me: *I am #TeamNobody*

We text for a while longer until I looked up, and my dad had pulled into the yard. He opened the door for me, and we walked inside.

"Kambridge, baby, I can't get your screams out of my head. Those screams are going to haunt me until I rectify it," he said, opening the refrigerator and taking a long swig of water from a bottle of water.

"Dad, I promise you that I am okay. I trust that you will protect me."

"I'm going to kill him," he said with finality.

He beckoned me over to him, and I took a seat at the bar. He placed an envelope in front of me. I opened it, and it was a check for twenty-two million dollars. I shook my head and slid it back across the table to him. He then slid it back to me.

"Um, this is yours. The moment I found out what your name was going to be, I started putting investments in your name, in case something like me going to jail happened. I projected that the investments would get a million dollars a year, and it did. You were originally supposed to get this on your twenty-fifth birthday, and you would have twenty-five million dollars, but I felt like this was the right time."

I was speechless. My mouth opened, but I couldn't form words. I was a millionaire. Just that fast. I rubbed my fingers over the check. I really can't believe this is real.

"You can keep this money for yourself," I said.

"Nah, Kam, I'm going to forever be good, and plus I know you'll always take care of an old man, if I shall ever need something."

All I could think to do was give him a hug. This was exciting news, and I couldn't wait to share this with my brother and sister.

∞

Tonight, I was going to get loose, and try to forget everything about today, including Malice. I told him to text me, but he never did. To stop torturing myself, I unfollowed Malice from my social media. I hope that he noticed that I did, and he unfollows me back. Once I got out the shower, I pulled my hair up into a bun on top of my head, with a few pieces left hanging down on each side. After doing my facial routine, I applied my make-up.

I looked at the red ensemble that I got from Agent Provocateur that I had laid across the sink. This lingerie set was going to kill them. We were going to make a video, and everything, like we were Charlie's Angels. I couldn't wait. I pulled on the red lace cheeky panties, and then the red thigh high fish net stockings. The lace bralette was so sexy, and it also had a piece that goes around my neck as well. The red sheer robe that went with it had fur around the edges. I felt so fucking sexy in this. I was going to pair this ensemble with my Christian Louboutin stilettos. Since it was cool tonight, I was going to put my long pea coat on over it, and in case my dad was up.

I gave myself a once over in my bathroom mirror and walked out of my bathroom. I jumped at the sight of my husband standing there looking at me, with papers in his hand.

"Can... can I help you?" I stuttered.

"Where are you headed?" he asked, trying not to sound jealous.

"Um, I was going to go visit someone," I toyed with him.

"Oh. Well, I was coming to bring you these. I don't know why I been sitting on them, but I finally signed them."

I nodded my head. He stared at me for a little while longer.

"Well, yeah, here these go," he sat the papers on my bed and slowly backed out of the room, keeping his eyes on me.

I went back in the bathroom because my eyes had watered. I didn't want the tears to fall and mess up my make-up, so I blotted my face.

"Calm down, Kambridge. This is what you wanted, right? Get yourself together girl," I gave myself a pep talk and let out a big sigh. "I love him, and I hate him." I groaned.

I walked back out the bathroom, and my soon-to-be ex-husband was standing there, again. He walked over to me and grabbed my chin, making me look at him. He wet his lips with the tip of his thick tongue. He gave me a peck on my lips. One more after that, and then another one before he slid his tongue in my mouth. We were exchanging so much saliva that it was coming out of the corner of our mouths. We pulled back and looked at each other.

Without speaking a word, we both knew what was going to happen. He slowly slid off my robe, and it hit the floor. Using his knee, he spread my legs wide and got on his knees. Malice started sucking on my pussy through my panties, making my pussy wetter than it already was. I tried to move my panties to the side, but he wasn't having it. He tapped my hand, making me move it out of the way. He continued to suck on my clit through my panties, making me lose my mind.

He tore the bottom of my panties and assaulted my clit. Between the wetness of my pussy and the saliva his mouth was producing, it sounded like Malice was smacking on a sucker or a jawbreaker or something. My knees were getting ready to give out on my ass. I looked down at him, and I could see the saliva running down the sides of his cheeks.

"Hmmmmm, shiiitttt," I groaned as my body was cumming for him.

After giving me the nut that I needed, he moved back and stood up. He took off his shirt, and his body was still to die for. Seeing my name across his collarbone turned me on just a little more. He unbuckled his pants and pulled them down along with his briefs. His dick stood at attention, and my mouth salivated at it. I grabbed it, but he placed his hand on top of mine and shook his head.

He laid me down on the bed, stood back, and stared at me. He bit his lip and shook his head. Malice got on top of me and started kissing me again.

"You taste this pussy?" he asked me in between kissing. "You gon' let another nigga taste that pussy?"

I shook my head. He placed his thick mushroom head at the wet opening of my pussy, and tried to push in, but my pussy locked him out.

"Shit, Mama, let me in," he whispered, and my pussy automatically puckered up for his ass.

He eased inside of me inch by inch, and he was stretching my walls out again. I placed my hand on his stomach, and then he covered my hand with his.

"You know at any time you want me to stop, Mama, I will."

He stroked me slow and deep.

"Uggh," I groaned when the base of his dick hit my pussy.

"Shit, Kam, this the best pussy in the world baby."

He grabbed my hands, raised them above my head, and started kissing me, while long stroking me. We both were moaning in each other's mouth. I wrapped my legs around his waist and lifted my ass up, so he could hit my G-spot. I looked at him, and his eyes were rolling to the back of his head.

"Kamm... Fucking Kam Bailey. Mothafuckkkaaa," he groaned as I felt his dick pulsating inside of me, letting me know that this nigga nutted, and inside of me.

He sat there for a second, and we stared at each other momentarily before he started sucking on my neck, hard. Making sure he was going to leave a hickey. He kissed me all over my chest, leaving hickies. He sucked on my gum drop nipples, making me wet again. He kissed down my stomach and started snacking my pussy again. Malice eats my pussy so loud.

My phone rang, but he didn't stop. It rang again, and he reached for it while he kept his head in position. He looked at it, and then turned it around.

"Answer it... put it on speaker," he ordered.

"No!" I exclaimed.

Since I didn't answer it, he did, and then put it on speaker and threw it up to me.

"H...h...hello," I stammered.

"Girl, what the hell are you doing? We are waiting on you. You trying to get dumb fine for a bunch of bitches. We ain't going to do shit, but eat and talk shit about these men," Shelly said.

"Um..." I started, and Malice started tongue fucking me. "Oowee," I whispered. "Shelly, I'm going... to be..."

"Bitch, what the fuck are you doing?"

My body was so weak, I was getting ready to drop the phone.

"Tell her what you doing, Kambridge," Malice said, and I knew she heard him.

"Ooweee, Kam, what y'all doing?"

"Umm, he... oh my god! He is eating my pussyyyyyy," I moaned, as I nutted so hard in his mouth. "Fuck, Shelly, I'll call... I'll call y'all when I'm on my way."

"Hell naw, slut. We are going to listen to this session. I feel like I'm there already."

Malice flipped me over, raised my ass up in the air, and kept my face down in the bed. He entered me so rough, and I moaned so loud. He grabbed my waist, got on his feet, and started pummeling my pussy so hard. Five strokes in, and I was squirting like crazy.

"Damn, Mama! You squirting already? You missed this dick,

didn't you?"

"DAMN! Kam, you be squirting??" Shelly said into the speaker.

I tried to hang the phone up, but Malice ordered me to leave it alone. This freaky ass nigga was getting off on this shit. He put both of my arms behind my back and continued to fuck me hard.

"Kam, girl! Your pussy so wet girl. I can hear that shit!" Shelly said.

"Ahhh, Malice!"

"Nah, what's my fucking name? You know better than that," he grunted.

"Daddy!" I groaned.

"Damn, right! What nigga gon' fuck you like this?"

"Nobodyyyy!" me and Shelly said at the same time.

"DADDY!"

"That's right! You know I like that shit loud. Get louder, Kam!"

"DADDYYYYYY!" I screamed as I came hard as hell.

Boom!

My door burst open, and my dad was standing there with a gun in his hand.

Prin... oh my god!"

"GET OUT, UNC! FUCK!" Malice yelled, but didn't stop.

My dad disappeared from the door just as quick as he came. Malice leaned over and sunk his teeth in my shoulder. He grunted, and I could feel him filling me up. He pulled out of me slowly, and we both fell to the bed, trying to catch our breath.

"Yasss. You better let her know, Malice."

Malice and I looked at each other and burst out laughing, before I hung up on Shelly.

"You owe me. This set cost two hundred dollars," I chuckled.

"You know I'll get you anything you want."

Minutes later, I drifted off to sleep with Malice playing in my hair.

Malice

$\mathcal{S}$taring at Kam while she slept made me realize this is where I belong. I swear to God, I didn't come over here to fuck this girl. I came over here to drop these papers off and leave, but when I saw her in this sexy ass shit, my dick rocked up. I came back in the room when she was talking to herself. Telling herself that she loves me and hates me. I know that the love can outweigh the hate. I continued to stare at her while she slept. The way her chest rose and fell, I could tell that this was some of the best sleep that she had gotten in a long time.

I picked her up and placed her in the bed the right way, and covered her up. I put the divorce papers in her desk drawer. I'm not going to mention them again, and if she does, I'll let her know where they are. When I walked downstairs, my uncle was sitting on the couch, downing a bottle of Hennessey.

"Unc, you aight?" I asked him.

"Nigga, hell naw! After I just saw the way you were assaulting my baby girl, no, I'm not alright," he confessed. "You were supposed to just be dropping off papers, and you got her calling you Daddy. I don't think I can do this Daddy shit," he complained.

"Unc, that's what she calls me. Malice when she mad. Phoenix when she is being serious, and Daddy any other time," I let him know. "But what's really wrong?"

"Mane, I can't sleep. Every time I close my eyes, I can hear my baby girl's screams in that courtroom. I probably won't rest well until that nigga is sleeping eternally."

"Unc, you know I'll handle that shit. No problem. I can't wait to get my hands on him to be honest. Mane, I'm going to go buy a big leather belt, and I'mma wear his ass out."

He started laughing. I went to the kitchen and grabbed two bottles of water. I handed him one. I pulled an Ambien out of my pocket and handed it to him.

"Look, I had been taking these to help me sleep since I can't sleep lately, since I been going through shit with my wife. This is going to help you sleep, and especially if you mix it with that alcohol, but don't drink no more. You're going to go into a deep sleep, and you'll probably get eight to ten hours of sleep."

He popped the pill in his mouth and drank the full bottle of water. He dapped me up and retired to his room. I walked back upstairs, and Kam still hadn't moved an inch. I went into her bathroom to wet a towel so I could wash the make-up off her face. While I was washing the make-up off her face, she didn't move at all. When I was done washing her face, I threw the towel in the hamper. I had been dependent on that Ambien to put me to sleep, but since my unc needed it more than me, I gave it to him. I cuddled up behind Kam, and instantly, my eyes started to lower. She took my arm and wrapped it around her. I fell asleep almost instantly.

∞

I woke up to Kam trying to squiggle out of the grip I had on her.

She got up and rushed to the bathroom to pee. I got up and followed her in the bathroom. We didn't say a word to each other. While I was peeing, she was looking at my dick.

"You wanna shake?" I asked.

She rolled her eyes at me, and I chuckled.

She started the shower and then started her brushing her teeth. I went into the drawer and grabbed a spare toothbrush that I put there when I was moving her shit in here. I started brushing my teeth too. We looked at each other in the mirror, and my wife looked like a leopard with the way I marked her body up. She got undressed and stepped in the shower. I walked into one of the guest rooms and grabbed an outfit for me to wear today, along with my shower things. I wasn't crazy; I knew to keep some things over here, because I knew I was going to be spending some nights over here, even if it was just to spend the night with my uncle.

I walked back into the bathroom and slid the glass door open.

"Can I join you?" I asked.

"If I said no, would you get in anyway?"

"Probably so."

"Well, why you ask, ugly?"

I chuckled at her and got in behind her. We washed in silence, until I started to speak.

"Kam, yesterday... in court, was a lot. If I had my pistol, I probably would have shot Kason. Baby, hearing you scream like that made me lose my damn mind. That's why I popped that shit off in the courtroom yesterday. I tried to steal his ass, but I ended up cracking that stupid ass lawyer of his. You make me so fucking crazy girl. Like, I don't want nobody to harm you, that's why me and Unc going to take that nigga out. I'm letting you know now."

"Don't go to jail over him, Phoenix. He's not worth it," she said not looking at me.

"But you're worth it. I'll do the rest of my life behind bars for you, Jessica Rabbit."

She laughed so hard, and I felt like I hadn't heard that in so long. She turned around and looked at me. She got on her knees and took me in her mouth. I had to catch the wall because I hadn't had my dick sucked in so damn long. She was swallowing my mans whole, even when he got rock hard.

"Fuuckkk," I groaned.

"Kam, I'm finna cum. Fuck."

She looked up at me and squinted like 'nigga what the fuck was that.'

"My bad. Mane, I ain't had my dick sucked in so long. Shit," I panted.

"You and that—"

"NO. Taryn and I are not fucking. Nothing. I'm not fucking another girl until I know for sure that me and you are done, and I have no more chances to get back with you. I mean, we just been chilling. She just been listening to me vent about your orange hair ass. She's been a support system to me. That's all."

She kissed her teeth before she replied, "She trying to be supportive right on that dick."

She made me laugh so hard. Double over laughing at that.

"You jealous? You think she want this dick?" I asked her while grabbing my mans, making him hard again.

She rolled her eyes and turned around. I slowly bent her over and slid inside of her tight ass pussy. She started throwing it back on me, and I had to hold on to the damn wall before she knocked me down.

"This my dick?" she asked.

"Hell yeah, lil' chocolate ass girl. Can't nobody else get this dick. This dick only get this hard for you."

"Shit, fuck me like this my dick then. Fuck me, bitch! Fuck me like this my dick and can't no other hoe get it."

I grabbed her waist and started slamming into her, hard as I could. Her calling me a bitch turned me on so much.

"Who's the bitch now, huh?" I grunted as I pumped inside of her.

I tried to hit her so hard that I knocked her fucking kidney off its hinges.

"Ahh, fuck!" she screamed, and I looked down at her coating my dick, making me cum again.

Boy, Kam, just don't know, but she pregnant. I wasn't no fool either. I brought the papers over last night because she was ovulating, and that was the time she was most likely to get pregnant. It pays to know your woman's body. Call me what you want, but this mothafucka is not getting away from me. Yes, I trapped my wife. She mine forever, and she might as well get used to it. Whether she files those papers or not, she was carrying a Bailey in her stomach again.

We rinsed off, got dressed, and went downstairs, and saw my unc and Olivia staring at each other, all weird like. Olivia looked like she wanted to cry, and my unc was looking at her with a blank look on his face.

"Good morning, people. We can leave and go back upstairs if you want. You guys are scaring me," Kam said.

"Kam, baby, sit down," Unc said.

I pulled her seat out for her, and I sat next to her.

"Um, this morning, Olivia woke up throwing up, and—"

"Oh my god! I'm going to be a big sister, again! Please tell me!" Kam squealed, holding her hands up to her mouth like she is a child.

"You're not mad?" Unc looked at her.

"No, why would I be? You get the chance to be a new dad all over... oh."

I guess she thought about that Trent would have to go back to jail in February.

"Unc, you know Olivia will be well taken care of. She is carrying legacy in her belly. Round the clock protection. You know that." I told him.

"I just feel like this is the second child that I am failing being behind bars. That shit hurts that I won't be there to raise him or her," Unc expressed.

"Unc! Chill with all that. Don't be stressing Miss Liv out. Aight?

We want her to carry a healthy baby."

"AHHHHH! TURN THAT UP! TURN THAT UP!" Kam screamed, while beating on the table.

Unc grabbed the remote off the table and turned the TV in the kitchen up.

JUST IN! Two fishermen found the car of Tracey Lewis, with her body still strapped inside, in Lake Michigan. At this moment, there is no foul play involved, but there is more to the story.

I could see the car being lifted out of the water and onto the tow truck. I looked at Kam to see if I can gauge her feelings, but her face was stoic. I rubbed her back to console her, but nothing. Her phone rang, and she answered it, placing it on speakerphone.

"You heard?" Kade asked into the phone, and he sniffed.

You could tell that he was crying and shit.

"Yeah, I just saw the news. I'm at home. Where are you?"

"I'm headed to get Kalena right now. I'm coming over there," he said, and hung up the phone.

"Kam, baby, say something," Unc said, after it being really quiet for ten minutes.

"Olivia, when are we going to make you a doctor's appointment?" Kam asked her.

"Um, can we talk about you? How are you feeling?" she asked her.

"I knew she was dead since the first day it came out that she was missing. Kason can fool everybody but me. He and that piece of shit ass lawyer of his had something to do with it. They all can burn in hell if you ask me. I'm pretty sure that's where she is."

"Kambridge, you will not speak about your mother in that tone. Do you understand me?" Unc scolded her.

"She ruined my life, Dad. I don't care. Instead of being a mom, she let me get my ass beat. She screwed my husband, and then tried to kill me. Like, she was mad at me because he married me. Like, she was going to leave Kason for Malice. Just... oh my god! I just don't care, nor do I want to talk about her... anymore. Please don't ask me how I feel about her. I'll be even happier when Kason is dead too," Kam snapped.

"That's it! Come here!" I yanked her out of her seat and pulled her upstairs. "What's your problem?" I asked her as soon as I slammed the door to her room.

"Malice, you don't understand. She ruined my life. My marriage. Everything. She tried to kill me for Pete's sake. Why on earth would you want me to feel sad about her dying? I'm not!" she snapped, and started pacing.

"Look at me, Kam. Nobody is asking you to feel sad or anything. We are just wanting you to be open about what you are feeling. We want you to know that we are very supportive of you and whatever you feel. We don't want you to shut us out."

She sighed and crossed her arms across her breasts. I could tell they were sore, because she was getting ready to come on her period in a couple of days, and them thangs were swollen. I pulled her arms from across her chest and pulled her into me. She buried her head in my chest and started crying.

"It's okay, baby. It's okay to cry. I'm here for you. Always," I comforted her.

"It's just all bad, man. I just want to go back to the day we got married in St. Maarten, or the day I opened my store, or the day I graduated from college. Those were the happiest days of my life," she whispered looking up at me.

"Can I take you back to the night of our marriage?" I winked.

"Uh, absolutely not. The house will absolutely have to be empty for that. The way you had my ass opened, sir... whew!"

I chuckled before I placed a kiss on her lips. We were getting all into it until we heard the doorbell ring. Kam rushed out of the room. I stayed behind to check my vibrating phone in my pocket.

TB: *I just watched the news. Did you see that they found your ex-wife's mom's body inside of her car?*

Me: *Yeah, we saw it this morning during breakfast. She's not 'ex' yet. Don't jinx it.*

TB: *What you mean by "we"?*

I squinted at the text message because I don't know where this tone was coming from.

Me: *We were having breakfast at her dad's house, and we saw it on TV.*

TB: *So, you stayed with her last night?*

Me: *This line of questioning is... interesting. You got something you want to get off your chest?*

TB: *Matter of fact, I do. You been prancing me around town... around the city... for the last month or so, and you over there laid up* *with her, like my feelings don't matter. You let this bitch tell you that she's happy y'all kid died, and you still sniffing behind her. She been asking for a divorce, and all you were supposed to be doing was dropping off the papers she so desperately wanted, and now y'all having breakfast this morning. You wild.*

Me: *First, you knew that my wife was going to come first from jump street. I haven't fucked you, nor kissed you. If we being honest, that night at the hotel was supposed to be a one night stand, but I was tired. I kept you around because you were cool, and you were letting me vent, but you crossed the line at calling my wife a bitch. Let me hurt your feelings some more, we fucked all last night too. Don't ever play me like that, ma. Matter of fact, you about to get your number blocked. Peace.*

Before she could reply, I placed her on the block list. She really had me hot to be honest. I slid my phone back in my pocket and went downstairs. I see that my brother and sister-in-law had made it, and they both were trying to console Kalena. She was so young, and she won't understand this shit for years to come.

"Brottheerr!" she called my name when she saw me.

She ran to me and hugged me so hard. I kissed her on her forehead and walked her back to where her sister was sitting.

"Um, guys, let's get some food in our bellies, ok. Korupt, Mayhem, and Angela are on their way over here. I know that you guys do not want to go out because the cameras are going to be in your face," Trent offered.

We all sat down to eat, and while everyone was having side conversations, I turned to Kam. I grabbed her hands.

"What are we doing, Kam? Are we going to work on us? I don't want—"

She placed a finger over my lips, and I got quiet.

"Nah, I need to know because I don't want to do this song and dance with you. I love you, but I won't chase you anymore. If we are going to work on us, then we need to get back in counseling."

"Okay, Daddy," she said quietly.

My eyes shifted from side to side because I wasn't expecting her to give in that easy. It had to be the hormone switch that she was going through right now. I didn't even have anything to say after that, so I ate until my people came through the door. They walked into the dining room, said their condolences, and then grabbed a plate to fix their food. This is how my life was supposed to be.

Kason

After that tape got released to the fucking press, nobody had been taking my phone calls. Nobody. I don't even understand how they got it when the fucking cord was still in my desk. It had to have been nobody but Shaw. After everything that I had done for him, that is the way that he repays me. I know Jackson's ass was happy that he could beat me and Elliot at something. When I was practicing law, he could never win a case against me, and he almost blew his top when I won the race for Judge over him. He hated Elliot too because he could never win a case against him either. I can only imagine that he is kicking back, laughing at my expense.

I was pacing in my office as soon as I heard the news that Tracey's body and car had been found. I took a big gulp of the Crown Royal that I had been sipping on all fucking morning. I had been calling Elliot, and he was not answering the phone either. I had been sending him text messages, and he was not answering those either. I took another gulp of the Crown Royal before calling him again, and got the voicemail again.

I took a deep breath before I called a number that I hadn't called in months. After ringing two times, a male's voice picked up. Definitely wasn't the person that I called.

"You got some mothafuckin' nerves callin' this number, my

nigga!" Big Will growled into the phone.

"Where is my daughter?" I slurred into the phone.

"Get the fuck off this phone. Call this number again, and I'll forget that she doesn't want me to kill you," he snapped and hung up the phone.

I called Elliot again, ten times in a row. Ten, and he did not answer the phone. A chill ran down my spine, and it made me feel like something bad was getting ready to happen. I knew that I had to move my gold again. I grabbed the key out of my desk drawer, and then my car keys. The moment I opened the door, two detectives were standing there, and my house was surrounded by the police.

"Going somewhere, Mr. Lewis?" one detective asked.

"No... well, yeah."

"Mr. Lewis, you are under arrest for the murder of Tracey Lewis. You have the right to remain—"

"I know my rights," I reminded him.

"Good. I really didn't feel like finishing them. Turn your murdering ass around. I'm sure it was you who probably tried to kill your step-daughter," he shook his head.

Roughly, he turned me around and forced me on my knees. He cuffed me hard as fuck, and I already know that these cuffs were going to leave marks. He drug me to the car as the other officers stormed my house. I could hear them throwing everything around, and I knew that my life was over.

The ride to the county jail was quiet. When they pulled up and ushered me out the car, I kept my head down, ignoring the reporters who were standing there waiting for me. They were asking question after question, and I was glad when the door closed, shutting out their noise. When they were processing me in, I felt like I was living in a horrible nightmare. I thought about all the wrong I had done to people over the last two decades. The people I had thrown in jail for longer than they were supposed to be in there. My wife that I had neglected so much, to the point where she felt that she needed to pay a nigga to fuck him. My children. This is God's way of paying me back. I was brought back to the present time when that guard stuck his finger in my asshole, instantly making me throw up. I had never felt anything like that.

"You might as well get used to that... murderer," the guard whispered.

Hell nah. I'd rather go out like a punk bitch before I let a nigga run his dick up in my ass. They threw me these god awful orange jump suits and threw me in a cold room. I was in this room for what felt like forever, before the detective walked in the room.

"We meet again, Mr. Lewis," Detective Parker smirked, and sat down in front of me, placing a manila folder on the desk.

"I'm not saying nothing until Elliot gets here," I said, and sat back in my chair.

"Ohhh, you haven't heard, huh?" he shook his head. "Your dear ol' lawyer, your buddy ol' pal Elliot, blew his brains out after Tracey's car and her body was found in Lake Michigan. He also left a note, rolling over on you and himself. I guess he had a conscience," he sighed with a chuckle.

"Bullshit!" I exclaimed.

He opened the folder, and I saw pictures of Elliot sitting at his desk in his house, with a bullet hole the size of a golf ball in his temple. I tried not to throw up at the sight of my longtime friend's brain matter splattered all over his desk. He took one picture out of the pile and pulled out a pair of reading glasses.

"Dear All. By the time you read this, I would have done something that I am not proud of. I need to right my wrongs. I walked in on Kason strangling Tracey to death, and I helped him cover up her murder, by pushing her car into Lake Michigan. I have also been privy to Kason locking up young men on trumped up charges, especially those that are drug related. I watched tapes in the Lewis household that show Kason abusing Kambridge until she could barely walk. One thing he didn't lie about, was the fact that he didn't poison Kambridge. He didn't, it was his wife, Tracey. All, I am sorry for those I have let down in the process of trying to keep a squeaky-clean image. All my love, Elliot Stone, Esq," he read the letter aloud.

That son of a bitch! I couldn't even formulate a fucking sentence, because there wasn't going to even be a trial because they had the tapes. My dumb ass forgot to get rid of the tapes. Hell, I never thought that I would need them. The only thing they would do is offer me a plea deal, and if I denied that, we would go to trial, and I for sure wouldn't win that. How could I be so fucking stupid?

"Tsk. Tsk. Tsk, you don't know what you've just done. All those cases you tried regarding drugs, will be overturned. All those young men you locked up, will be released back into the streets. You fucked up royally. Do you have anything you want to say?"

"Get me a lawyer," I managed to squeeze out.

I could feel that my blood pressure had risen to stroke levels.

"Matter of fact, you have a lawyer, who came down here specifically for you. Matter of fact, you made bail. He'll be in here momentarily," he smirked.

"How did I make bail? I never even made a phone call to anyone. Who is the lawyer that wants to help me?"

I felt like this was a set up.

Detective Parker turned the recorder off and then glared at me.

"Kason Lewis, you are the worst type of man. Granting you bail solidifies your death out on the street. You wouldn't even make it to the trial, if there was one. You don't have to surrender your passport, or any of that. The moment you walk out on the streets, you better watch your back. You have more enemies on the streets than you have behind here. Good luck!" Detective Parker warned me, and turned the recorder back on.

He gathered up the pictures and placed them back in the folder. Moments later, Connor walked in the door with a cast on each of his arms. I heard about Malice breaking both of his arms for hemming up Kambridge.

"Connor, you bailed me out?" I asked with surprise, especially since I wasn't always nice to the boy.

"I sure did. Are you ready to roll?" he asked.

"Yes, let me get changed, and I will meet you out front."

I got changed back into my clothes so fast, and walked out front. Everybody was mugging me, and it felt like everything was moving in slow motion. Walking into the sea of people, flashing cameras, people throwing things, and yelling obscenities, did not phase me one bit. Once I was safely in Connor's car, people were beating on his car windows, blocking the road and everything.

"Thank you, son," I said to him.

"Don't thank me."

The car was quiet for the longest, until he said something as we were pulling into my yard.

"You know, Judge Lewis, I wanted to mirror your life. I wanted the hot wife, great kids, big house, nice cars, and everything, but you just ruined that for me. You never treated me like your son, and I know that you secretly hated me. I know that it was you who essentially ruined me and Kam's relationship. It was you who put in her head that I wouldn't marry her because she was black... and you know what... you were absolutely right. I only tolerated her because she had good mouth, and I knew that with your recommendation, I would be a shoe-in for whatever company I wanted to work with once I got my license, but you ruined that. Knowing that I was associated with you in any capacity, has me blackballed. I'll never be able to have a career because of you. Get the fuck out of my car, and I can't wait until your body is floating in Lake Michigan," Connor spoke with so much venom in his voice.

I couldn't reply to him, so I eased out of the car. I didn't have to use a key to walk in the house, because the door was already cracked open. Everything was everywhere. There were holes in the walls. I don't know what they were looking for in the walls, but they wouldn't find anything. I walked along the hallway, rubbing my fingers along the wall, trying my best to picture things the way they were when my household was semi happy. I made it to my office and everything was torn down and flipped over. The house I once thought was a home, was torn apart.

I walked down to the basement, turned the light on, and just like the rest of the house, it was a mess. There was a box of baby clothes that had been thrown around. I reached down to pick up a Gucci baby set that belonged to Kam when she was just a toddler. Tracey never got rid of anything. I instantly started crying. In just a matter of months, everything went from sugar to shit. I used the set to wipe my eyes. My eyes landed on the orange extension cord, and I instantly knew what I had to do.

I got the cord, walked to the top of the stairs, and tied the cord in a tight knot. I walked back to the bottom of the stairs, grabbed a chair, and placed it right under the dangling cord. I wrapped it around my neck as tight as I could. I closed my eyes, counted to three, and then kicked the chair from under me. I instantly started getting light headed, and then I heard feet coming down the stairs.

"Oh no you mothafuckin' don't, bitch! Cut that bitch down," I heard a voice say before I passed out.

Trent

I stared at this mothafucka going in and out of consciousness. This mothafucka really and truly tried to go out like a punk bitch. He should have been a man and took that shit on the chin. I did twenty-two years, and not once did I think about killing myself at all. I called in a few old favors so I could get Kason out on bail. I found Connor in a bar, damn near drinking his life away, and I told him that I needed him to go pick Kason up from jail. At first, he told me no, but with a little threat, he easily changed his mind.

Korupt had a little homie standing across the street, waiting to let us know when he pulled up in his yard. I swear he wasn't even in his house for thirty minutes before he tried to kill himself. There is no way I was going to let him kill himself without beating his ass first.

"Wake yo' ass up," Korupt said, kicking the chair.

When he woke up and realized that me, Korupt, Mayhem, and Malice were staring at him, he started yelping for help.

"Oh please, nigga. You know can't nobody hear your ass," Mayhem said.

I started pacing in front of him, trying to contain my anger.

"Life. You locked me up for life, Kason. Had my daughter never met my nephew, she would have never known who I was until she turned twenty-five because of the trust I had for her. Twenty-two years of my life gone, because you a hating ass nigga. A part of me wanted to take your ass out with a single shot to the head, but nah. That's too easy. I'm going to untie you, and I want you to fight me. This been a long time coming," I said, sitting the gun on the chair I was sitting in. I tightened up the sweats that I was wearing and rolled my neck around, cracking it.

I untied him, stepped back, and gave him the chance to stand up. He held his hands up in surrender mode.

"Look, Trent, I don't want to fight—"

Pop!

I popped him right in the mouth, cutting off his sentence. Only thing he did was hold his hand up to his bleeding mouth. I flexed my hand inward and outward, because I hit that nigga in his mouth hard as fuck.

"Trent, please, bro—"

Pop! Pop!

I hit him with a two-piece that brought him down to his knees. His mouth and nose were leaking.

"I stopped being your bro the minute you stole from my real brother," I snapped.

Pop! Crack!

I kicked him so hard in his rib cage, that I heard his ribs crack. He fell flat on the floor of his basement.

"Agghhhh" he groaned out. "Just kill me, please," he begged.

"Shut the fuck up, and get up and fight me like a man, Kason. You beat my daughter until she could barely walk. You had her screaming for help."

Pop!

I kicked him in his mouth, and he coughed up blood, spitting out teeth as well.

"Get up, Kason," I growled. "Fight me."

"I don't wanna fight you," he groaned out, trying to get up, but kept falling from the pain that I had inflicted on him. "Please, just kill me."

I squatted in front of him and pulled my phone out. I called my daughter, and she answered on the first ring.

"Hey, Dad!" she said, all warm and inviting.

Hearing her voice on the phone always gives me the feels.

"Hey, Princess. Someone got something they want to say to you. He can barely talk, so you have to listen closely."

I put the phone on speakerphone. She got real quiet on the phone, as if she already knew what was going on. We left the women at the house with Kade. He knew where we were going, but he said he didn't want to come with us.

"Kam..." *cough cough.* I'm so sorry. I'm sorry."

Pop!

I punched him in his mouth again.

"What the fuck are you sorry for, bitch ass nigga?"

"I'm sorry... sorry for hurting you all those years. I loved... you.

I just hated that... you didn't come from me. I was jealous. You look like him. I hated that..." *cough cough* "I loved you. I had a weird way of showing it, but... I did love you," he managed to get out.

I took the phone off the speakerphone.

"Hey, Princess. Ask my baby mama do she want some food when I come home," I chuckled.

"No, Dad. I think she's fine. We literally just ate two hours ago."

"Okay, Princess. I'll be home soon. I love you."

"Love you more. Don't hurt him too bad," she said, and hung up the phone.

"See... she just saved your life... again, but you know all those bruises you put on my daughter, you about to get put on you," I said to him, and his eyes gaped open. "Oh yeah, you're going to wish you were dead when they are done with you."

We both looked at Mayhem, Malice, and Korupt, and they were standing there with big leather belts in their hands, and he looked like he had seen a ghost.

Patting him on his shoulder, I said, "Take care, Kason." I stood up and started up the stairs.

"Take it away, boys," I told them.

Smack! Smack! Smack!

All you could hear was the belts tearing into his skin and him screaming bloody murder. I closed the basement door, and Detective Parker was sitting in the chair, twisting around.

"Thank you, fam," I dapped him up.

"You know that you are a free man after this, right? Every case that he has tried will be overturned, by law. Your whole team will be complete again," Detective Parker informed me, and I became overwhelmed. I needed to go out to the truck.

"Look, go down there and make sure they don't kill the man. I'm going out there to the truck."

I walked out there to the truck and slid inside. The only thing that I could do was thank God. I thank God that I will be able to get out and be with my daughter and my unborn. This is what I been praying for the last twenty-two years. I been praying to get to know Kam, but now I get to spend the rest of my life with her. I didn't expect to fall in love either, but I did. Olivia and I started as sex buddies, and now I want to marry her. Seems quick, but damn, she makes me feel good. In just a couple of months, I have told her everything about me, and she has disclosed everything about her, including her husband not signing the paperwork. With a little reinforcement, he will sign them.

"Damn, we beat that nigga bloody. I feel good," Malice said, as they slid inside the truck.

"I wanna marry Olivia," I blurted out.

"Why you say it like that? You looking for our approval? She makes you happy, and you make her happy. I say go for it," Korupt said.

"Unc, I don't know. I married your tack head ass daughter in two months, and look where we at," he laughed.

"I got an eyeful of where y'all at last night. Don't talk me to death, nigga," I said to him, cringing at the thought of how nasty he was hitting my daughter from the back.

He rubbed his chin and started laughing.

"Unc, I say go for it. Life is too short not to try shit, get it wrong, and then get it right. You got a lot wrong in your day, and if you think Olivia is your 'right', then go for it," Mayhem said. "Same goes for you, Malice. Kam ain't leaving your ass alone. I saw all the hickies on her body, which meant y'all got real personal when you were just supposed to be dropping those papers off. Y'all either need to get it together, or leave each other alone. Do you understand me?"

Malice looked at him like he was getting ready to come across the seat.

"You don't scare me, Phoenix. You know that. If you want to square up, then we can do that. Do you understand me? Love her or leave her alone. Point, blank, period. I know I'm only talking to a brick wall, but you get what I'm saying," he said to him.

The whole way back to the house, Mayhem and Malice argued about who can beat up who, knowing good and well that Mayhem can dust his ass. My nephew is quiet, but deadly, and that's why everybody knows not to play with him.

When we walked into the house, and it was smelling good as fuck. We all found a bathroom to get washed up in and walked back into the living room.

"Kade, you ain't been letting these women talk bad about us have you?" I asked him, and he laughed a little.

"Nah, I been holding down the fort. Is everything uh..."

"Everything is fine. Everything will be fine," I assured him.

The rest of the day, we were laughing and talking. Finding out I was having another kid, and I was going to be free, was one of the best days that I had in a long time, and a day that I will never forget. After everyone had gone to their respective houses, I got some of the best sleep that night that I had gotten in a long time.

Kam

One week later...

This past week has been exhausting. I really need to get on planning a trip for Shelly and I, for her stepping in over the last few months for me. She hasn't asked me for a dime, but I told her to make sure that she is paying herself. I looked at the accounts, and she hadn't taken a dime out for herself. She always says that she doesn't need the money, and that it helps her stay out of trouble. Anything that helps Shelly stay out of trouble is a good deal for me.

That night after everyone had gone home, I was scared to ask my dad if he killed Kason, but he told me that he didn't before I completed the question, but he wishes that he was dead. Two days after that, Kade and Kalena went to identify Tracey's mangled her body. The sea creatures had done a number on her body, Kade told me, but he could still tell that it was her. The coroner said that she died by strangulation. We were called down to the station that evening so we can watch the tapes with Detective Parker. I was mortified to see myself getting beat the way that Kason was beating me. The fact that I was looking at my mom killing me slowly on camera, made me sick to my stomach. My dad was rocking back and forth so fast to the point where I had to hold him. You could see Kason and Tracey arguing before he choked her out, and that's where Elliot came in. They looked like they were arguing for a while, before they started wiping down Tracey's body. I couldn't watch anymore after that.

Now, here we are sitting at this memorial service for her. I don't know why I'm here, but I am. We are having something small at the burial site. It's a closed casket funeral. A few of her co-workers came to say a few words on her behalf. Everybody was dressed in all black, and I'm standing at the back next to Malice in an all-white lace dress, sipping on some Bacardi 151 Rum out of a flask. Some of the strongest alcohol. I needed to be numb for this stupid shit. The stupid men convinced me to come.

"Do you think that you should slow down," Malice leaned over and whispered in my ear.

"Nope," I said, and turned the flask up again.

"Kam, it'll be over in five minutes. Give me the flask," he ordered.

"Nope!" I said with much force, causing a few people to turn around.

"Aye, if you make a mothafuckin' scene out here, I'mma make a movie. Now give me the damn flask," he growled in my ear.

I pushed the flask in his hand, and he put it in his back pocket. He crossed his hand in front of him. I looked him up and down, while he kept his head focused on the casket in front of us. He has on some sleek black shoes, some black chino's, and a white, tailored button down shirt. He had on a gold chain around his neck that matched his wedding ring. His wedding ring. He had a tan line now. He hasn't taken it off since he put it on.

That night after everyone left and went home, Mayhem came back to talk to me. Malice didn't stay with me that night because I wanted a night alone...to think. He explained to me that Malice was in love with me, and there is nothing that I could do to change that. I was Malice's first love, and that's why he's acting crazy like that over me. He told me that Malice won't leave me alone until I file the divorce papers. Honestly, I liked that Malice was groveling at my feet. He told me that he had told Malice to leave me alone, but he told him that he wasn't. Mayhem told me that Malice had become a better person because of me. He's more focused now than he had ever been. He doesn't make plans without thinking about me, and how I would feel about it.

After that talk, it made me see the silver lining in the situation. If I hadn't met Malice, I would still be getting my ass beat on a daily. If I hadn't met Malice, I would still be with Connor and still feeling unappreciated. If I hadn't met Malice, I wouldn't love myself. Basically, because of Malice, my life got better, whether I wanted to believe it or not, and that was all I needed to think about before I ripped up the divorce papers, but he doesn't know it yet.

"We commit Sister Tracey Lewis's body to ground, earth to earth, ashes to ashes, dust to dust, looking for the blessed hope and the glorious appearing of the great God in our Savior Jesus Christ, who shall change the body of our humiliation and fashion it anew, in the likeness of His own body of glory, according to the working of His mighty power wherewith He is able to subdue all things unto Himself," the pastor said.

The men started to work Tracey's body into the ground, and I still didn't feel anything. Malice put his arm around my shoulder, but I didn't need comforting. I didn't know what I needed, but it wasn't comforting. Kade and Olivia were comforting Kalena, while I continued to stare at the men lowering her casket. I walked towards the truck that I rode in, with Malice on my heels.

"Can we help you?" I asked Taryn, who was standing near the truck.

"I'm just here to support my friend."

"Supporting your friend in the loss of his wife's mom. Ok. Girl. Gone."

"Taryn, you need to leave. I told you I wanted nothing to do with you after you disrespected my wife," Malice said with some bass in his voice.

"Wait, what now? She disrespected who? Me?" I pointed to myself.

Before she could pop another word out of her mouth, I dived on her ass. I was hitting her with everything that I had in my body.

Pow! Pow! Pow!

"Disrespect now, hoe," I snapped before punching her in her mouth again.

Malice finally picked me up off her.

"My husband said you need to leave, then you need to leave. Point blank period."

Malice put me in the truck, and then he slammed the door. I looked out the window, and saw that no one was even making their way over to the truck. I guess they figured that Malice had it all under control.

"What the fuck is wrong with you? You can't be out here fighting like that, ma. That's not cute at all," he let me know.

"I ain't trying to be cute. If we gon' work this shit out, you might as well take me to that white bitch house, so I can whoop her ass too," I said pulling my hair up in a tight ball.

"She's dea... wait, what?" he glared at me.

He glared at me, but I am mirroring his glare because I wanted to know what he was getting ready to say.

"You first? What was that you were about to say? She's what?"

"She's dead," he whispered.

My hands went to my mouth to cover up it up from screaming loud.

"What do you mean, she's dead? I haven't seen anything on the news regarding her—"

"You won't."

"Malice?" I called his name. My eyes were asking the question that I'm not sure if I wanted to know the answer to.

"Yes. I did," he calmly said, while staring into my eyes.

I didn't know what to say. I scooted away from him, but he scooted towards me.

He grabbed the collar of my dress and pulled me on his lap, making me straddle him. He looked up to me with tears in the corners of his eyes.

"Kam, don't you ever fear me. I'll never hurt you. That bitch ruined my life, so she had to go. If I had to do it again, I would. Nothing, or no one, will ever come in between us. I mean that shit. You said that we were going to make this work, and I'm so thankful. I'll do whatever I have to do to rebuild your trust in me. Understand me? Look at me."

"Daddy, you killed for me?" I asked, as I could feel my pussy getting wet.

My period just went away two days ago, and I was needing to feel him inside of me.

"Hell yeah, ma. Blew that hoe brains out for you," he smirked, and placed a kiss on my lips.

"Babe, I am turned into a hoodrat, ghetto bitch. You telling me that just made my pussy wet."

"Oh it did?" he grinned.

He raised me up a little, and he unzipped his pants. His dick came out of his boxers with ease. He moved my panties to the side and gave my clit a squeeze, making me groan a little.

"Slide on this mothafucka, my lil' hoodrat," he whispered.

I raised up and slowly slid down on Phoenix's nine piece. Our moans were quieted once we started tongue kissing each other.

I managed to look out the window to see my dad, Olivia, Mayhem, and Malice's parents walking towards the truck, so I started bouncing on him quick. I needed a nut.

"Fuck! Kam... What the fuck you doingggg?" Malice groaned as I bounced on him like a jack rabbit.

"Our parents are coming this way, and I'm trying to get my... ahh. Fuck."

"Keep bouncing ma, I'm there, baby. Keep bouncing ma, I'm there..." he growled. "I'm there... I'm there," his voice went up an octave, before I felt his dick jumping inside of me.

He took the hand towel out of his pocket and caught the nut that was coming out of me. He cleaned his dick off. We both got situated only ten seconds before the people who were riding with us got in the truck. We tried to act normal, but Malice's face was flushed, and I was looking out the window trying not to look guilty. The moment Korupt fixed the rearview mirror, we locked eyes for a moment, and he smirked.

"If I didn't know any better, I would say that my children are guilty of something," Korupt said from the front.

"Dad, ain't nobody guilty of nothing," Malice said.

"Guilty dog barks every time," he laughed.

Even if we weren't given away, his remark gave us away.

The following Monday...

I pulled up at work, happy to be there, but instantly felt bad when I saw Dontay's car in the parking lot. I feel like I don't owe him anything since he knew I was married from jump street. He hadn't contacted me at all, and I hadn't tried to contact him. Before I walked into my store, I walked into his studio to see him. He was in the mirror dancing as always, and when he saw me, he instantly turned his nose up like I was annoying him, which almost prompted me to walk back out.

"Hey, Dontay," I spoke, but he ignored me, kind of hurting my feelings.

I walked over to him, but he moved back.

"What the fuck you want, Kam? Let me guess, you coming in here to tell me that you are going to work shit out with your husband. If so, you ain't got to tell me, because I see it all over the gossip blogs. You don't care that the nigga fucked your mom, huh?"

"Dontay—"

"Don't call my fucking name. Once a cheater, always a cheater, and you know that. Mane, get the fuck out of my studio, and I don't ever wanna see you again. I cut your part from the recital anyway."

"Damn, you that mad, nigga? Phoenix wasn't just some nigga off the street. He is my husband. So, why the fuck you mad? We went on one date, and it was cut short by my husband, and your ass didn't even try to get up and defend me, so how would we have been together anyway, huh? You weren't even willing to get your ass whooped for me. I was coming over here to apologize, but fuck you," I snapped, and burst out the door of his studio.

I walked into my store, and Shelly was giving me a weird look while she was talking on the phone. As soon as she hung up, she was looking at me waiting for me to talk.

"Girl, what is going on?"

"I went over to Dontay's studio to kind of apologize for kind of throwing him to the side, and he tried me girl. I had to the curse his ass the fuck out."

Shelly laughed and shook her head.

"Do we have some orders?"

"Nah, not yet."

I got on the computer, and went into my work email, and had close to a thousand emails.

"Aye, Shelly, you weren't checking my work emails?"

"No. I didn't know your password for that email. I tried a few times, but I couldn't crack it."

"You didn't check the security question?"

"Nah, my bad girl. I hope nothing important is in there."

I scrolled, deleted, scrolled, and deleted some more. It wasn't anything but sales on equipment.

"OH MY GOD!" I screamed.

"What bitch!" Shelly ran from the back. "You made me mess up my damn shirt."

"I forgot to tell you that I am a millionaire," I laughed.

"Bitch, me too," she laughed.

"No, I'm dead ass. My dad gave me the check from all the investments he put in my name. It was for twenty-two million dollars. So much shit been going on, I forgot to tell you. Looking at all those emails, I completely just got the dopest idea for a Christmas present for Malice."

"Damn girl. Life is really looking up for you, and I swear I am so happy for you. You deserve all this shit, and more, but what's the present?"

"I'm going to buy the building back from Cat's estate and fix it up for Rich Cutz! Mayhem told me that after Catherine bought the building, Malice kind of got discouraged and damn near stopped going to school. Luckily, Mayhem fucks with smart bitches, and they had been doing Malice's work online for him. He said that he was okay, now that we were going to work on our marriage. So, he went back to school today. Thank God!" I said.

"Girl, that's such a dope ass idea. You gon' get pregnant that night."

"Girl, I don't know. I don't think that we are ready for kids right now. We are trying to work on our marriage right now. Maybe in about two or three years, child," I smiled at the thought of having a couple of lil' Phoenix's running around.

I continued to delete the messages out of my computer, when I saw a subject line that read, 'I'LL BE DEAD WHEN YOU READ THIS.'

It was from an unknown email address. A part of me wanted to delete it, but another part of me wanted to read it as well.

"Shelly, come look at this," I said to her.

I clicked on it, and we both started reading in silence.

Dear Kambridge,

Sorry if I'm all over the place, but I'm freestyling and typing as my thoughts come. The subject of this came out of nowhere. I just feel like dying, so it fit perfectly.

I pray that this email finds you in good health. As a mom, I know

I failed you. I know that I didn't treat you the way that you should be treated as a daughter. I failed you because I didn't get you away from that monster the first time he hit you. I begged Kason for a divorce, so I could live happily ever after with Trent, but he told me he would kill me before he let that happen. Honestly, I loved your (real) father. Trent was everything, but I was so afraid to leave Kason because I didn't want him to hurt Trent, and he still ended up getting life in prison... because he loved me. When I was with Trent, I hadn't felt anything like that from Kason in years. I'm crying typing this because Trent made me feel things that Kason NEVER made me feel. Now, I'm kicking myself because we would have been a family, but I know that will never happen now.

Kam, I failed you because I didn't protect you from getting your heart broken. The moment I knew about Malice, I should have told you what he was, but I was selfish. I wanted him because he made me feel something physically, I hadn't felt from Kason in decades. I'm sorry that I had moments of insanity by wanting my daughter's husband. Honestly, he felt like shit when he found out that you were my daughter. He cancelled my appointments that same day, but I continued to call him to try and see him. He didn't budge, and he blocked me every time. One of my co-workers he was messing with as well, got blocked. I can really say that he didn't cheat on you when you got married to him.

The selfishness and jealousy in me made me hack your iCloud, and I saw that you and Malice had gotten married. Kalena never told me. The insane part of me made me watch the videos of you two in your phone, making love. This is going to be weird, but please don't stop reading. The way he looks at you when he is making love to you, is unmatched. Kason stopped looking at me like that twenty-five years ago. The way he bites his lips when he is drilling inside of you, tells me that he is completely obsessed with you, and no one could ever have that effect on him. I was so jealous that it wasn't me, that I drove to your store and damaged it. Kambridge, I am so sorry. Please forgive me.

Daughter, I am so sorry for causing you to have to have a kidney transplant. I mixed a bunch of mercury from broken thermometers together, and I would wipe your room down with it. That's why they found a thermometer in your room. I wanted to make it seem like an accident. I was having an insane moment, but I am so happy that Trent could get out and help you. Trent is such a good man, and I know that he would have been an even better father, had it not been snatched away from him. Try not to be so hard on him. He'll get it right, eventually.

Kason was so sneaky to the point where he thought I didn't know about his stupid ass trying to start a drug ring. That won't work because Korupt has this whole city on lock, and other surrounding cities. Also, he stole something from Korupt, and I know where he put it. It's at a storage. I put the address and number on an envelope along with a key inside. It's in the side of your Celine purse. Kason's dumb ass put it in Kalena's name. He's so smart until he's dumb.

In closing, Kam I'll never forgive myself, so I don't expect you to, at least not yet. I betrayed you in the worst way. I just want to let you know that I love you so much, even though you think I don't. Also, please forgive Malice. He is in love with you, and will do anything for you. You both need the love that only you two can give each other. Forgive him.

All my love,

Tracey Lewis.

"Your mom was sick, Kambridge. Oh my god! She ruined your shop over some dick that she was paying for," Shelly spoke.

I was fuming. How dare she just casually admit fucking up my shop? How dare she just casually admit watching me and husband fuck, like that shit wasn't creepy or incestuous, or something like that. It gotta be something like that, because who the fuck watches their kid fuck... WHO? I printed out three copies of the email.

"Shelly, I'm leaving," I said.

The moment I walked outside, Malice was pulling up. Just the person that I wanted to see.

"Hey boo.... what's wrong?" he asked getting out the car.

"Get back in, we are going to your parents' house."

As soon as we got back in the car, I started reading him the stupid email, starting with the subject line. The email was even dated the day before her death.

"Wooowwwwww, your mom was sick in the head. The only good part in that letter was when she told you to forgive me. I mean..."

"Too soon, Phoenix," I snapped at him.

Twenty minutes later, we were pulling into the gates of a beautiful home. I mean very beautiful home. I could appreciate it more if I wasn't fuming.

"You grew up in this home?" I asked.

"Yes... that's right... you never been here before, but yes, this is my parents' home."

Wow, I thought to myself.

A maid opened the door for us and told us that Mr. Bailey was in his office.

"When the door is closed, we are supposed to—" Malice started.

I burst into the door just as Mr. Bailey was lighting a blunt. He looked at me with a crazy look on his face, then looked past me at Malice.

"Dad, I told her that—"

"Read this," I cut Malice off, and slammed the print out in front of his face.

Before he could puff the blunt, I took it out of his mouth and started pulling on it.

"You don't see your father over here?"

I turned around to see my dad looking at me all weird like. I walked over to him and kissed him on his cheek, and handed him the other copy.

"Princess, what is this?"

I didn't reply to him, I just continued to pull on the strong ass blunt that Mr. Bailey had. Malice came over and took the blunt out of my hand, and he started pulling on it.

"What in the fuck?" Mr. Bailey asked, as his eyes continued to scan the paper.

"Yep. That's the same expression that I had."

"This is fucking crazy. Your mother was a sick individual, Kambridge. I am so sorry."

"I have the envelope, and I want to go with you. Thanks."

I pulled the envelope out, and put it in front of him. He pressed into the intercom and told Mayhem to come down, because we were getting ready to leave.

∞

Me, Malice, Mayhem, and our dads were standing in front of this storage building. Korupt was playing with the lock, but it wouldn't open. He kept playing with it until it opened. Mayhem and Malice had their guns out, ready to fire if they needed to. When it opened, all our eyes bucked, and our mouths fell open. It was the gold... It was shiny. I felt like I needed to put on my shades to look at this.

"Wow, Dad, what are you going to do with all of this?" Malice asked.

"Shit, I don't even know yet, but I'm going to move it, ASAP."

We continued to marvel at the gold for the next few minutes, before we left. Now, I feel like these chapters of Kason and Tracey were finally closed.

Trent

$\mathcal{L}$ ife is crazy. I get out to save my daughter, only to find love, and find out that I don't have to go back into that hellhole. The warden called me a week ago, and told me that I didn't have to report back, unless I wanted to come and get my things. I had been processed out, and I am a completely free man. I hadn't told Olivia yet, but I'm planning something very special for her.

Me, my nephews, and my brother had taken a trip to New York to go to this family owned diamond place that we used to frequent, back when we first got put on and was rocking the diamonds. The minute we walked in, the little white lady looked at me with a shocked look on her face.

"AHH! Henry! Henry! Henry!" she screamed.

Henry came around the corner quickly with his shotgun in his hand, but then dropped it when he saw it was me and Korupt.

"Trent... Trent... is that you?" he asked, putting on his glasses.

They both came around the corner and hugged me so tight. Caroline started to cry.

"Hey, Mama Caroline! Stop crying. Come on now," I said.

They then hugged Korupt as well.

"This must be Mr. Phoenix and Mr. Pryor. Ohhh, I haven't seen you guys since you were little tiny babies," Caroline said wiping her tears.

Malice and Mayhem looked super confused.

"Um, boys, these are your grand-godparents, if that makes sense. I met them through my dad when he brought me here. These are also me and Korupt's godparents. Our dads told us if something was to ever happen to them, we were supposed to take our moms and come to New York to be with Henry and Caroline, but of course, your uncle and I were hardheaded, so we stayed and set up shop. If something had happened to me, your mom was going to take y'all and move here, but luckily, y'all never needed to move here."

"But we never met them," Malice said.

"That was the point!" Korupt said.

"I'm so happy to see my two grown men. I've been watching the news and seeing everything that was going on. I wanted to call, but you know... the agreement. What can I do for you?"

"We know you meant well, ma. We are here to visit, and I also need a ring. I'm going to propose to my baby mama. She's the one," I said.

"What you mean 'she's the one.' You thought that sick woman was 'the one' too, and look where that got you," she snarled.

"Ma, I promise you. She is the one. You can come meet her and talk with her. You can also meet Kambridge as well," I said to her.

"You know, this is one crazy situation. Trent, your daughter is married to your brother's son, which would make them cousins, if

Paxton was your real brother."

"Keep it all in the family, Mama," I joked.

She slapped my arm and went around the back to bring out the big boys. Henry went and locked the door, so no other patrons could come in. He dimmed the lights in the place, so we would be able to get a good look at the diamonds. We all took a seat at the round table. Caroline came back with pretty ass rings, and I felt like I wanted to get them all for her. Let her get a ring for every day of the week.

We each studied the rings for about an hour, until I came across the perfect ring. This was it. This Oval cut ring was perfect. It would look nice on her finger.

"This is it, Mama. This one right here. How much is this one?"

"Yes, son. This one is perfect. I like it. 4.5 carat, Oval S12. This diamond alone is fifty-five thousand, with the whole ring set, I can let it go for seventy thousand," she said.

"Oowee, that's a good price. I'll take it," I said, happy with the choice that I had made.

"Ms. Caroline, what about this ring right here? This is perfect for my wife. I want to upgrade her ring and give her a wedding where my uncle can walk her down the aisle, and properly give her away to me," Malice said, looking at me.

Caroline held her hand to her chest and blushed at the declaration of love that Malice professed for my daughter.

"Phoenix, this is the 5.55 carat, Radiant Cut. This diamond is eighty-five thousand, and with the ring set, I can give it to you for a hundred and twenty thousand."

"I'll take it," he said not even hesitating.

"Damn! Y'all mothafuckas just had to put the pressure on a nigga. You know I can't come home without a fucking ring; now I'm pissed," Korupt said shaking his head. "Mane, Mayhem pick a ring out for your mama that costs more than Kambridge's ring. If you don't, I'll have to hear that shit all fucking night. 'How you let your son outdo you? I want another ring Korupt. I want this... and I want that...' he mocked Angela.

"Here is this one, and get these put in an earring set," Mayhem offered.

"Oowee, that is my favorite diamond. This is the 7 carat I S12, and this diamond alone is a hundred and fifteen grand. The ring set would be a hundred and seventy-five thousand. I actually think this is enough, son. You can save the earrings for another occasion."

Korupt thought about it for a moment, and then he agreed with her.

"How are you guys paying for this? Cash? Credit?"

"Mom, I got something even better."

He reached into his bag and pulled out multiple gold bars and gave it to her. Her eyes lit up.

"Hold up. You got it back? Do you know that this is worth like thrice as much now? You don't even have to give me this many."

"Ma, you been taking care of us for so long. It's time to let us take care of you. Take this. It's time for you to retire anyway. You and Henry are how old? Eighty? You know these niggas out here these days are ruthless now. I don't want you two to get hurt," Korupt said.

"First, we are eighty-five, and we are healthy as an ox. We eat healthy, and we take daily walks. So, mind your business, son. Plus, we not ready to give this business over just yet. When we are, you will know. I promise," Henry laughed.

We chatted for a few more hours before we left and headed back home. I was ready to get in between my woman's legs.

∞

1 week later...

I was running just a little late to the doctor's office because the DMV was packed as fuck. Olivia left from work to go to the doctor's appointment. I had to go get my license back so I won't go back to jail for some goofy shit. As soon as I pulled into the parking lot, I saw Olivia engaging into a shouting match with Mario. I knew how he looked from the pictures, because I looked into him. I threw the car in park, got my piece out of the glove compartment, and approached them. They were so engaged into the shouting match, to the point where they didn't even hear or see me coming up.

"Olivia, that man don't want you. He was in prison all his fucking life. He can't offer you shit but dick," Mario snapped. "Then you get pregnant by this nigga. He's a fucking grandpa already. Like, he is seventy years old. You are fucking wrinkly balls and dick. He probably gotta take Viagra."

"Well, Grandpa got the best dick I ever had. I be screaming and shouting when he in this pussy. At least he knows how to make me squirt. He loves me, and I love him. We are going to raise this baby together, and all I need for you to do, is sign these fucking papers," she yelled back.

"Bitch, I ain't signing shit," he said, getting ready to hit her.

Click!

I got both of their attention, and Olivia jumped behind me. I placed a sloppy kiss on her mouth.

"You will sign those papers, and if I ever hear you refer to my fiancée as a bitch again, this Grandpa will blow your brains out. Go get the papers out the car and bring them back over here. Thanks," I said to him.

"Baby go inside, and I'll be right in, okay," I said to her.

When she walked away, I smacked her on her ass and watched it bounce. That baby was making them titties plump, and that ass even fatter. I been hitting that pussy every night since I found out that she was pregnant. Damn!

"Here. I don't want any trouble," Mario rushed back over to me.

"It was trouble when you came at my baby mama," I said, hitting him with the butt of the gun, knocking him to the ground. I squatted next to him. "Oh, and I'm fifty-five, and I don't take Viagra, but from what I heard, maybe that's what you needed. Have a good day, Mario. Come near me or my girl again, and you will get more than a hit to the head."

I walked in the clinic just as they were calling Olivia to the back. I followed right behind her into the exam room. A beautiful woman walked in and flashed us the biggest smile.

"Good afternoon, Ms. Bradshaw and Mr. Wilson. How are you two doing? I'm Dr. Rose. Is this both of your first pregnancy?"

"Yes," we answered at the same time. "Well, I have a daughter, but I wasn't there for the pregnancy, really," I continued.

"Oh okay, I see. Let's get you undressed, and I'll be back in here in just a few minutes."

"Um, Daddy, out there, you called me your fiancée, was that something to make him mad, or?"

"Shhhh," I said.

The doctor came back in before she could say anything, and she squinted her eyes at me.

"Since this is your first appointment, I'm going to take pictures of your cervix to make sure that everything is okay in there, and then I'm going to let you hear your little baby's heartbeat."

After the doctor did everything that she needed to do, she let me hear the baby's heart beat, and I swear the tears came out of nowhere.

"Ms. Bradshaw, you are approximately eight weeks, and your due date is May tenth," Dr. Rose said.

"That would be the perfect Mother's Day present," Olivia started crying.

We got the ultrasound pictures and left the doctor's office with our next appointment and headed home. I trailed her home, and I couldn't help but to think that I was going to be a new dad. I was really in my feelings about this.

When we walked in the house, the house was dimmed with

dozens and dozens of red roses and petals everywhere, with slow music playing. I had Kam and Shelly decorate the house for us. The slow music was playing in the background, and she turned and looked at me. She placed a kiss on my cheek and then on my lips. She started stroking my dick through the jeans that I was wearing, and I could feel the precum oozing out of my dick. I walked her upstairs and slowly started to undress her. Her baby bump was so fucking sexy. I got on my knees and placed kisses on her baby bump and then kissed all the way down to this heaven on earth.

I flicked my tongue all over her pearl that was peeking out at me, and her knees started to get weak. I laid her back on the bed while I continued to assault her clit. She was losing her mind. I pulled the ring out my pocket and placed it on my pinky and then got undressed.

I eased inside of her wet pussy, and my dick almost let off early at the sound of it and the way it closed around my dick. Her pussy was tight and wet as fuck.

"Dadddddyyyy," she moaned. "Right there. Oh my god. Right there," she moaned.

"Right where? Here?" I dug deeper in her.

"Yes... Yes... Right there."

I leaned over and grabbed her hands, pushing them above her head. I placed small kisses on her lips, while I stroked her pussy.

"Ma, you wanna marry a nigga? You wanna be Mrs. Wilson?"

"Yess, Daddy! I doooo. Oh my goddd! I'm cumming," she moaned out.

I pulled the ring off my finger and put it on hers. She was so busy shaking she didn't even realize that I put the ring on her finger, but I kept up the rhythm.

"I'm about to cum baby girl. Fuuckk," I groaned.

After I drained my dick inside of her, I pulled out and fell next to her, trying to catch my breath.

"Fuck! I could never get tired of that dick," she laughed.

"I hope not because you stuck with me for life," I informed her.

She looked at me and said, "There is no other place I'd rather be."

She used her left hand to wipe the sweat from my forehead, and she saw the diamond on her hand. Her mouth fell open, and she stared at me. She closed her mouth, looked at the ring again, and her mouth opened again.

"This... is... fucking... perfect. What the fuck? How the fuck? Daddy, oh my god!"

"Calm down before you have a heart attack. I know you told your parents about me, but I'm going to ask your dad just out of respect, but I just wanted you to know that I am serious as fuck about you. Have you told him that you were pregnant yet?"

"Yes, I have. I told him all about you, but he told me more about you... more than I knew. Apparently, he knows that you are a protector, so he's not worried, but I can't wait for you to formally meet him."

Olivia rolled on top of me and started dancing and singing.

"I'm getting married. I'm getting married. I'm getting married. Oh, let me take care of you."

She slid down and took my dick in her mouth and went to work. Damn, she was already sucking dick different. I could get used to this shit. Me and Liv had sex on and off for the next couple of hours, until we eventually took an evening nap.

Kam

$\mathcal{I}$ had been working myself sick trying to get Rich Cutz fixed up because Christmas was just one month away. When I tell you that the building was horrible… it would have cost Malice wayyyy more money to fix it up. No one knew what I was doing besides Shelly, so I would have the contractors to call Shelly, and she would call me. Malice would kill me if random men were calling my phone, especially since we had been very open and honest with each other lately, about everything. The only thing that nigga was worried about was Dontay and if anything happened between us. I blocked Dontay from all my social media in front of him, so he would know that there was nothing going on with us. He blocked Taryn from social media, even though he already had her blocked from his phone. He showed me the messages where she got real disrespectful towards me, and I am so glad that he didn't fuck that bitch, because her ass would try to turn up pregnant, and I'll have to beat her ass.

Me, Olivia, Shelly, and Angela were out getting last minute Thanksgiving stuff. We are going to have one big Thanksgiving dinner. Olivia's family is coming over, and Malice's family will be there. Shelly wanted to eat with us, so her mom and dad will be there as well. They cool as fuck, so they ain't going to be on no crazy shit.

"Can I tell y'all something, and Angela, you have to PROMISE not to tell your son," I said, and looked at her.

"Chile, if you cheated on my son..."

"Nothing like that, but..." I pulled my dress tight on my stomach, and there was a little bump.

"No!" she said.

I nodded my head and pulled an ultrasound out my purse. I was throwing up last week, and I went got a pregnancy test. It said that I was pregnant, and I immediately booked an appointment. Turns out, I was pregnant with twins. TWINS! God took one and then gave me two. I pray that it is a boy and a girl, so we can wait for like five more years before we have another kid.

They looked at the ultrasound, and Angela started crying, which made Olivia cry. Her hormones always have her crying, and I really don't want that to happen to me.

"Is that two babies?" Olivia whispered.

"Yes. I'm going to tell him next month for his graduation present. Hopefully, I don't get too big between now and then. Well, his graduation is in two weeks so nothing should change too drastically," I replied.

Yes. My baby is finally getting his bachelor's. The first couple months of his last semester were crazy, but he made it through, and I was so proud of him.

"Oh my god! This is so crazy. How far along are you? Hopefully you are close to my due date," Olivia beamed with excitement.

"Girl, and run my daddy crazy with three babies at the same

time? His kid and grandkids. We definitely have to get a bigger house," I laughed. "My due date is in June though."

"I can't wait to be an Aunt! I'm going to spoil them so much!" Shelly said rubbing my little bump.

We were in the store for another hour, picking up things and talking about the baby shower and the nurseries. Angela talking about she wanted to decorate since she doesn't do anything else. She even wanted to do our baby showers together. I told her that I didn't mind, because I really didn't have any friends besides Shiana, Aiysha, and Shelly.

When we walked into the house, you could hear the men yelling at the TV. This place really sounded and felt like the holidays. The house smelled of pumpkin spice and food that we were letting marinate. This was going to be a great holiday, and the first time that I really felt like I was surrounded by loved ones.

"Hey ladies," the men spoke.

"Kade, where is Kalena?" I asked him when I noticed that she wasn't sitting where she was when we left.

"She's upstairs. She was tired, or something."

I went upstairs to my room, and Kalena was laying in the bed crying.

"Kalena, what's wrong?"

"How could Mom and Dad be so sick? You are so beautiful and so kind, and you just never let it waver you, and then you met Malice. He makes you so happy. I know I'm rambling. I just... I'm tired. I haven't really slept. I want to leave private school and be around more people like me. I want to go to public school because they won't pick on me for the color of my skin. The friends I did have all abandoned me when I needed them the most," she cried.

"It's okay. Just finish out the school year, and I'll talk to Kade to see what we can do about getting you in a different school at the beginning of the year. Is that okay? And snap back on them white hoes. Trust me. You snap on one, and they'll leave you alone. I promise."

She flashed me a smile, and I knew that she was going to be okay.

"I'm going back downstairs. You should come down and help us prepare. We could always use a second set of hands."

She got up and followed me down the stairs, and we got ready for Thanksgiving dinner tomorrow.

∞

Thanksgiving Day

I couldn't fuck my husband this morning the way I wanted to because we had a house full of people, but he did let me ride that dick slow. I got up and took a shower. While I was in the shower, Phoenix came and got in with me. I held my breath because I prayed that he didn't notice the change in my body.

"You okay, Mama?" he asked me, as he started rubbing my back.

"Yes. I'm fine. How are you this morning?"

"I'm good. Feel like I ain't showered with your ass in weeks, that's all. Love seeing the water all over your body," he laughed. "Kam, I don't know if this offensive or not, but I am glad that you have gained all that weight back that you lost when you were in that hospital, because you had turned into a stick. Now, you getting thick on me, and a nigga is loving this shit," he said grabbing my waist.

"You better love it, or I'll find a nigga that do," I laughed.

"Aye, don't play like that. You already know I'll body that nigga."

I waved him off and got out the shower, leaving him in there to rinse off. I put on some leggings and one of Malice's button down t-shirts with my Puma slides. I looked in the mirror and did all the motions that I will most likely do downstairs, so I would know if people would be able to tell if I was pregnant or not. I was so lucky to hide the morning sickness from him, because Malice is normally gone by the time I wake up, because he had to be in class a whole hour before I had to be at work.

It smelled so good downstairs. The ladies were already down there making sure everything was great. I don't know what the smell was, but my damn babies didn't agree with the shit, so I had to run in the bathroom around the corner and puke my guts out. I pray that my babies act right during this dinner.

"Everything okay, baby?" Olivia asked.

"Yes. These kids don't like the smell of something in here," I whispered.

"Oh lord!" Angela said.

"It'll be alright. He won't find out," Shelly said.

"You're pregnant?" Kalena whispered with a look of excitement on her face.

"Yes, with twins. I told them yesterday. I'm going to tell Malice after his graduation. So don't say anything."

"Oh my god!" she squealed lowly. "I'm so excited. You told Kade?"

"Told Kade what?"

We all whipped around to see Kade coming in the kitchen, looking like he stepped off a damn magazine.

"That his favorite food is almost ready," Angela said, saving me, because I couldn't think of anything fast.

Kalena helped me set the table while Olivia and Angela were placing some of the food in the middle. The doorbell rang, and I knew that it was Mr. and Mrs. Long. I hadn't seen them in a long time. I opened the door, and Shelly was standing there with her parents. She looked just like her mom. I invited them in, and they took a seat at the table.

Moments after that, the doorbell rang again, and it was Olivia's parents and her sister. We hadn't been around each other much, but I could tell that she was cool, but I was kind of sideeying her after I read that text message from her, talking about me. I'm sure that we would get past it, eventually.

Twenty minutes later, the rest of the men stumbled downstairs, rubbing their stomachs as if they had been working all day. The nerve of their asses. They took their seats, and we fixed their plates and then our own. At least Tracey taught me something. Fix your husband's plate first and then yours, because he is the head of your household. After I fixed my plate, I sat down right next to my husband, and on the other side of me was my dad.

"So, I guess we can go around and say what we are thankful for," my dad said. "I'll start. I'm thankful that God saw fit to free me from that place. I'm thankful that I got a chance to start being a father to my daughter, Kam. She was my first true love, and I am so happy that she is okay with sharing me with Olivia and her little sibling that's on the way. I'm thankful for Olivia and my unborn. I'm thankful for my brother for holding down the fort and always having my back when I needed him the most, and for my new family and friends," my dad said, and sat down.

Everyone went around the table and said what they were thankful for, and then it stopped on my husband. I needed to see what he had to say.

"I am thankful for... everything and every moment that has led me to be sitting next to this very beautiful woman. She is the light of my life, and I swear I don't know what I would do without her. I am also thankful for my new family and new friends."

I smirked at him and sipped on the water to wet my throat, because the list of things that I was thankful for was long. I stood up and cleared my throat.

"First, thank you all for coming here and sharing your Thanksgiving with our family. I am thankful for my dad, for bullying his way out of prison to help me in my time of need. If it wasn't for him, I would probably be dead right now, and I am forever indebted to him. Kade," I sniffed because I knew my dumb self was getting ready to cry, "I am so thankful for you for being the man that I needed in my life. I am thankful for you stepping in when I needed you the most.

The foot massages. The talks. The wiping of my tears and the nursing of my bruises, you were there. I can't ever imagine life without my big brother. Kalena, I am thankful to be your big sister. I love you so much. Shelly, I am so thankful that you stepped in and took care of my store when I wasn't at my best. I don't know how I can repay you, but I am still working on that trip for us. Mr. and Mrs. Bailey, I am thankful that you guys accepted me into your family as your daughter. Mayhem, I'm thankful for that night—"

"What night?" Malice interrupted me.

"Shut up, dude, and let me finish. I'm thankful that you came over that night to talk to me, helping me understand how Malice and I make each other better. You made me look at the silver lining in all of this. Basically, thank you for pushing me to do something I was going to do anyway, rip up those divorce papers, and Olivia, I'm thankful that you had my best interest at heart, and even more thankful that you gave my dad a chance to be a dad, from the very beginning stages."

I turned and looked at my husband, who looked like he was waiting for my speech about him.

"Mr. Phoenix Bailey, I remember that day you waltzed your disrespectful self into my store, not knowing under all that disrespect was a gentle giant. I'm just thankful for you... without you, I would have never fully learned to love myself. Without you, I wouldn't have known what true love is. Without you, I wouldn't be who I am today... stronger, wiser, and a better thinker. I'm thankful that you decided that you wanted to grow old with me. I love you so much."

"It's all love baby. I wasn't letting your ass go anyway. Divorce papers or no divorce papers," he said, and everybody laughed.

The rest of the dinner went great. Everybody, including my fat ass, had two and three helpings of food. We didn't even have nothing left to put up or even to have leftovers tomorrow. I was low-key mad, because you know dressing is not good until the day after Thanksgiving. Either way, I'm glad that I got to spend this holiday with people who mean the most to me.

Surprisingly, my dad got along with Olivia's parents just as well. I could see how her parents were smiling in his face every time he said something. I have learned that my dad was very charming, and that's probably how he got all the women that he got when he was younger. Looking around at my huge loving family, I couldn't help but to smile to myself. Everything truly had come up.

Malice

Graduation Day...

Today was the day that I had been waiting on since I signed up for school two years ago. Having an associate's degree wasn't enough, I had to go for the bachelor's. A part of me was upset that I wasn't going to have Rich Cutz up and running like I had planned too, but it's just a minor setback for a major come back. I was even more pissed when I saw that somebody had bought the building and was doing major ass work on it. I didn't have it in me to even try and find out who bought the building from Catherine's estate. Maybe it was just a sign that I needed to have my business elsewhere, although I really wanted that building.

I hardly slept last night because I was so nervous about today. I looked over at my wife, who was laying halfway on her side and halfway on her stomach, gripping the pillow like she always does when I don't hold her. She looked so peaceful with her orange ass hair. She really was the love of my life, and I can't ever see myself without her. I nudged her, and she stirred awake.

"Still can't sleep, Daddy?" she asked sleepily.

"Nah, not really. You know my graduation is first... at nine, and I have to be at the school at eight. It's six right now. I guess I never thought that I would get this far. I still feel like I haven't accomplished a lot. I don't know."

"Phoenix Allen Bailey, don't you start doubting yourself. You made it further than people you went to middle school or high school with. You made it pretty far without the help of your parents, although you had to do some disgusting shit to do it, you did it. I'm proud of you, and I need you to be proud of you too, baby," she said, with her eyes still closed.

Kam always knows what to say to make things better, and that's one of the reasons why I loved her. She had been sleeping a lot lately, which made me wonder if she was pregnant, but if she was, she would tell me. I can't wait until she is though. I'mma keep her ass barefoot and pregnant. She just doesn't know it yet. I closed my eyes to get at least an hour or so of sleep before I had to head to the school.

∞

"Congratulations, son!" my daddy said, pulling me into a big embrace!

This hug felt the greatest from him because he didn't support me from the beginning, but over these last few months, my life has changed. The day my wife tried to commit suicide, it was like my dad did a complete 180. He's been texting me daily when I'm not around, just to see how I'm doing. We don't talk about the drug game anymore. He's really been the dad that I should have had from the very beginning.

"You look good. My son got a damn degree. I'm so proud of you for doing something that I have never done. You are the first person in the family with a degree, and I'm just... happy. Thank you for never giving up, even when I was pushing you to," my dad got choked up.

"Is that my husband, looking all educated and shit?" I heard my wife say from behind me.

I turned around and started posing for her as she took pictures of me and stuff. She hugged me tight.

"I'm so proud of you. I can't wait to have your degree framed and placed with all your accolades. I'm so glad that you didn't give up," she said with water in her eyes.

"Congratulations, bro! You look good. I'm proud of you for sticking to it," Mayhem said, dapping me up then pulling me into a hug.

I was so happy that my family was there, because when I first started this journey, I wasn't so sure that I would have anyone here for me besides my brother, and maybe my mother. To have these people cheering for me when my name was called made a nigga get emotional as I shook the president's hand and received my degree.

"Malice... congratulations," we all whipped our heads around, and it was Taryn standing there with flowers.

"Okay, BITCH! I don't think you got the message last mothafuckin' time when I knocked your head off," Kam said, pulling her hair up in a ponytail.

"Taryn, move around ma. I was trying to be your friend, but you disrespected my wife. It was over with after that," I said to her.

"YOU WASN'T SAYING THAT WHEN YOU WAS DEEP IN MY PUSSY TWO WEEKS AGO!" she yelled, and I looked at her like she was crazy. My eyebrows furrowed because this bitch was lying.

"Kam, I never fucked—" I started, but she cut me off by holding up her hand.

"What his dick look like, huh?"

"You know what his dick look like, bitch! I wasn't paying attention because it was inside of me," she chuckled.

"His dick is unique. It has a very unique look. You would know what it looked like if you fucked him, because my nigga likes fucking with lights on. You got a nice ass, and if you fucked my husband, he would love to see that ass jiggle on his dick," Kam said, making my eyes get big at how vulgar she was being in front of these people. The cameras were recording, waiting for something to pop off.

"Bitch, fuck you! Mentally ill ass bitch!" she snapped.

"Oh hell no!" Shelly said, and before I knew it, she got out of her heels and dived on Taryn.

Taryn was holding her own, but Shelly managed to tussle her to the ground and got on top of her. The crowd was laughing and pointing at her.

"Talk that shit now, bitch!" Shelly said while pounding on her face. "Talk shit about my sister again, and I'll kill you hoe! Leave... my... brother-in-law alone." *POP!* "He don't want you." *POP!* "He never wanted you." *POP! POP!*

My dad pulled Shelly off her, and she put back on her shoes. Some bystanders helped Taryn to her feet, and her face was knotted up. I would have felt bad had she not came and lied on me. Shelly started reapplying her lipstick, like she didn't just beat that girl ass, which made everybody laugh.

"Where we are eating at?" I asked. "I'm hungry as hell."

We all piled into the trucks and headed to Gibson's Bar and Steakhouse. The moment we walked in, my stomach started growling even harder. We had reserved the back room where it was just me and my family. We had two waitresses working on our table.

"Yo, I can't wait to get in your guts tonight," I whispered to Kam, and she grinned while squeezing my dick.

The waitresses brought our drinks back while two other waitresses brought in balloons... pink and blue balloons, and gave everyone a card. I noticed that Shelly was recording us. I opened my card and I read it aloud.

"Could be pink, could be blue, all I know is that there are two. Bailey twins soon come."

Behind the card was a picture of an ultrasound, and I was overcome with emotions. The tears came out of nowhere.

"Awwww, don't cry baby," my wife said rubbing my back.

"Ma, you pregnant with twins for real?" I asked her, while rubbing her little bump. This is why she started looking healthy again. My baby was pregnant with my baby...babies.

She nodded her head, and I started crying again.

"Wait, so my uncle about to have a baby and grandbabies at the same time. Unc, you about to be stressed out. Those big black braids are about to turn gray," Mayhem laughed.

"Congratulations kids!" Unc said.

After the shock wore off me about to be a dad, we dug in our food. It was like I fell even more in love with my wife. I kept stealing looks at her, and she looked so beautiful. Like, I really couldn't have picked a sexier woman to procreate with and give my last name. The ring was burning a hole in my pocket, and I felt like there was no better moment than now to ask her to renew our vows in front of our family and friends, so I stood up.

"I have an announcement to make," I took the ring box out my pocket, twirled it around in my hand, and the cameras went up again. "Um, when I put the first ring on my wife's finger, I promised her that if she stuck with me, I would upgrade her ring. I told her that every day wouldn't be pretty, and there would be days that she wouldn't like me, but if she continued to love me, we could make it through everything. Granted, these last few months were NOT pretty. We both said things we didn't mean, we both did things we shouldn't have done, but overall, it brought us back to each other, where we're supposed to be," I said, and then turned to my wife and got on one knee. "Kambridge, I should have done this the right way in the beginning. Will you meet me at the altar again for a ceremony for our family and friends?" I asked her.

"Yes, Daddy! Yes!"

I slid the ring on her finger, and I could see the lump grow in her throat.

"Whoa! Dear Jesus! Wow! This ring is marvelous. Oh my god! I mean, I loved my first one, but THIS one! Damn!" she laughed.

After the proposal, we laughed and talked at the restaurant for the next few hours. I honestly don't think that life could get much better than this. My wife is pregnant with twins, and I just proposed to her again. Life...is...good.

Kason

*L*ife with no possibility of parole. Life with no possibility of parole. Life with no possibility of parole. I really can't believe that was the only deal they could possibly get for me. I will spend the rest of my life in here. The only way to keep me safe is to have me away from the general population. My first week here, I got my ass whooped every night. Every night. They didn't let up, and I had to beg the warden to move me away from general population.

I ate alone. I had my own cell and even watched an hour of TV a day, alone. I only saw three people a day. Six months ago, if someone had told me that I would spend the rest of my life in jail, I would have told them that they were lying. A few days ago, I got a letter from Shaw, telling me that he wasn't sorry for turning over that device to Murphy, because Kam didn't deserve the way I was beating on her, and that he hopes I rot in jail for the rest of my life.

On the news, they showed where Malice had graduated and got his bachelor's in business. They showed a whole video of him walking across the stage, and then with his family and my family. I laughed to myself because I had really tried to keep them apart, and they ended up being closer. I saw clips that she is pregnant with twins, and he gave her another ring. I'll be glad when they stop airing this story, but since this story was so big, and had so many twists and turns, anytime one of them does anything remotely good, they'll air it, and then remind us who they were.

Another segment I saw where they were letting some of the men out that I had put in jail. Granted, some of them deserve to be there, but because of my fuck up, they are getting out. It's such a shame that they don't know that Korupt's team is about to be bigger and stronger.

I was staring at the ceiling when the CO came to my cell and told me that I had a visitor. I looked into the small mirror they had nailed to the wall. The scars that Mayhem, Korupt, and Malice unleashed on me had me looking like Freddie Krueger. They tore my body up, and I felt everything that Kambridge felt when I was whooping on her. The CO walked me to the vistor's room, and I saw Kade and Kalena sitting there. I wanted to hug them both, but they kept sitting down, so I wasn't going to force it. I sat down in front of them, and we both exchanged glares.

"Dad, why?" Kalena asked.

"I should have reacted differently, and there are some things that you won't be able to understand right now," I said.

"No, I can understand. Why did you do it?"

"I should have divorced your mom before—" I started.

"Before your murdered her. You should have divorced her before your murdered her," Kade said cutting me off.

"Yes, but I loved your mom. I hated that she cheated on me with the one guy who hated my guts, and vice versa. I took it out on Kambridge, and I was stupid for doing that. I was less of a man for doing that. I'm going to pray every night that she forgives me, and one day she comes and speaks to me, but I know that won't happen soon. Just tell her that I love her, and she will forever be my daughter. I take full responsibility for the role I played in Tracey's death, and how I treated Kambridge. Kade... please take care of your sisters. You are all they got," I said to them, got up from the table, and left them sitting there.

I couldn't take it anymore. I couldn't take sitting in front of my kids, knowing that I took their mother away from them, out of anger and pure jealousy. I went back to my cell and laid there. A part of me wanted to take the sheets and wrap them around my neck to get away from this world, but if it didn't work the first time, I don't want to chance it again. I'm going to get right with God and pray that when I die, he'll have mercy on my soul.

Kambridge

Christmas...

The smell of food woke me and my kids up. I sat up in the bed and stretched a little bit. I looked at my husband, and he was sitting up against the headboard. He was looking at me with a look of disgust.

"Um, Merry Christmas to you too. Why are you looking at me like you want to kill me?" I asked him with my nose scrunched up.

This man was really looking at me like I had shit on me. I was trying to figure out what I had done.

"Kambridge, I'm going to ask you one time, and if you lie to me, I swear to God, I'mma crack your fucking face open," he snarled.

I started laughing, but when I realized that he wasn't playing, I instantly got serious.

"Phoenix, what the fuck is wrong with you?" I asked him.

"Where the fuck were you last night?" he asked.

"What are you talking about?" I asked.

Last night, after putting it on his ass, he was out like a light. I made sure that he was snoring loudly, and I snuck out to go see the finishing touches on Rich Cutz. Y'all, when I tell you the place looks fucking amazing. It's going to blow his mind. The building is huge. On one side, there are six stations where niggas can cut hair, and the other side is eight stations where bitches can do hair. I'mma have to screen them hoes though when they try to work up in there, because if one of them try Malice, they are going to get their wig split.

In the back, there are rooms where a barber or a stylist can get private rooms, if they want to pay the booth rent for private areas. You can get waxes, facials, and other things skin related. Of course, my make-up booth is in the back. I have a private area in the back for when I do make-up on clients. You could even get your nails and toes done in Rich Cutz. Yeah, I'm going all out. My make-up business is going to be called KaePaints, because I am going to be painting faces on.

On the other side of the building there are three big screen TVs where everyone in the shop would be able to see them, two pool tables, a huge fish tank, which had nothing but exotic fish in it, and a spades table. The floors were marble, and so were the walls. There were chandeliers, and all the mirrors had LED lights around them. Listen, I went all out for my husband. He'll be paying me back for years to come for this shit, but it's going to be worth seeing the smile on his face versus seeing the scowl that's on his face right now.

"Kam, don't fucking play games with me. I told you that you only had one time to answer this question. When I woke up and went to the bathroom, your ass was gone. I thought that maybe you were downstairs, but you weren't. You weren't nowhere to be found. Looked in the garage, and my car was gone. Where the fuck did you go in MY car, last night? Don't fucking lie to me!" he snapped.

"Malice, what are you insinuating?" I asked him.

"I ain't insinuating nothing. I'm just asking you where the fuck you went. You are stalling, which means you're trying to figure out a lie. You weren't at Shelly's because she was at the Christmas Eve party. I checked her social media. So, where the fuck was you? You cheating on me? Are those really my twins?" he laughed, while trying to light a blunt. He was shaking so bad, and I could tell that I was getting to him.

"Phoenix, obviously you had a bad dream, and you need to go back to sleep and wake up on the right side of the bed. It's Christmas, and I am not going to let you ruin my Christmas early this morning. Go take a shower and come downstairs. I'm sure breakfast is ready."

"I ain't have no fucking dream Kambridge. I woke up, and your lil' black ass was gone. Keep fucking with me, and I promise to God, I'll kill you."

I straddled his lap and stared at him as he inhaled on the blunt.

"Kam, move, because I ain't trying to blow smoke in your face. You don't need to be getting a contact pregnant with my kids, mane."

"Now wait a minute. Two minutes ago, you said they weren't yours, but now they yours. Which one is it?"

"Move, dog! Before I knock you out," he said, trying to move me off him.

I put my hand behind my back and started stroking his dick through his boxers, and I could feel him getting hard. My pussy was already wet because these kids kept my hormones going, and I loved when he got aggressive with me.

"You really want me to move?"

He squinted his eyes at me as he blew the smoke out in my face.

I was already naked, so I raised up and slid down on his dick. I got on my feet and started going up and down slowly.

"You want me to move, baby?" I moaned out.

"Sssss, nah, baby. Keep going," he whispered.

"You think I'll give this pussy away? Huh? You think I'll let another nigga get this wet...tight...warm ass pussy," I said starting to speed up.

"Heelll nah. This my mothafuckin' pussy. Ma, you about to make me bust."

Before I could even get my nut, I could feel Phoenix dick pulsate inside of me.

"Man, you need to hurry up and have those damn kids, ma! I be trying to hold my cum, but that wet pussy be gripping me up. Why the fuck do kids make you wetter? I need to google that shit."

I got up off him, went to take care of my morning hygiene, and put on some clothes before going downstairs to see my dad and Olivia setting the table. I was starving and was ready to eat. I was also so very excited to take Malice to see his present soon.

"Good morning, people!" I spoke. "Merry Christmas!"

"Merry Christmas!" they both said at the same time.

I could smell the pine from the real Christmas tree that we had. I sat at the table, waiting for my dad to bring me my plate. After he sat my plate down, he set a blue box down in front of me.

"This is from Olivia and me. Um, I didn't know what to get you because you have everything in the world, so I hope you like it."

I opened the box, and it was a Pandora bracelet. It had a charm that had 'dad's love' on it and another charm that said, 'step-mother's love'. My heart was so full, and it made me so happy.

"I love it!" I exclaimed.

I gave him a brown folder, and I hoped that it made him happy. It was something so small, but I knew it would mean so much to him. He opened it and read for a little while, and then he looked up at me.

"You changed your last name...to Wilson?" he asked.

"Yes. So, it's Kambridge Wilson-Bailey, now."

He gave me the biggest hug.

"Olivia, I really didn't know what to get you because I don't really know what you like, so I hired a decorator to make my little sibling's room look perfect."

"Oh my god! Now I can scratch that off my list. You are the best, Kam!" she said hugging me.

Malice finally drug his stupid ass downstairs, and Kade and Kalena came down behind him as well. They had been staying in the extra guest rooms for the last few days.

"Merry Christmas, everybody!" Kade said.

"Kade, Kalena, sit! I want you to open your presents!" I exclaimed.

I got their presents from under the tree. They opened them and both seemed so happy with their presents. I got them both custom Rolexes, but Kade got a trip for two to Italy, and I gave Kalena an extra five thousand dollars. You know teenagers are very fickle.

"What's this key to?" Malice said, holding up the key from his box.

"Who told you to open up your gift anyway?"

"Shit! It had my damn name on it. What's this key to?"

"It's the key to my heart. Make sure you don't lose it."

The whole time everyone was eating breakfast, I could tell that the key was bothering Malice, because he kept twirling it around in his hand, and me leaving last night, but he was trying to hold it in. I told him to get dressed so we can go for a ride. I told Mayhem to make sure all his little thug friends and parents were at the address at one o'clock.

I sent my people a text and told them where to meet us because I was going to ride him around first, so he wouldn't think anything was off.

I went upstairs, and Malice was sitting on the bed.

"Kam, you not going to tell me where you went last night?" he asked.

"Baby, I'm going to tell you after we get dressed, okay?"

He shook his head and went in the bathroom. He slammed the door in my face, so I had to go to a guest room and get ready. I swear to God, I was going to kill him afterwards because he is acting so stank.

An hour later, I was waiting downstairs for Malice. He came downstairs in a pair of blue Levi jeans, a white long sleeve t-shirt that had his chest out, and a pair of black boots. When he made it downstairs, he pulled on his pea coat and a scarf. Listen to me, I don't know what it is about men in scarfs and pea coats, but he looked so fucking sexy.

As soon as we were in the car, he started with the questions.

"Ma, where were you last night?" he asked. "Mane, you got me ready to go helm that Chris Brown ass nigga up. Were you with him?"

"Malice. Baby. No, I was not with another man last night. Where is my Christmas present?"

"I ain't giving you shit until you tell me where the fuck you were!"

I ignored him and continued to drive around the city, until I threw a bandana in his lap and told him to cover his eyes.

"Nah, ma! I can't close my eyes because you are careless. A nigga could run up on us, and just nah..."

"Put the bandana on!" I spoke through gritted teeth.

"Aight, a nigga come up and murk us, I'mma choke you out when we get to heaven."

I laughed at him as we pulled up to Rich Cutz. Everyone was waiting outside for us. I knew they were freezing, but it's going to be so worth it once they stepped inside. I opened the door for him and led him out. I stood him in front of the crowd of people, and I pulled the tarp off the sign out front.

"Malice, you still got the key to my heart?"

"Yeah, yeah, yeah."

"Take the bandana off!"

He took the bandana off, and his mouth hit the floor while everyone cheered. I couldn't quite gauge his reaction.

Malice

*M*y eyes had to be deceiving me. I'm looking at a bad ass sign that said Rich Cutz and KaePaints.

"Son, say something!" my dad said from behind me.

All I could do was go hug my wife and place a sloppy kiss on her lips.

"Baby, thank you for this. I swear I'm going to fix this place up, and you won't have to spend a dime of your money," I said.

She laughed as I fumbled with the key to try and open the door. When I opened the door, I turned the lights on, and my knees got weak. I literally fell to my knees as I took in the view of this place. While I was still on my knees trying to catch my breath, my wife was walking around and showing people the place.

"Bro, you got a mothafuckin' keeper, dog!" Retro said, dapping me up, and pulling me up off the floor. "I'mma be up in here every mothafuckin' day, chilling. Mane, come look around."

"Nigga, I never expected this shit. Damn!" I said still trying to wrap my head around this shit.

"Niiggaaa, come look over here," Spice said.

I walked to the other side, and it was the fish tank that I told my wife I wanted one day. I mean, I told her this months ago, and I thought that she had forgot. The big screen TVs she had hanging from the wall were dope as fuck. Now, we can watch all the football games at the same time when they come on. She had a sitting area where niggas could come and talk shit.

I finally made my way to the back, dragging my hands along the marble walls. I finally saw what KaePaints was. This lil' heffa had her own station in my shop. She had some pictures of the different make-up looks that she did on herself and Shelly. She was only charging sixty dollars for a full face and eyelashes.

"How dare you? How you know I want to work with you?" I said leaning against the door frame, looking at my pregnant wife wiping off her counter.

"Technically, you won't be working with me. I have my own little place back here. I won't even hear none of the dirty talk that you men will be talking up front," she said, turning around looking at me with her hand on her hip.

"Kambridge," I said walking in and closing the door behind me. I got on my knees in front of her and looked up at her. My eyes watered, and I tried to blink back my tears, but I couldn't. She makes me so weak and vulnerable. I don't even care about crying in front of her. This was my wife. The love of my life. "I don't know how I could ever repay you for doing this for me. My heart almost stopped when I walked in here. I'm sorry for this morning and thinking you was cheating on me. I just don't want to ever lose you."

"Baby, the only way you could repay me is to make this shop boom like a mothafucka. Make me and your kids proud of you," she said wiping my tears away. "Although, you did go overboard thinking I would leave my bed to go sleep with another man, AFTER I had sex with you. Is you crazy?"

"Ma, I'm crazy as fuck over your chocolate ass. Oh, Merry Christmas."

I pulled the box out of my pocket and handed it to her. She opened it and marveled over the pear shape, two carat earrings that I got for her. I could tell that this woman loved diamonds, and I shouldn't have started this shit. She immediately put her earrings in and pulled her hair up in her ponytail so she could show them off. She turned around to look at herself in the mirror.

"Baby, I love them so much. Who knew you had such good taste?"

I stood up and got behind her. The minute my dick brushed against her ass, he got hard. I slowly rolled down her leggings and started playing with her clit. She bit her big ass bottom lip, so she wouldn't make any noises.

"You feel my mans?" I whispered in her ear.

She nodded her head. I unbuttoned my pants and let them fall right in the middle of my thigh. I eased in my wife's goodness, and she let out a hushed sigh. Usually, I would make her ass get loud, but I ain't want to embarrass her too bad. Boy, pregnant pussy really is the best. My wife's pussy got wet before, but she gets reallllll wet now.

Splat! Splat!

"She talking to me baby," I said, and bit down on her neck.

"Daddy, you feel so good. Oh my god!"

"Kam, I love you so much! You mean the world to me. Fuck! I can't last long for shit in this pussy no more," I groaned, as I shot my load inside of her, but I kept going because I was going to make her nut.

"Spread your cheeks baby. Let me go deeper."

She reached behind her and spread her ass cheeks, and I dug so deep inside of her, and she started squirting.

"Oowwee, Kam, stop squirting girl, before I have your ass hollering back here," I warned her.

"I cannnn'ttt. You keep hitting my spot, baby! Sssssss," she moaned as she squirted again.

"Aight bet! Now, I'm about to show out."

I pulled her away from the mirror and bent her over her chair and started wearing her ass out, and she was trying to keep quiet.

"Nah, what's my fucking name! What the fuck I tell you? You wanted Daddy to beat this pussy up, didn't you? That's what you wanted, ain't it?" I growled.

"Yesss, Daddy! Daddy! Ahhhh! Fuck me! Fuck me!" she moaned, and started throwing it back, matching my strokes.

"Oh, so you grown now? You throwing it back it like that?" I smirked as I continued to fuck her... hard. "I like the way you twerk on this dick. That shit makes Daddy cum."

She ain't have to twerk that long because I felt those walls constrict, and my dick couldn't take no more tightness, and I came in her. After I was finished cumming inside of her, we went into her bathroom and got cleaned up.

After we got cleaned up, we walked back out front, and surprisingly no one was even paying attention to us. She walked me over to my booth, and on my station was my name on a gold plate and our wedding picture in a frame.

"Come on, ma! Why you got the wedding picture in the shop mane? Everybody in here know I got the baddest bitch." I laughed when she smacked me in my stomach and walked away to mingle with the crowd.

I'm twenty-eight years old, and I have never had a Christmas like this. This Christmas will be a Christmas that I will never forget. I sat in my barber chair, and this shit was comfortable than a mothafucka. I watched as the crowd marveled at my new place. I had succeeded at everything I had never dreamed that I would succeed in. Find love, have my own shop, get married, and have kids. What more could a nigga want?

EPILOGUE...

Kam

1 year later...

So much could happen in a year. The day after Christmas, my dad took Olivia to the courthouse and married her with her parents and me and Malice as their witnesses. He decided that he didn't want to go into the new year without Olivia having his last name. It was the cutest thing. I could tell that they were truly in love with each other, and I was happy that my dad had found love.

Kade is still Kade. My big brother. My protector. My best friend. He still works for Mayhem, and now Malice, as his accountant and business manager. So, he's doing well for himself. I told him that he needs to stop burying himself into work and find somebody and get married. He told me about the Lency chick, but she couldn't even stick around when times got hard for him and our family. So, I told him that he dodged a bullet. I was sad for him because he was really feeling her. If I saw her, I would probably knock her out, just because. Kalena was now in public school and loving it more than the private school that both Kade and I graduated from. She had a lot of friends now, and I was so happy for her. Boys are scared to ask her out on a date because of her brother and brother-in-law. She doesn't like that too much, but I had to let her know, if a man is scared to date you because of your brothers, then they are weak and you don't need them anyway.

My in-laws are still crazy as hell, and Korupt is still running the dope game. He was glad that he got his gold back, and I convinced him to fix up the block that Malice's shop was on. He did, and he ended up opening a gym and a place where kids can hang out at after school. This whole block was neutral, and no drug selling or any of that would happen on this block.

Shelly, my best friend, has calmed down a whole LOT! She's not giving her body to random men anymore. She has done a whole one-eighty. She's still the general manager of my store, and business was so great that she had to hire two more people to help her out. We also had to move my store right next to Rich Cutz, because Malice said he didn't want to have to kill Dontay, or as he called him 'that dancing ass nigga,' or my favorite one 'that Chris Brown ass nigga'. I told him that he really didn't have to worry, because Dontay really wasn't a threat to me, and he didn't say anything to me after that heated exchange we had in his studio.

Kason. Last the news reported, he had converted to Islam, and now spends his time studying and preaching the Quran to prisoners. Connor... well, Connor got what he wanted with Holly. I saw them out a few months ago, and they looked a hot ass mess. Holly was pregnant, and they looked homeless. You know Connor got on the internet and told everybody that I was the reason that he couldn't find a job. Then proceeded to tell all white people not to ever date black people. That was so funny. That's the reason why they won't prosper because they are racist. I wish I would have known that before, but a leopard can't change their spots, even though he hid his for so long.

Mayhem Bailey. The man who knows nothing about love, essentially saved my marriage. I would never be able to thank him enough. Over the last year, Phoenix and I had been setting him up on dates, but none of them were working out for him. Eventually, he will find somebody to love him past that wall he got built up, but for now, he's still dicking and dismissing them.

As for me, Kambridge Wilson-Bailey, on Mother's Day, when I was big as a house with the twins, Phoenix and I had the perfect vow renewal service in his parent's backyard. It was so perfect, and everybody loved it. Kade started from the beginning of the aisle and walked me to the middle of the aisle to my dad. I latched on to his arm, and they both gave me away to Phoenix. I couldn't stop crying during the whole thing. Everyone enjoyed the reception until my step-mother went into labor. My dad panicked, and he almost fell out from either excitement or nervousness, but he managed to get her to the hospital in one piece. When the family made it to the hospital, Olivia had given birth to Trent Wilson, Jr. I already knew that he was going to look like me. He was the cutest eight-pound chocolate baby.

Two weeks later, I had given birth to two healthy babies, Phoebe and Phoenix Bailey, Jr. They came out looking exactly like their daddy, and I was so mad about it. They didn't get anything from me. When they opened their eyes, they even had their daddy's brown eyes. I just wanted to give the whole babies away. Since they been born, Phoenix has been very hands on with everything.

With some of the money, I completed renovated the house. Call me crazy, but I wanted all of us under the same roof. There was a suite added for Kade and Kalena, a suite for Mayhem if he wanted to stay, and a suite for Angela and Korupt, if they ever wanted to stay over. The house was so huge that we could go days without seeing each other, if we didn't meet in the kitchen every day for dinner. Life was good as fuck, and there was nothing that I could complain about.

I walked in Rich Cutz, and it was booming. Every stylist and barber had somebody in the chair, and at least two people waiting for them to finish. There were people on the pool table and the spades table. Rich Cutz has been doing so good. Last month, his business was named Business of the Year in two magazines. This place was full of white, black, and brown people. Everybody got along in here, just like Phoenix wanted it to be.

"Hey, Mrs. Bailey. He in the back," Spice said.

I spoke to everyone as I walked in the back to my husband's office. As I approached the door, I could hear him talking to Phoebe and Phoenix Jr.

"Besides your mom, you two are the best things that could have ever happened to me. You two are my hearts in human form. Never knew something could be perfect," he said.

I walked in the door, and he looked up at me, smiling. I took Phoebe out of her car seat and placed her on my breast, so she could feed. My breasts were overflowing with milk, and I needed to get it out before they burst.

"Hey, Daddy! You have any clients today?" I asked him, as I sighed from the relief I was getting from Phoebe taking the pressure off my full breast.

"I had them earlier this morning, and I got like five more later today. Kam, sometimes, I still can't believe that this is my life. I'm married with two kids. My wife made me the best man that I could be, and of course that pussy tamed a nigga," he laughed.

I shook my head at him. He's still everything that he was the first day I met him...except the male escort. That's him. That's Malice. A Malice love is the best love that I could have ever come across.

THE END!!!

MESSAGE FROM THE AUTHORESS!!!!

Hey Y'all! Thank you so much for being patient with me as I get this book out. I can't thank you enough for the constant love and support. When you get finish reading, please be kind, and leave me a review. I must thank God for blessing me with this talent that I just discovered in 2016, and Porscha Sterling for helping me give my talent the vision. My Royalty sisters, I thank you for all the constant support and laughs. Last, but certainly not least, I must thank my readers. Without you all, I wouldn't have a reason to write. Thanks for keeping me on my toes and helping me become a better writer. Kam and Malice's story may be over, but it definitely may not be the last you hear from them.

With Love,

Bianca

CONNECT WITH ME ON MY ON SOCIAL MEDIA

Facebook Readers Group:

https://www.facebook.com/groups/AuthoressBianca/

Facebook Like Page: www.facebook.com/AuthoressBianca

Instagram: @AuthoressBianca

Other novels by Bianca

https://www.amazon.com/author/bianca

Subscribe to my Website: www.authoressbianca.com

Looking for a publishing home?

Royalty Publishing House, Where the Royals reside, is accepting submissions for writers in the urban fiction genre. If you're interested, submit the first 3-4 chapters with your synopsis to submissions@royaltypublishinghouse.com.

Check out our website for more information: www.royaltypublishinghouse.com.

Text ROYALTY to 42828 to join our mailing list!

To submit a manuscript for our review, email us at submissions@royaltypublishinghouse.com

Text RPHCHRISTIAN to 22828 for our CHRISTIAN ROMANCE novels!

Text RPHROMANCE to 22828 for our INTERRACIAL ROMANCE novels!

Do You Like CELEBRITY GOSSIP?

Check Out QUEEN DYNASTY!
Visit Our Site: www.thequeendynasty.com

Get LiT!

Download the LiT eReader app today and enjoy exclusive content, free books, and more

CPSIA information can be obtained
at www.ICGtesting.com
Printed in the USA
LVOW13s1746071117
555373LV00013B/1135/P